P9-CMS-522

THE CRIME WAVE AT BLANDINGS

Books by

P. G. WODEHOUSE

A Damsel in Distress
Big Money
Bill the Conqueror
Blandings Castle
Carry On, Jeeves!
Divots
Fish Preferred
Golf Without Tears
He Rather Enjoyed It
Hot Water
If I Were You
Indiscretions of Archie
Jeeves
Laughing Gas
Leave It to Psmith
Meet Mr Mulliner
Money for Nothing
Mostly Sally
Mr Mulliner Speaking
Mulliner Nights
Nothing but Wodehouse
Sam in the Suburbs
The Crime Wave at Blandings
The Little Warrior
The Small Bachelor
Three Men and a Maid
Very Good, Jeeves
Young Men in Spats

P. G. WODEHOUSE

THE CRIME WAVE AT BLANDINGS

THE BOOK LEAGUE OF AMERICA, INC.
New York 1937

PRINTED AT THE *Country Life Press*, GARDEN CITY, N. Y., U. S. A.

CONTENTS

THE CRIME WAVE AT BLANDINGS

THE DAY on which Lawlessness reared its ugly head at Blandings Castle was one of singular beauty. The sun shone down from a sky of cornflower-blue, and what one would really like would be to describe in leisurely detail the ancient battlements, the smooth green lawns, the rolling parkland, the majestic trees, the well-bred bees and the gentlemanly birds on which it shone.

But those who read thrillers are an impatient race. They chafe at scenic rhapsodies and want to get on to the rough stuff. When, they ask, did the dirty work start? Who were mixed up in it? Was there blood, and, if so, how much? And—most particularly—where was everybody and what was everybody doing at whatever time it was? The chronicler who wishes to grip must supply this information at the earliest possible moment.

The wave of crime, then, which was to rock one of Shropshire's stateliest homes to its foundations broke out towards the middle of a fine summer afternoon, and the persons involved in it were disposed as follows:

Clarence, ninth Earl of Emsworth, the castle's owner and overlord, was down in the potting shed, in conference with Angus McAllister, his head gardener, on the subject of sweet peas.

His sister, Lady Constance, was strolling on the terrace with a swarthy young man in spectacles, whose name was Rupert Baxter and who had at one time been Lord Emsworth's private secretary.

Beach, the butler, was in a deck chair outside the back premises of the house, smoking a cigar and reading Chapter Sixteen of *The Man With The Missing Toe.*

George, Lord Emsworth's grandson, was prowling through the shrubbery with the air gun which was his constant companion.

Jane, his lordship's niece, was in the summerhouse by the lake.

And the sun shone serenely down—on, as we say, the lawns, the battlements, the trees, the bees, the best type of bird and the rolling parkland.

Presently Lord Emsworth left the potting shed and started to wander towards the house. He had never felt happier. All day his mood had been one of perfect contentment and tranquillity, and for once in a way Angus McAllister had done nothing to disturb it. Too often, when you tried to reason with that human mule, he had a way of saying "Mphm" and looking Scotch, and then saying "Grmph" and looking Scotch again, and after that just fingering his beard and looking Scotch without speaking, which was intensely irritating to a sensitive employer. But this afternoon Hollywood yesmen could have taken his correspondence course, and Lord Emsworth had none of that uneasy feeling, which usually came to him on these occasions, that the moment his back was turned his own sound, statesmanlike policies would be shelved and some sort of sweet-pea New Deal put into practice as if he had never spoken a word.

He was humming as he approached the terrace. He had his programme all mapped out. For perhaps an hour, till the day had cooled off a little, he would read a Pig book in the library. After that he would go and take a sniff at a rose or two and possibly do a bit of snailing. These mild pleasures were all his simple soul demanded. He wanted nothing more. Just the quiet life, with nobody to fuss him.

And now that Baxter had left, he reflected buoyantly, nobody did fuss him. There had, he dimly recalled, been some sort of trouble a week or so back —something about some man his niece Jane wanted to marry and his sister Constance didn't want her to marry —but that had apparently all blown over. And even when the thing had been at its height, even when the air had been shrill with women's voices and Connie had kept popping out at him and saying, "Do *listen,* Clarence!" he had always been able to reflect that, though all this was pretty unpleasant, there was nevertheless a bright side. He had ceased to be the employer of Rupert Baxter.

There is a breed of granite-faced, strong-jawed businessman to whom Lord Emsworth's attitude towards Rupert Baxter would have seemed frankly inexplicable. To these Titans a private secretary is simply a Hey-you, a Hi-there, a mere puppet to be ordered hither and thither at will. The trouble with Lord Emsworth was that it was he and not his secretary who had been the puppet. Their respective relations had always been those of a mild reigning monarch and the pushing young devil who has taken on the dictatorship. For years, until he had mercifully tendered his resignation to join an American named Jevons, Baxter had worried Lord Emsworth, bossed him, bustled him, had always been after him to do things and remember things and sign things. Never a moment's peace. Yes, it was certainly delightful to think that Baxter had departed forever. His going had relieved this Garden of Eden of its one resident snake.

Still humming, Lord Emsworth reached the terrace. A moment later, the melody had died on his lips, and he was rocking back on his heels as if he had received a solid punch on the nose.

"God bless my soul!" he ejaculated, shaken to the core.

His pince-nez, as always happened when he was emotionally stirred, had leaped from their moorings. He recovered them and put them on again, hoping feebly that the ghastly sight he had seen would prove to have been an optical illusion. But no. However much he blinked, he could not blink away the fact that the man over there talking to his sister Constance was Rupert Baxter in person. He stood gaping at him with a horror which would have been almost excessive if the other had returned from the tomb.

Lady Constance was smiling brightly, as women so often do when they are in the process of slipping something raw over on their nearest and dearest.

"Here is Mr Baxter, Clarence."

"Ah," said Lord Emsworth.

"He is touring England on his motor bicycle and, finding himself in these parts, of course he looked us up."

"Ah," said Lord Emsworth.

He spoke dully, for his soul was heavy with foreboding. It was all very well for Connie to say that Baxter was touring England, thus giving the idea that in about five minutes the man would leap on his motor bicycle and dash off to some spot a hundred miles away. He knew his sister. She was plotting. Always ardently pro-Baxter, she was going to try to get Blandings Castle's leading incubus back into office again. Lord Emsworth would have been prepared to lay the odds on this in the most liberal spirit. So he said "Ah."

The monosyllable, taken in conjunction with the sagging of her brother's jaw and the glare of agony behind his pince-nez, caused Lady Constance's lips to tighten. A disciplinary light came into her fine eyes. She looked like a female lion tamer about to assert her personality with one of the troupe.

"Clarence!" she said sharply. She turned to her companion. "Would you excuse me for a moment, Mr Baxter? There is something I want to talk to Lord Emsworth about."

She drew the pallid peer aside, and spoke with sharp rebuke.

"Just like a stuck pig!"

"Eh?" said Lord Emsworth. His mind had been wandering, as it so often did. The magic word brought it back. "Pigs? What about pigs?"

"I was saying that you were looking like a stuck pig. You might at least have asked Mr Baxter how he was."

"I could see how he was. What's he doing here?"

"I told you what he was doing here."

"But how does he come to be touring England on motor bicycles? I thought he was working for an American fellow named something or other."

"He has left Mr Jevons."

"What!"

"Yes. Mr Jevons had to return to America, and Mr Baxter did not want to leave England."

Lord Emsworth reeled. Jevons had been his sheet anchor. He had never met that genial Chicagoan, but he had always thought kindly and gratefully of him, as one does of some great doctor who has succeeded in insulating and confining a disease germ.

"You mean the chap's out of a job?" he cried aghast.

"Yes. And it could not have happened at a more fortunate time, because something has got to be done about George."

"Who's George?"

"You have a grandson of that name," explained Lady Constance with the sweet, frozen patience which she so often used when conversing with her brother. "Your heir, Bosham, if you recollect, has two sons, James and George. George, the younger, is spending his summer holidays here. You may have noticed him about. A boy of twelve with auburn hair and freckles."

"Oh, George? You mean George? Yes, I know George. He's my grandson. What about him?"

"He is completely out of hand. Only yesterday he broke another window with that air gun of his."

"He needs a mother's care?" Lord Emsworth was

vague, but he had an idea that that was the right thing to say.

"He needs a tutor's care, and I am glad to say that Mr Baxter has very kindly consented to accept the position."

"What!"

"Yes. It is all settled. His things are at the Emsworth Arms, and I am sending down for them."

Lord Emsworth sought feverishly for arguments which would quash this frightful scheme.

"But he can't be a tutor if he's galumphing all over England on a motor bicycle."

"I had not overlooked that point. He will stop galumphing over Engand on a motor bicycle."

"But——"

"It will be a wonderful solution of a problem which was becoming more difficult every day. Mr Baxter will keep George in order. He is so firm."

She turned away, and Lord Emsworth resumed his progress towards the library.

It was a black moment for the ninth Earl. His worst fears had been realised. He knew just what all this meant. On one of his rare visits to London he had once heard an extraordinarily vivid phrase which had made a deep impression upon him. He had been taking his after-luncheon coffee at the Senior Conservative Club, and some fellows in an adjoining nest of armchairs had started a political discussion, and one of them had said about something or other that, mark his words, it was the "thin end of the wedge." He recognised what was happening now as the "thin end of the wedge." From Baxter as a temporary tutor to Baxter as a permanent secretary would, he felt, be so short a step that the contemplation of it chilled him to the bone.

A shortsighted man whose pince-nez have gone astray at the very moment when vultures are gnawing at his bosom seldom guides his steps carefully. Anyone watching Lord Emsworth totter blindly across the terrace would have foreseen that he would shortly collide with something, the only point open to speculation being with what he would collide. This proved to be a small boy with ginger hair and freckles who emerged abruptly from the shrubbery carrying an air gun.

"Coo!" said the small boy. "Sorry, Grandpapa."

Lord Emsworth recovered his pince-nez and, having adjusted them on the old spot, glared balefully.

"George! Why the deuce don't you look where you're going?"

"Sorry, Grandpapa."

"You might have injured me severely."

"Sorry, Grandpapa."

"Be more careful another time."

"Okay, big boy."

"And don't call me 'big boy.' "

"Right ho, Grandpapa. I say," said George, shelving the topic, "who's the bird talking to Aunt Connie?"

He pointed—a vulgarism which a good tutor would have corrected—and Lord Emsworth, following the finger, winced as his eye rested once more upon Rupert Baxter. The secretary—already Lord Emsworth had mentally abandoned the qualifying "ex"—was gazing out over the rolling parkland, and it seemed to his lordship that his gaze was proprietorial. Rupert Baxter, flashing his spectacle over the grounds of Blandings Castle, wore—or so it appeared to Lord Emsworth—the smug air of some ruthless monarch of old surveying conquered territory.

"That is Mr Baxter," he replied.

"Looks a bit of a ——," said George critically.

The expression was new to Lord Emsworth, but he recognised it at once as the ideal description of Rupert Baxter. His heart warmed to the little fellow, and he might quite easily at this moment have given him sixpence.

"Do you think so?" he said lovingly.

"What's he doing here?"

Lord Emsworth felt a pang. It seemed brutal to dash the sunshine from the life of this admirable boy. Yet somebody had to tell him.

"He is going to be your tutor."

"Tutor?"

The word was a cry of agony forced from the depths of the boy's soul. A stunned sense that all the fundamental decencies of life were being outraged had swept over George. His voice was thick with emotion.

"Tutor?" he cried. "*Tew*-tor? Ter-YEW-tor? In the middle of the summer holidays? What have I got to have a tutor for in the middle of the summer holidays? I do call this a bit off. I mean, in the middle of the summer holidays. Why do I want a tutor? I mean to say, in the middle of . . ."

He would have spoken at greater length, for he had much to say on the subject, but at this point Lady Constance's voice, musical but imperious, interrupted his flow of speech.

"Gee-orge."

"Coo! Right in the middle——"

"Come here, George. I want you to meet Mr Baxter."

"Coo!" muttered the stricken child again and, frowning darkly, slouched across the terrace. Lord Emsworth proceeded to the library, a tender pity in his heart for this boy who by his crisp summing up of Rupert Baxter had revealed himself so kindred a spirit. He knew just how George felt. It was not always easy to get anything into Lord Emsworth's head, but he had grasped the substance of his grandson's complaint unerringly. George, about to have a tutor in the middle of the summer holidays, did not want one.

Sighing a little, Lord Emsworth reached the library and found his book.

There were not many books which at a time like this could have diverted Lord Emsworth's mind from what weighed upon it, but this one did. It was Whiffle on *The Care of the Pig* and, buried in its pages, he forgot everything. The chapter he was reading was that noble one about swill and bran mash, and it took him completely out of the world, so much so that when some twenty minutes later the door suddenly burst open it was as if a bomb had been exploded under his nose. He dropped Whiffle and sat panting. Then, although his pince-nez had followed routine by flying off, he was able by some subtle instinct to sense that the intruder was his sister Constance, and an observation beginning with the words "Good God, Connie!" had begun to leave his lips, when she cut in short.

"Clarence," she said, and it was plain that her nervous system, like his, was much shaken, "the most dreadful thing has happened!"

"Eh?"

"That man is here."

"What man?"

"That man of Jane's. The man I told you about."

"What man did you tell me about?"

Lady Constance seated herself. She would have preferred to have been able to do without tedious explanations, but long association with her brother had taught her that his was a memory that had to be refreshed. She embarked, accordingly, on these explanations, speaking wearily, like a schoolmistress to one of the duller members of her class.

"The man I told you about—certainly not less than a hundred times—was a man Jane met in the spring, when she went to stay with her friends, the Leighs, in Devonshire. She had a silly flirtation with him, which of course she insisted on magnifying into a great romance. She kept saying they were engaged. And he hasn't a penny. Nor prospects. Nor, so I gathered from Jane, a position."

Lord Emsworth interrupted at this point to put a question.

"Who," he asked courteously, "is Jane?"

Lady Constance quivered a little.

"Oh, Clarence! Your niece Jane."

"Oh, my *niece* Jane? Ah! Yes. Yes, of course. My niece Jane. Yes, of course, to be sure. My——"

"Clarence, please! For pity's sake! Do stop doddering and listen to me. For once in your life I want you to be firm."

"Be what?"

"Firm. Put your foot down."

"How do you mean?"

"About Jane. I had been hoping that she had gotten over this ridiculous infatuation—she has seemed perfectly happy and contented all this time—but no. Apparently they have been corresponding regularly, and now the man is here."

"Here?"

"Yes."

"Where?" asked Lord Emsworth, gazing in an interested manner about the room.

"He arrived last night and is staying in the village. I found out by the merest accident. I happened to ask George if he had seen Jane, because I wanted Mr Baxter to meet her, and he said he had met her going towards the lake. So I went down to the lake, and there I discovered her with a young man in a tweed coat and flannel knickerbockers. They were kissing one another in the summerhouse."

Lord Emsworth clicked his tongue.

"Ought to have been out in the sunshine," he said disapprovingly.

Lady Constance raised her foot quickly, but instead of kicking her brother on the shin merely tapped the carpet with it. Blood will tell.

"Jane was defiant. I think she must be off her head. She insisted that she was going to marry this man. And, as I say, not only has he not a penny, but he is apparently out of work."

"What sort of work does he do?"

"I gather that he has been a land agent on an estate in Devonshire."

"It all comes back to me," said Lord Emsworth. "I remember now. This must be the man Jane was speaking to me about yesterday. Of course, yes. She asked me to give him Simmons' job. Simmons is retiring next month. Good fellow," said Lord Emsworth sentimentally. "Been here for years and years. I shall be sorry to lose him. Bless my soul, it won't seem like the same place without old Simmons. Still," he said, brightening, for he was a man who could make the best of things, "no doubt this new chap will turn out all right. Jane seems to think highly of him."

Lady Constance had risen slowly from her chair. There was incredulous horror on her face.

"Clarence! You are not telling me that you have promised this man Simmons' place?"

"Eh? Yes, I have. Why not?"

"Why not! Do you realize that directly he gets it he will marry Jane?"

"Well, why shouldn't he? Very nice girl. Probably make him a good wife."

Lady Constance struggled with her feelings for a space.

"Clarence," she said, "I am going out now to find Jane. I shall tell her that you have thought it over and changed your mind."

"What about?"

"Giving this man Simmons' place."

"But I haven't."

"Yes, you have."

And so, Lord Emsworth discovered as he met her eye, he had. It often happened that way after he and Connie had talked a thing over. But he was not pleased about it.

"But, Connie, dash it all——"

"We will not discuss it any more, Clarence."

Her eye played upon him. Then she moved to the door and was gone.

Alone at last, Lord Emsworth took up his Whiffle on *The Care of the Pig* in the hope that it might, as had happened before, bring calm to the troubled spirit. It did, and he was absorbed in it when the door opened once more.

His niece Jane stood on the threshold.

Lord Emsworth's niece Jane was the third prettiest girl in Shropshire. In her general appearance she resembled a dewy rose, and it might have been thought that Lord Emsworth, who yielded to none in his appreciation of roses, would have felt his heart leap up at the sight of her.

This was not the case. His heart did leap, but not up. He was a man with certain definite views about roses. He preferred them without quite such tight lips and determined chins. And he did not like them to look at him as if he were something slimy and horrible which they had found under a flat stone.

The wretched man was now fully conscious of his position. Under the magic spell of Whiffle he had been able to thrust from his mind for awhile the thought of what Jane was going to say when she heard the bad news; but now, as she started to advance slowly into the room in that sinister, purposeful way characteristic of so many of his female relations, he realized what he was in for, and his soul shrank into itself like a salted snail.

Jane, he could not but remember, was the daughter of his sister Charlotte, and many good judges considered Lady Charlotte a tougher egg even than Lady Constance or her younger sister, Lady Julia. He still quivered at some of the things Charlotte had said to him in her time; and, eyeing Jane apprehensively, he saw no reason for supposing that she had not inherited quite a good deal of the maternal fire.

The girl came straight to the point. Her mother, Lord Emsworth recalled, had always done the same.

"I should like an explanation, Uncle Clarence."

Lord Emsworth cleared his throat unhappily.

"Explanation, my dear?"

"Explanation was what I said."

"Oh, explanation? Ah, yes. Er—what about?"

"You know jolly well what about. That agent job. Aunt Constance says you've changed your mind. Have you?"

"Er . . . Ah . . . Well . . ."

"Have you?"

"Ah . . . Well . . . Er . . ."

"Have you?"

"Well . . . Er . . . Ah . . . Yes."

"Worm!" said Jane. "Miserable, crawling, cringing, gelatine-backboned worm!"

Lord Emsworth, though he had been expecting something along these lines, quivered as if he had been harpooned.

"That," he said, attempting a dignity which he was

far from feeling, "is not a very nice thing to say. . . ."

"If you only knew the things I would like to say! I'm holding myself in. So you've changed your mind, have you? Ha! Does a sacred promise mean nothing to you, Uncle Clarence? Does a girl's whole life's happiness mean nothing to you? I never would have believed that you could have been such a blighter."

"I am not a blighter."

"Yes, you are. You're a life blighter. You're trying to blight my life. Well, you aren't going to do it. Whatever happens, I mean to marry George."

Lord Emsworth was genuinely surprised.

"Marry George? But Connie told me you were in love with this fellow you met in Devonshire."

"His name is George Abercrombie."

"Oh, ah?" said Lord Emsworth, enlightened. "Bless my soul, I thought you meant my grandson George, and it puzzled me. Because you couldn't marry him, of course. He's your brother or cousin or something. Besides, he's too young for you. What would George be? Ten? Eleven?"

He broke off. A reproachful look had hit him like a shell.

"Uncle Clarence!"

"My dear?"

"Is this a time for drivelling?"

"My dear!"

"Well, is it? Look in your heart and ask yourself. Here I am, with everybody spitting on their hands and dashing about trying to ruin my life's whole happiness, and instead of being kind and understanding and sympathetic you start talking rot about young George."

"I was only saying——"

"I heard what you were saying, and it made me sick. You really must be the most callous man that ever lived. I can't understand you, of all people, behaving like this, Uncle Clarence. I always thought you were fond of me."

"I am fond of you."

"It doesn't look like it. Flinging yourself into this foul conspiracy to wreck my life."

Lord Emsworth remembered a good one.

"I have your best interests at heart, my dear."

It did not go very well. A distinct sheet of flame shot from the girl's eyes.

"What do you mean, my best interests? The way Aunt Constance talks, and the way you are backing her up, anyone would think that George was someone in a straw hat and a scarlet cummerbund that I'd picked up on the pier at Blackpool. The Abercrombies are one of the oldest families in Devonshire. They date back to the Conquest, and they practically ran the Crusades. When your ancestors were staying at home on the plea of war work of national importance and wangling jobs at the base, the Abercrombies were out fighting the paynim."

"I was at school with a boy named Abercrombie," said Lord Emsworth musingly.

"I hope he kicked you. No, no, I don't mean that. I'm sorry. The one thing I'm trying to do is to keep this little talk free of—what's the word?"

Lord Emsworth said he did not know.

"Acrimony. I want to be calm and cool and sensible. Honestly, Uncle Clarence, you would love George.

You'll be a sap if you give him the bird without seeing him. He's the most wonderful man on earth. He got into the last eight at Wimbledon this year."

"Did he, indeed? Last eight what?"

"And there isn't anything he doesn't know about running an estate. The very first thing he said when he came into the park was that a lot of the timber wanted seeing to badly."

"Blast his impertinence," said Lord Emsworth warmly. "My timber is in excellent condition."

"Not if George says it isn't. George knows timber."

"So do I know timber."

"Not so well as George does. But never mind about that. Let's get back to this loathsome plot to ruin my life's whole happiness. Why can't you be a sport, Uncle Clarence, and stand up for me? Can't you understand what this means to me? Weren't you ever in love?"

"Certainly I was in love. Dozens of times. I'll tell you a very funny story——"

"I don't want to hear funny stories."

"No, no. Quite. Exactly."

"All I want is to hear you saying that you will give George Mr Simmons' job, so that we can get married."

"But your aunt seems to feel so strongly——"

"I know what she feels strongly. She wants me to marry that ass Roegate."

"Does she?"

"Yes, and I'm not going to. You can tell her from me that I wouldn't marry Bertie Roegate if he were the only man in the world——"

"There's a song of that name," said Lord Emsworth, interested. "They sang it during the war. No, it wasn't 'man.' It was 'girl.' If you were the only . . . How did it go? Ah, yes. 'If you were the only girl in the world and I was the only boy' . . ."

"Uncle Clarence!"

"My dear?"

"Please don't sing. You're not in the taproom of the Emsworth Arms now."

"I have never been in the taproom of the Emsworth Arms."

"Or at a smoking concert. Really, you seem to have the most extraordinary idea of the sort of attitude that's fitting when you're talking to a girl whose life's happiness everybody is sprinting about trying to ruin. First you talk rot about young George, then you start trying to tell funny stories, and now you sing comic songs."

"It wasn't a comic song."

"It was, the way you sang it. Well?"

"Eh?"

"Have you decided what you are going to do about this?"

"About what?"

The girl was silent for a moment, during which moment she looked so like her mother that Lord Emsworth shuddered.

"Uncle Clarence," she said in a low, trembling voice, "you are not going to pretend that you don't know what we've been talking about all this time? Are you or are you not going to give George that job?"

"Well——"

"Well?"

"Well——"

"We can't stay here forever, saying 'well' at one another. Are you or are you not?"

"My dear, I don't see how I can. Your aunt seems to feel so very strongly . . ."

He spoke mumblingly, avoiding his companion's eye, and he had paused, searching for words, when from the drive outside there arose a sudden babble of noise. Raised voices were proceeding from the great open spaces. He recognised his sister Constance's penetrating soprano, and mingling with it his grandson George's treble "coo." Competing with both, there came the throaty baritone of Rupert Baxter. Delighted with the opportunity of changing the subject, he hurried to the window.

"Bless my soul! What's all that?"

The battle, whatever it may have been about, had apparently rolled away in some unknown direction, for he could see nothing from the window but Rupert Baxter, who was smoking a cigarette in what seemed a rather overwrought manner. He turned back, and with infinite relief discovered that he was alone. His niece had disappeared. He took up Whiffle on *The Care of the Pig* and had just started to savour once more the perfect prose of that chapter about swill and bran mash, when the door opened. Jane was back. She stood on the theshold, eyeing her uncle coldly.

"Reading, Uncle Clarence?"

"Eh? Oh, ah, yes. I was just glancing at Whiffle on *The Care of the Pig!*"

"So you actually have the heart to read at a time like

this? Well, well! Do you ever read Western novels, Uncle Clarence?"

"Eh? Western novels? No. No, never."

"I'm sorry. I was reading one the other day, and I hoped that you might be able to explain something that puzzled me. What one cowboy said to the other cowboy."

"Oh yes?"

"This cowboy—the first cowboy—said to the other cowboy—the second cowboy—'Gol dern ye, Hank Spivis, for a sneaking, ornery, low-down, double-crossing, hornswoggling skunk.' Can you tell me what a sneaking, ornery, low-down, double-crossing, hornswoggling skunk is, Uncle Clarence?"

"I'm afraid I can't, my dear."

"I thought you might know."

"No."

"Oh."

She passed from the room, and Lord Emsworth resumed his Whiffle.

But it was not long before the volume was resting on his knee while he stared before him with a sombre gaze. He was reviewing the recent scene and wishing that he had come better out of it. He was a vague man, but not so vague as to be unaware that he might have shown up in a more heroic light.

How long he sat brooding, he could not have said. Some little time, undoubtedly, for the shadows on the terrace had, he observed as he glanced out of the window, lengthened quite a good deal since he had seen them last. He was about to rise and seek consolation from a ramble among the flowers in the garden below, when the door opened—it seemed to Lord Emsworth, who was now feeling a little morbid, that that blasted door had never stopped opening since he had come to the library to be alone—and Beach, the butler, entered.

He was carrying an air gun in one hand and in the other a silver salver with a box of ammunition on it.

Beach was a man who invested all his actions with something of the impressiveness of a high priest conducting an intricate service at some romantic altar. It is not easy to be impressive when you are carrying an air gun in one hand and a silver salver with a box of ammunition on it in the other, but Beach managed it. Many butlers in such a position would have looked like sportsmen setting out for a day with the birds, but Beach still looked like a high priest. He advanced to the table at Lord Emsworth's side, and laid his cargo upon it as if the gun and the box of ammunition had been a smoked offering, and his lordship a tribal god.

Lord Emsworth eyed his faithful servitor sourly. His manner was that of a tribal god who considers the smoked offering not up to sample.

"What the devil's all this?"

"It is an air gun, m'lord."

"I can see that, dash it! What are you bringing it here for?"

"Her ladyship instructed me to convey it to your lordship—I gathered for safekeeping, m'lord. The weapon was until recently the property of Master George."

"Why the deuce are they taking his air gun away from the poor boy?" demanded Lord Emsworth hotly.

Ever since the lad had called Rupert Baxter a —— he had been feeling a strong affection for his grandson.

"Her ladyship did not confide in me on that point, m'lord. I was merely instructed to convey the weapon to your lordship."

At this moment, Lady Constance came sailing in to throw light on the mystery.

"Ah, I see Beach has brought it to you. I want you to lock that gun up somewhere, Clarence. George is not to be allowed to have it any more."

"Why not?"

"Because he is not to be trusted with it. Do you know what happened? He shot Mr Baxter!"

"What!"

"Yes. Out on the drive just now. I noticed that the boy's manner was sullen when I introduced him to Mr Baxter and said that he was going to be his tutor. He disappeared into the shrubbery, and just now, as Mr Baxter was standing on the drive, George shot him from behind a bush."

"Good!" cried Lord Emsworth, then prudently added the word "gracious."

There was a pause. Lord Emsworth took up the gun and handled it curiously.

"Bang!" he said, pointing it at a bust of Aristotle which stood on a bracket by the bookshelves.

"Please don't wave the thing about like that, Clarence. It may be loaded."

"Not if George has just shot Baxter with it. No," said Lord Emsworth, pulling the trigger, "it's not loaded." He mused awhile. An odd, nostalgic feeling was creeping over him. Far-off memories of his hot boyhood had begun to stir within him. "Bless my soul," he said. "I haven't had one of these things in my hand since I was a child. Did you ever have one of these things, Beach?"

"Yes, m'lord, when a small lad."

"Bless my soul, I remember my sister Julia borrowing mine to shoot her governess. You remember Julia shot the governess, Connie?"

"Don't be absurd, Clarence."

"It's not absurd. She did shoot her. Fortunately women wore bustles in those days. Beach, don't you remember my sister Julia shooting the governess?"

"The incident would no doubt have occurred before my arrival at the castle, m'lord."

"That will do, Beach," said Lady Constance. "I do wish, Clarence," she continued as the door closed, "that you would not say that sort of thing in front of Beach."

"Julia did shoot the governess."

"If she did, there is no need to make your butler a confidant."

"Now, what was that governess's name? I have an idea it began with——"

"Never mind what her name was or what it began with. Tell me about Jane. I saw her coming out of the library. Had you been speaking to her?"

"Yes. Oh yes. I spoke to her."

"I hope you were firm."

"Oh, very firm. I said, 'Jane . . .' But listen, Connie, damn it, aren't we being a little hard on the girl? One doesn't want to ruin her whole life's happiness, dash it."

"I knew she would get round you. But you are not to give way an inch."

"But this fellow seems to be a most suitable fellow. One of the Abercrombies and all that. Did well in the Crusades."

"I am not going to have my niece throwing herself away on a man without a penny."

"She isn't going to marry Roegate, you know. Nothing will induce her. She said she wouldn't marry Roegate if she were the only girl in the world and he was the only boy."

"I don't care what she said. And I don't want to discuss the matter any longer. I am now going to send George in, for you to give him a good talking-to."

"I haven't time."

"You have time."

"I haven't. I'm going to look at my flowers."

"You are not. You are going to talk to George. I want you to make him see quite clearly what a wicked thing he has done. Mr Baxter was furious."

"It all comes back to me," cried Lord Emsworth. "Mapleton!"

"What *are* you talking about?"

"Her name was Mapleton. Julia's governess."

"Do stop about Julia's governess. Will you talk to George?"

"Oh, all right, all right."

"Good. I'll go and send him to you."

And presently George entered. For a boy who has just stained the escutcheon of a proud family by shooting tutors with air guns, he seemed remarkably cheerful. His manner was that of one getting together with an old crony for a cosy chat.

"Hullo, Grandpapa," he said breezily.

"Hullo, my boy," replied Lord Emsworth with equal affability.

"Aunt Connie said you wanted to see me."

"Eh? Ah! Oh! Yes." Lord Emsworth pulled himself together. "Yes, that's right. Yes, to be sure. Certainly I want to see you. What's all this, my boy, eh? Eh, what? What's all this?"

"What's all what, Grandpapa?"

"Shooting people and all that sort of thing. Shooting Baxter and all that sort of thing. Mustn't do that, you know. Can't have that. It's very wrong and—er—very dangerous to shoot at people with a dashed great gun. Don't you know that, hey? Might put their eye out, dash it."

"Oh, I couldn't have hit him in the eye, Grandpapa. His back was turned and he was bending over, tying his shoelace."

Lord Emsworth started.

"What! Did you get Baxter in the seat of the trousers?"

"Yes, Grandpapa."

"Ha, ha . . . I mean, disgraceful . . . I—er—I expect he jumped?"

"Oh yes, Grandpapa. He jumped like billy-o."

"Did he, indeed? How this reminds me of Julia's governess. Your aunt Julia once shot her governess under precisely similiar conditions. She was tying her shoelace."

"Coo! Did *she* jump?"

"She certainly did, my boy."

"Ha, ha!"

"Ha, ha!"

"Ha, ha!"

"Ha, h—— Ah . . . Er—well, just so," said Lord Emsworth, a belated doubt assailing him as to whether this was quite the tone. "Well, George, I shall of course impound this—er—instrument."

"Right ho, Grandpapa," said George, with the easy amiability of a boy conscious of having two catapults in his drawer upstairs.

"Can't have you going about the place shooting people."

"Okay, chief."

Lord Emsworth fondled the gun. That nostalgic feeling was growing.

"Do you know, young man, I used to have one of these things when I was a boy."

"Coo! Were guns invented then?"

"Yes, I had one when I was your age."

"Ever hit anything, Grandpapa?"

Lord Emsworth drew himself up a little haughtily.

"Certainly I did. I hit all sorts of things. Rats and things. I had a very accurate aim. But now I wouldn't even know how to load the dashed affair."

"This is how you load it, Grandpapa. You open it like this, and shove the slug in here, and snap it together again like that and there you are."

"Indeed? Really? I see. Yes. Yes, of course, I remember now."

"You can't kill anything much with it," said George, with a wistfulness which betrayed an aspiration to higher things. "Still, it's awfully useful for tickling up cows."

"And Baxter."

"Yes."

"Ha, ha!"

"Ha, ha!"

Once more, Lord Emsworth forced himself to concentrate on the right tone.

"We mustn't laugh about it, my boy. It's no joking matter. It's very wrong to shoot Mr Baxter."

"But he's a ——"

"He is a ——" agreed Lord Emsworth, always fair-minded. "Nevertheless . . . remember, he is your tutor."

"Well, I don't see why I've got to have a tutor right in the middle of the summer holidays. I sweat like the dickens all through the term at school," said George, his voice vibrant with self-pity, "and then plumb spang in the middle of the holidays they slosh a tutor on me. I call it a bit thick."

Lord Emsworth might have told the little fellow that thicker things than that were going on in Blandings Castle, but he refrained. He dismissed him with a kindly, sympathetic smile and resumed his fondling of the air gun.

Like so many men advancing into the sere and yellow of life, Lord Emsworth had an eccentric memory. It was not to be trusted an inch as far as the events of yesterday or the day before were concerned. Even in the small matter of assisting him to find a hat which he had laid down somewhere five minutes ago, it was nearly always useless. But by way of compensation for this it was a perfect encyclopaedia on the remote past. It rendered his boyhood an open book to him.

Lord Emsworth mused on his boyhood. Happy days, happy days. He could recall the exact uncle who had given him the weapon, so similar to this one, with which Julia had shot her governess. He could recall brave, windswept mornings when he had gone prowling through the stable yard in the hope of getting a rat—and many a fine head had he secured. Odd that the passage of time should remove the desire to go and pop at things with an air gun. . . .

Or did it?

With a curious thrill that set his pince-nez rocking gently on his nose, Lord Emsworth suddenly became aware that it did not. All that the passage of time did was to remove the desire to pop temporarily—say for forty years or so. Dormant for a short while—well, call it fifty years—that desire, he perceived, still lurked unquenched. Little by little it began to stir within him now. Slowly but surely, as he sat there fondling the gun, he was once more becoming a potential popper.

At this point, the gun suddenly went off and broke the bust of Aristotle.

It was enough. The old killer instinct had awakened. Reloading with the swift efficiency of some hunter of the woods, Lord Emsworth went to the window. He was a little uncertain as to what he intended to do when he got there, except that he had a very clear determination to loose off at something. There flitted into his mind what his grandson George had said about tickling up cows, and this served to some extent to crystallise his aims. True, cows were not plentiful on the terrace of Blandings Castle. Still, one might have wandered there. You never knew with cows.

There were no cows. Only Rupert Baxter. The ex-secretary was in the act of throwing away a cigarette.

Most men are careless in the matter of throwing away cigarettes. The world is their ash tray. But Rupert Baxter had a tidy soul. He allowed the thing to fall to the ground like any ordinary young man, it is true, but immediately he had done so his better self awakened. He stooped to pick up the object that disfigured the smooth, flagged stones, and the invitation of that beckoning trousers' seat would have been too powerful for a stronger man than Lord Emsworth to resist.

He pulled the trigger, and Rupert Baxter sprang into the air with a sharp cry. Lord Emsworth reseated himself and took up Whiffle on *The Care of the Pig*.

Everybody is interested nowadays in the psychology of the criminal. The chronicler, therefore, feels that he runs no risk of losing his grip on the reader if he pauses at this point to examine and analyse the workings of Lord Emsworth's mind after the penetration of the black act which has just been recorded.

At first, then, all that he felt as he sat turning the pages of his Whiffle was a sort of soft, warm glow, a kind of tremulous joy such as he might have experienced if he had just been receiving the thanks of the nation for some great public service.

It was not merely the fact that he had caused his late employee to skip like the high hills that induced this glow. What pleased him so particularly was that it had been such a magnificent shot. He was a sensitive man, and though in his conversation with his grandson George he had tried to wear the mask, he had not been completely able to hide his annoyance at the boy's careless assumption that in his air-gun days he had been an indifferent marksman.

"Did you ever hit anything, Grandpapa?" Boys say these things with no wish to wound, but nevertheless they pierce the armour. "Did you ever hit anything, Grandpapa?" Forsooth! He would have liked to see George stop putting finger to trigger for forty-seven years, and then, first crack out of the box, pick off a medium-sized secretary at a distance like that! In rather a bad light, too.

But after he had sat for awhile, silently glowing, his mood underwent a change. A gunman's complacency after getting his man can never remain for long an unmixed complacency. Sooner or later there creeps in the thought of Retribution. It did with Lord Emsworth. Quite suddenly, whispering in his ear, he heard the voice of Conscience say:

"What if your sister Constance learns of this?"

A moment before this voice spoke, Lord Emsworth had been smirking. He now congealed, and the smile passed from his lips like breath off a razor blade, to be succeeded by a tense look of anxiety and alarm.

Nor was this alarm unjustified. When he reflected how scathing and terrible his sister Constance could be when he committed even so venial a misdemeanour as coming down to dinner with a brass paper fastener in his shirt front instead of the more conventional stud, his imagination boggled at the thought of what she would do in a case like this. He was appalled. Whiffle on *The Care of the Pig* fell from his nerveless hand, and he sat looking like a dying duck. And Lady Constance, who now entered, noted the expression and was curious as to its cause.

"What is the matter, Clarence?"

"Matter?"

"Why are you looking like a dying duck?"

"I am not looking like a dying duck," retorted Lord Emsworth with what spirit he could muster.

"Well," said Lady Constance, waiving the point, "have you spoken to George?"

"Certainly. Yes, of course I've spoken to George. He was in here just now and I—er—spoke to him."

"What did you say?"

"I said"—Lord Emsworth wanted to make this very clear—"I said that I wouldn't even know how to load one of those things."

"Didn't you give him a good talking-to?"

"Of course I did. A very good talking-to. I said, 'Er—George, you know how to load those things and I don't, but that's no reason why you should go about shooting Baxter.' "

"Was that all you said?"

"No. That was just how I began. I——"

Lord Emsworth paused. He could not have finished the sentence if large rewards had been offered to him to do so. For, as he spoke, Rupert Baxter appeared in the doorway, and he shrank back in his chair like some Big Shot cornered by G-men.

The secretary came forward limping slightly. His eyes behind their spectacles were wild and his manner emotional. Lady Constance gazed at him wonderingly.

"Is something the matter, Mr Baxter?"

"Matter?" Rupert Baxter's voice was taut and he quivered in every limb. He had lost his customary suavity and was plainly in no frame of mind to mince his words. "Matter? Do you know what has happened? That infernal boy has shot me *again!*"

"What!"

"Only a few minutes ago. Out on the terrace."

Lord Emsworth shook off his palsy.

"I expect you imagined it," he said.

"Imagined it!" Rupert Baxter shook from spectacles to shoes. "I tell you I was on the terrace, stooping to pick up my cigarette, when something hit me on the . . . something hit me."

"Probably a wasp," said Lord Emsworth. "They are very plentiful this year. I wonder," he said chattily, "if either of you are aware that wasps serve a very useful purpose. They keep down the leatherjackets, which, as you know, inflict serious injury upon——"

Lady Constance's concern became mixed with perplexity.

"But it could not have been George, Mr Baxter. The moment you told me of what he had done, I confiscated his air gun. Look, there it is on the table now."

"Right there on the table," said Lord Emsworth, pointing helpfully. "If you come over here, you can see it clearly. Must have been a wasp."

"You have not left the room, Clarence?"

"No. Been here all the time."

"Then it would have been impossible for George to have shot you, Mr Baxter."

"Quite," said Lord Emsworth. "A wasp, undoubtedly. Unless, as I say, you imagined the whole thing."

The secretary stiffened.

"I am not subject to hallucinations, Lord Emsworth."

"But you are, my dear fellow. I expect it comes from exerting your brain too much. You're always getting them."

"Clarence!"

"Well, he is. You know that as well as I do. Look at that time he went grubbing about in a lot of flowerpots because he thought you had put your necklace there."

"I did not——"

"You did, my dear fellow. I daresay you've forgotten it, but you did. And then, for some reason best known to yourself, you threw the flowerpots at me through my bedroom window."

Baxter turned to Lady Constance, flushing darkly. The episode to which his former employer had alluded was one of which he never cared to be reminded.

"Lord Emsworth is referring to the occasion when your diamond necklace was stolen, Lady Constance. I was led to believe that the thief had hidden it in a flowerpot."

"Of course, Mr Baxter."

"Well, have it your own way," said Lord Emsworth agreeably. "But bless my soul, I shall never forget waking up and finding all those flowerpots pouring in through the window, and then looking out and seeing Baxter on the lawn in lemon-coloured pajamas with a wild glare in his——"

"Clarence!"

"Oh, all right. I merely mentioned it. Hallucinations —he gets them all the time," he said stoutly, though in an undertone.

Lady Constance was cooing to the secretary like a mother to her child.

"It really is impossible that George should have done this, Mr Baxter. The gun has never left this——"

She broke off. Her handsome face seemed to turn suddenly to stone. When she spoke again the coo had gone out of her voice and it had become metallic.

"Clarence!"

"My dear?"

Lady Constance drew in her breath sharply.

"Mr Baxter, I wonder if you would mind leaving us for a moment. I wish to speak to Lord Emsworth."

The closing of the door was followed by a silence, followed in its turn by an odd, whining noise like gas escaping from a pipe. It was Lord Emsworth trying to hum carelessly.

"Clarence!"

"Yes? Yes, my dear?"

The stoniness of Lady Constance's expression had become more marked with each succeeding moment. What had caused it in the first place was the recollection, coming to her like a flash, that when she had entered this room she had found her brother looking like a dying duck. Honest men, she felt, do not look like dying ducks. The only man whom an impartial observer could possibly mistake for one of these birds *in extremis* is the man with crime upon his soul.

"Clarence, was it you who shot Mr Baxter?"

Fortunately there had been that in her manner which led Lord Emsworth to expect the question. He was ready for it.

"Me? Who, me? Shoot Baxter? What the deuce would I want to shoot Baxter for?"

"We can go into your motives later. What I am asking you now is—did you?"

"Of course I didn't."

"The gun has not left the room."

"Shoot Baxter, indeed! Never heard anything so dashed absurd in my life."

"And you have been here all the time."

"Well, what of it? Suppose I have? Suppose I had wanted to shoot Baxter? Suppose every fibre in my being had egged me on, dash it, to shoot the feller? How could I have done it, not even knowing how to load the contrivance?"

"You used to know how to load an air gun."

"I used to know a lot of things."

"It's quite easy to load an air gun. I could do it myself."

"Well, I didn't."

"Then how do you account for the fact that Mr Baxter was shot by an air gun which had never left the room you were in?"

Lord Emsworth raised pleading hands to heaven.

"How do you know he was shot with this air gun? God bless my soul, the way women jump to conclusions is enough to . . . How do you know there wasn't another air gun? How do you know the place isn't bristling with air guns? How do you know Beach hasn't an air gun? Or anybody?"

"I scarcely imagine that Beach would shoot Mr Baxter."

"How do you know he wouldn't? He used to have an air gun when he was a small lad. He said so. I'd watch the man closely."

"Please don't be ridiculous, Clarence."

"I'm not being half as ridiculous as you are. Saying I shoot people with air guns. Why should I shoot people with air guns? And how do you suppose I could have potted Baxter at that distance?"

"What distance?"

"He was standing on the terrace, wasn't he? He specifically stated that he was standing on the terrace. And I was up here. It would take a most expert marksman to pot the fellow at a distance like that. Who do you think I am? One of those chaps who shoot apples off their sons' heads?"

The reasoning was undeniably specious. It shook Lady Constance. She frowned undecidedly.

"Well, it's very strange that Mr Baxter should be so convinced that he was shot."

"Nothing strange about it at all. There wouldn't be anything strange if Baxter was convinced that he was a turnip and had been bitten by a white rabbit with pink eyes. You know perfectly well, though you won't admit it, that the fellow's a raving lunatic."

"Clarence!"

"It's no good saying 'Clarence.' The fellow's potty to the core, and always has been. Haven't I seen him on the lawn at five o'clock in the morning in lemon-coloured pajamas, throwing flowerpots in at my window? Pooh! Obviously, the whole thing is the outcome of the man's diseased imagination. Shot, indeed! Never heard such nonsense. And now," said Lord Emsworth, rising firmly, "I'm going out to have a look at my roses. I came to this room to enjoy a little quiet reading and meditation, and ever since I got here there's been a constant stream of people in and out, telling me they're going to marry men named Abercrombie and saying they've been shot and saying I shot them and so on and so forth. . . . Bless my soul, one might as well try to read and meditate in the middle of Piccadilly Circus. Tchah!" said Lord Emsworth, who had now got near enough to the door to feel safe in uttering this unpleasant exclamation. "Tchah!" he said, and adding "Pah!" for good measure made a quick exit.

But even now his troubled spirit was not to know peace. To reach the great outdoors at Blandings Castle, if you start from the library and come down the main staircase, you have to pass through the hall. To the left of this hall there is a small writing room. And outside this writing room Lord Emsworth's niece Jane was standing.

"Yoo-hoo," she cried. "Uncle Clarence."

Lord Emsworth was in no mood for yoo-hooing nieces. George Abercrombie might enjoy chatting with this girl. So might Herbert, Lord Roegate. But he wanted solitude. In the course of the afternoon he had had so much female society thrust upon him, that if Helen of Troy had appeared in the doorway of the writing room and yoo-hooed at him, he would merely have accelerated his pace.

He accelerated it now.

"Can't stop, my dear, can't stop."

"Oh yes you can, old Sure-Shot," said Jane, and Lord Emsworth found that he could. He stopped so abruptly that he nearly dislocated his spine. His jaw had fallen and his pince-nez were dancing on their string like leaves in the wind.

"Two-Gun Thomas—the Marksman of the Prairie—he never misses. Kindly step this way, Uncle Clarence," said Jane. "I would like a word with you."

Lord Emsworth stepped that way. He followed the girl into the writing room and closed the door carefully behind him.

"You—you didn't see me?" he quavered.

"I certainly did see you," said Jane. "I was an interested eyewitness of the whole thing from start to finish."

Lord Emsworth tottered to a chair and sank into it, staring glassily at his niece. Any Chicago businessman of the modern school would have understood what he was feeling and would have sympathised with him.

The thing that poisons life for gunmen, and sometimes makes them wonder moodily if it is worth while going on, is this tendency of the outside public to butt in at inconvenient moments. Whenever you settle some business dispute with a commercial competitor by means of your submachine gun, it always turns out that there was some officious witness passing at the time, and there you are, with a new problem confronting you.

And Lord Emsworth was in a worse case than his spiritual brother of Chicago would have been, for the latter could always have solved his perplexities by rubbing out the witness. To him this melancholy pleasure was denied. A prominent Shropshire landowner, with a position to keep up in the county, cannot rub out his nieces. All he can do, when they reveal that they have seen him wallowing in crime, is to stare glassily at them.

"I had a front seat for the entire performance," proceeded Jane. "When I left you, I went into the shrubbery to cry my eyes out because of your frightful cruelty and inhumanity. And while I was crying my eyes out, I suddenly saw you creep to the window of the library, with a hideous look of low cunning on your face, and young George's air gun in your hand. And I was just wondering if I couldn't find a stone and bung it at you, because it seemed to me that something along those lines was what you had been asking for from the start, when you raised the gun and I saw that you were taking aim. The next moment there was a shot, a cry, and Baxter weltering in his blood on the terrace. And as I stood there, a thought floated into my mind. It was: What will Aunt Constance have to say about this when I tell her?"

Lord Emsworth emitted a low gurgling sound, like the death rattle of that dying duck to which his sister had compared him.

"You—you aren't going to tell her?"

"Why not?"

An aguelike convulsion shook Lord Emsworth.

"I implore you not to tell her, my dear. You know what she's like. I should never hear the end of it."

"She would give you the devil, you think?"

"I do."

"So do I. And you thoroughly deserve it."

"My dear!"

"Well, don't you? Look at the way you've been behaving. Working like a beaver to ruin my life's happiness."

"I don't want to ruin your life's happiness."

"You don't? Then sit down at this desk and dash off a short letter to George, giving him that job."

"But——"

"What did you say?"

"I only said 'But——' "

"Don't say it again. What I want from you, Uncle Clarence, is prompt and cheerful service. Are you ready? 'Dear Mr Abercrombie . . .' "

"I don't know how to spell it," said Lord Emsworth, with the air of a man who has found a way out satisfactory to all parties.

"I'll attend to the spelling. A-b, ab; e-r,er; c-r-o-m, crom; b-i-e, bie. The whole constituting the word 'Abercrombie', which is the name of the man I love. Got it?"

"Yes," said Lord Emsworth sepulchrally, "I've got it."

"Then carry on. 'Dear Mr Abercrombie. Pursuant'—One p, two u's—spread 'em about a bit—an r, an s, and an ant—'Pursuant on our recent conversation——' "

"But I've never spoken to the man in my life."

"It doesn't matter. It's just a form. 'Pursuant on our recent conversation, I have much pleasure in offering you the post of land agent at Blandings Castle, and shall be glad if you will take up your duties immediately. Yours faithfully, Emsworth.' E-m-s-w-o-r-t-h."

Jane took the letter, pressed it lovingly on the blotting pad and placed it in the recesses of her costume.

"Fine," she said. "That's that. Thanks most awfully, Uncle Clarence. This has squared you nicely for your recent foul behaviour in trying to ruin my life's happiness. You made a rocky start, but you've come through magnificently at the finish."

Kissing him affectionately, she passed from the room, and Lord Emsworth, slumped in his chair, tried not to look at the vision of his sister Constance which was rising before his eyes. What Connie was going to say when she learned that in defiance of her direct commands he had given this young man . . .

He mused on Lady Constance, and wondered if there were any other men in the world so sister pecked as he. It was weak of him, he knew, to curl up into an apologetic ball when assailed by a mere sister. Most men reserved such craven conduct for their wives. But it had always been so, right back to those boyhood days which he remembered so well. And too late to alter it now, he supposed.

The only consolation he was able to enjoy in this dark hour was the reflection that, though things were bad, they were unquestionably less bad than they might have been. At the least, his fearful secret was safe. That rash moment of recovered boyhood would never now be brought up against him. Connie would never know whose hand it was that had pulled the fatal trigger. She might suspect, but she could never know. Nor could Baxter ever know. Baxter would grow into an old white-haired, spectacled pantaloon, and always this thing would remain an insoluble mystery to him.

Dashed lucky, felt Lord Emsworth, that the fellow

had not been listening at the door during the recent conversation. . . .

It was at this moment that a sound behind him caused him to turn and, having turned, to spring from his chair with a convulsive leap that nearly injured him internally. Over the sill of the open window, like those of a corpse emerging from the tomb to confront its murderer, the head and shoulders of Rupert Baxter were slowly rising. The evening sun fell upon his spectacles, and they seemed to Lord Emsworth to gleam like the eyes of a dragon.

Rupert Baxter had not been listening at the door. There had been no necessity for him to do so. Immediately outside the writing-room window at Blandings Castle there stands a rustic garden seat, and on this he had been sitting from beginning to end of the interview which has just been recorded. If he had been actually in the room, he might have heard a little better, but not much.

When two men stand face to face, one of whom has recently shot the other with an air gun, and the second of whom has just discovered who it was that did it, it is rarely that conversation flows briskly from the start. One senses a certain awkwardness—what the French call *gêne*. In the first half minute of this encounter the only thing that happened in a vocal way was that Lord Emsworth cleared his throat, immediately afterwards becoming silent again. And it is possible that his silence might have prolonged itself for some considerable time had not Baxter made a movement as if about to withdraw. All this while he had been staring at his former employer, his face an open book in which it was easy for the least discerning eye to read a number of disconcerting emotions. He now took a step backwards, and Lord Emsworth's aphasia left him.

"Baxter!"

There was urgent appeal in the ninth Earl's voice. It was not often that he wanted Rupert Baxter to stop and talk to him, but he was most earnestly desirous of detaining him now. He wished to soothe, to apologise, to explain. He was even prepared, should it be necessary, to offer the man his old post of private secretary as the price of his silence.

"Baxter! My dear fellow!"

A high tenor voice, raised almost to A in alto by agony of soul, has a compelling quality which it is difficult even for a man in Rupert Baxter's mental condition to resist. Rupert Baxter had not intended to halt his backward movement, but he did so, and Lord Emsworth, reaching the window and thrusting his head out, was relieved to see that he was still within range of the honeyed word.

"Er—Baxter," he said, "could you spare me a moment?"

The secretary's spectacles flashed coldly.

"You wish to speak to me, Lord Emsworth?"

"That's exactly it," assented his lordship, as if he thought it a very happy way of putting the thing. "Yes, I wish to speak to you." He paused, and cleared his throat again. "Tell me, Baxter—tell me, my dear fellow—were you—er—were you sitting on that seat just now?"

"I was."

"Did you by any chance overhear my niece and myself talking?"

"I did."

"Then I expect—I fancy—perhaps—possibly—no doubt you were surprised at what you heard?"

"I was astounded," said Rupert Baxter, who was not going to be fobbed off with any weak verbs at a moment like this.

Lord Emsworth cleared his throat for the third time.

"I want to tell you all about that," he said.

"Oh?" said Rupert Baxter.

"Yes. I—ah—welcome this opportunity of telling you all about it," said Lord Emsworth, though with less pleasure in his voice than might have been expected from a man welcoming an opportunity of telling somebody all about something. "I fancy that my niece's remarks may—er—possibly have misled you."

"Not at all."

"They may have put you on the wrong track."

"On the contrary."

"But, if I remember correctly, she gave the impression—by what she said—my niece gave the impression by what she said—anybody overhearing what my niece said would have received the impression that I took deliberate aim at you with that gun."

"Precisely."

"She was quite mistaken," said Lord Emsworth warmly. "She had got hold of the wrong end of the stick completely. Girls say such dashed silly things . . . cause a lot of trouble . . . upset people. They ought to be more careful. What actually happened, my dear fellow, was that I was glancing out of the library window . . . with the gun in my hand . . . and without knowing it I must have placed my finger on the trigger, for suddenly, without the slightest warning . . . you could have knocked me down with a feather . . . the dashed thing went off. By accident."

"Indeed?"

"Purely by accident. I should not like you to think that I was aiming at you."

"Indeed?"

"And I should not like you to tell—er—anybody about the unfortunate occurrence in a way that would give her—I mean them—the impression that I aimed at you."

"Indeed?"

Lord Emsworth could not persuade himself that his companion's manner was encouraging. He had a feeling that he was not making headway.

"That's how it was," he said after a pause.

"I see."

"Pure accident. Nobody more surprised than myself."

"I see."

So did Lord Emsworth. He saw that the time had come to play his last card. It was no moment for shrinking back and counting the cost. He must proceed to that last fearful extremity which he had contemplated.

"Tell me, Baxter," he said, "are you doing anything just now, Baxter?"

"Yes," replied the other with no trace of hesitation. "I am going to look for Lady Constance."

A convulsive gulp prevented Lord Emsworth from speaking for an instant.

"I mean," he quavered, when the spasm had spent itself, "I gathered from my sister that you were at liberty at the moment—that you had left that fellow what's his name—the American fellow—and I was hoping, my dear Baxter," said Lord Emsworth, speaking thickly, as if the words choked him, "that I might be able to persuade you to take up—to resume—in fact, I was going to ask you if you would care to become my secretary again."

He paused and, reaching for his handkerchief, feebly mopped his brow. The dreadful speech was out, and its emergence had left him feeling spent and weak.

"You were?" cried Rupert Baxter.

"I was," said Lord Emsworth hollowly.

A great change for the better had come over Rupert Baxter. It was as if those words had been a magic formula, filling with sweetness and light one who until that moment had been more like a spectacled thundercloud than anything human. He ceased to lower darkly. His air of being on the point of shooting out forked lightning left him. He even went so far as to smile. And if the smile was a smile that made Lord Emsworth feel as if his vital organs were being churned up with an egg whip, that was not his fault. He was trying to smile sunnily.

"Thank you," he said. "I shall be delighted."

Lord Emsworth did not speak.

"I was always happy at the castle."

Lord Emsworth did not speak.

"Thank you very much," said Rupert Baxter. "What a beautiful evening."

He passed from view, and Lord Emsworth examined the evening. As Baxter had said, it was beautiful, but it did not bring the balm which beautiful evenings usually brought to him. A blight seemed to hang over it. The setting sun shone bravely on the formal garden over which he looked, but it was the lengthening shadows rather than the sunshine that impressed themselves upon Lord Emsworth.

His heart was bowed down with weight of woe. Oh, says the poet, what a tangled web we weave when first we practise to deceive, and it was precisely the same, Lord Emsworth realised, when first we practise to shoot air guns. Just one careless, offhand pop at a bending Baxter, and what a harvest, what a retribution! As a result of that single, idle shot he had been compelled to augment his personal staff with a land agent, which would infuriate his sister Constance, and a private secretary, which would make his life once again the inferno it had been in the old, bad Baxter days. He could scarcely have got himself into more trouble if he had gone blazing away with a machine gun.

It was with a slow and distrait shuffle that he eventually took himself from the writing room and proceeded with his interrupted plan on going and sniffing at his roses. And so preoccupied was his mood that Beach, his faithful butler, who came to him after he had been sniffing at them for perhaps half an hour, was obliged to speak twice before he could induce him to remove his nose from a Gloire de Dijon.

"Eh?"

"A note for you, m'lord."

"A note? Who from?"

"Mr Baxter, m'lord."

If Lord Emsworth had been less careworn, he might have noticed that the butler's voice had not its customary fruity ring. It had a dullness, a lack of tone. It was the voice of a butler who has lost the bluebird. But, being in the depths and so in no frame of mind to analyse the voice production of butlers, he merely took the envelope from its salver and opened it listlessly, wondering what Baxter was sending him notes about.

The communication was so brief that he was enabled to discover this at a glance.

LORD EMSWORTH,

After what has occurred, I must reconsider my decision to accept the post of secretary which you offered me.

I am leaving the castle immediately.

R. BAXTER.

Simply that, and nothing more.

Lord Emsworth stared at the thing. It is not enough to say that he was bewildered. He was nonplussed. If the Gloire de Dijon at which he had recently been sniffing had snapped at his nose and bitten the tip off, he could scarcely have been more taken aback. He could make nothing of this.

As in a dream, he became aware that Beach was speaking.

"Eh?"

"My month's notice, m'lord."

"Your what?"

"My month's notice, m'lord."

"What about it?"

"I was saying that I wish to give my month's notice, m'lord."

A weak irritation at all this chattering came upon Lord Emsworth. Here he was, trying to grapple with this frightful thing which had come upon him, and Beach would insist on weakening his concentration by babbling.

"Yes, yes, yes," he said. "I see. All right. Yes, yes."

"Very good, m'lord."

Left alone, Lord Emsworth faced the facts. He understood now what had happened. The note was no longer mystic. What it meant was that for some reason that trump card of his had proved useless. He had thought to stop Baxter's mouth with bribes, and he had failed. The man had seemed to accept the olive branch, but later there must have come some sharp revulsion of feeling, causing him to change his mind. No doubt a sudden twinge of pain in the wounded area had brought the memory of his wrongs flooding back upon him, so that he found himself preferring vengeance to material prosperity. And now he was going to blow the gaff. Even now the whole facts in the case might have been placed before Lady Constance. And even now, Lord Emsworth felt with a shiver, Connie might be looking for him.

The sight of a female form coming through the rose-bushes brought him the sharpest shudder of the day, and for an instant he stood pointing like a dog. But it was not his sister Constance. It was his niece Jane.

Jane was in excellent spirits.

"Hullo, Uncle Clarence," she said. "Having a look at the roses? I've sent that letter off to George, Uncle Clarence. I got the boy who cleans the knives and boots to take it. Nice chap. His name is Cyril."

"Jane," said Lord Emsworth, " a terrible, a ghastly thing has happened. Baxter was outside the window of the writing room when we were talking, and he heard everything."

"Golly! He didn't!"

"He did. Every word. And he means to tell your aunt."

"How do you know?"

"Read this."

Jane took the note.

"H'm," she said, having scanned it. "Well, it looks to me, Uncle Clarence, as if there was only one thing for you to do. You must assert yourself."

"Assert myself?"

"You know what I mean. Get tough. When Aunt Constance comes trying to bully you, stick your elbows out and put your head on one side and talk back at her out of the corner of your mouth."

"But what shall I say?"

"Good heavens, there are a hundred things you can say. 'Oh yeah?' 'Is zat so?' 'Hey, just a minute,' 'Listen, baby,' 'Scram' . . ."

" 'Scram'?"

"It means 'Get the hell outa here.' "

"But I can't tell Connie to get the hell outa here."

"Why not? Aren't you master in your own house?"

"No," said Lord Emsworth.

Jane reflected.

"Then I'll tell you what to do. Deny the whole thing."

"Could I, do you think?"

"Of course you could. And then Aunt Constance will ask me, and I'll deny the whole thing. Categorically. We'll both deny it categorically. She'll have to believe us. We'll be two to one. Don't you worry, Uncle Clarence. Everything 'll be all right."

She spoke with the easy optimism of youth, and when she passed on a few moments later seemed to be feeling that she was leaving an uncle with his mind at rest. Lord Emsworth could hear her singing a gay song.

He felt no disposition to join in the chorus. He could not bring himself to share her sunny outlook. He looked into the future and still found it dark.

There was only one way of taking his mind off this dark future, only one means of achieving a momentary forgetfulness of what lay in store. Five minutes later Lord Emsworth was in the library, reading Whiffle on *The Care of the Pig*.

But there is a point beyond which the magic of the noblest writer ceases to function. Whiffle was good—no question about that—but he was not good enough to purge from the mind such a load of care as was weighing upon Lord Emsworth's. To expect him to do so was trying him too high. It was like asking Whiffle to divert and entertain a man stretched upon the rack.

Lord Emsworth was already beginning to find a difficulty in concentrating on that perfect prose, when any chance he might have had of doing so was removed. Lady Constance appeared in the doorway.

"Oh, here you are, Clarence," said Lady Constance.

"Yes," said Lord Emsworth in a low, strained voice.

A close observer would have noted about Lady Constance's manner, as she came into the room, something a little nervous and apprehensive, something almost diffident, but to Lord Emsworth, who was not a close observer, she seemed pretty much as usual, and he remained gazing at her like a man confronted with a ticking bomb. A dazed sensation had come upon him. It was in an almost detached way that he found himself speculating as to which of his crimes was about to be brought up for discussion. Had she met Jane and learned of the fatal letter? Or had she come straight from an interview with Rupert Baxter in which that injured man had told all?

He was so certain that it must be one of these two topics that she had come to broach that her manner as she opened the conversation filled him with amazement. Not only did it lack ferocity, it was absolutely chummy. It was as if a lion had come into the library and started bleating like a lamb.

"All alone, Clarence?"

Lord Emsworth hitched up his lower jaw and said, yes, he was all alone.

"What are you doing? Reading?"

Lord Emsworth said, yes, he was reading.

"I'm not disturbing you, am I?"

Lord Emsworth, though astonishment nearly robbed him of speech, contrived to say that she was not disturbing him. Lady Constance walked to the window and looked out.

"What a lovely evening."

"Yes."

"I wonder you aren't out of doors."

"I was out of doors. I came in."

"Yes. I saw you in the rose garden." Lady Constance traced a pattern on the window sill with her finger. "You were speaking to Beach."

"Yes."

"Yes, I saw Beach come up and speak to you."

There was a pause. Lord Emsworth was about to break it by asking his visitor if she felt quite well, when Lady Constance spoke again. That apprehension in her manner, that nervousness, was now well marked. She traced another pattern on the window sill.

"Was it important?"

"Was what important?"

"I mean, did he want anything?"

"Who?"

"Beach."

"Beach?"

"Yes. I was wondering what he wanted to see you about."

Quite suddenly there flashed upon Lord Emsworth the recollection that Beach had done more than merely hand him Baxter's note. With it—dash it, yes, it all came back to him—with it he had given his month's notice. And it just showed, Lord Emsworth felt, what a morass of trouble he was engulfed in that the fact of this superb butler handing in his resignation had made almost no impression upon him. If such a thing had happened only as recently as yesterday, it would have constituted a major crisis. He would have felt that the foundations of his world were rocking. And he had scarcely listened. "Yes, yes," he had said, if he remembered correctly. "Yes, yes, yes. All right." Or words to that effect.

Bending his mind now on the disaster, Lord Emsworth sat stunned. He was appalled. Almost since the beginning of time, this superbutler had been at the castle, and now he was about to melt away like snow in the sunshine—or as much like snow in the sunshine as was within the scope of a man who weighed sixteen stone in the buff. It was frightful. The thing was a nightmare. He couldn't get on without Beach. Life without Beach would be insupportable.

He gave tongue, his voice sharp and anguished.

"Connie! Do you know what's happened? Beach has given notice!"

"What!"

"Yes! His month's notice. He's given it. Beach has. And not a word of explanation. No reason. No . . ."

Lord Emsworth broke off. His face suddenly hardened. What seemed the only possible solution of the mystery had struck him. Connie was at the bottom of this. Connie must have been coming the grande dame on the butler, wounding his sensibilities.

Yes, that must be it. It was just the sort of thing she would do. If he had caught her being the Old English Aristocrat once, he had caught her a hundred times. That way of hers of pursing the lips and raising the eyebrows and generally doing the daughter-of-a-hundred-earls stuff. Naturally no butler would stand it.

"Connie," he cried, adjusting his pince-nez and staring

keenly and accusingly, "what have you been doing to Beach?"

Something that was almost a sob burst from Lady Contance's lips. Her lovely complexion had paled, and in some odd way she seemed to have shrunk.

"I shot him," she whispered.

Lord Emsworth was a little hard of hearing.

"You did what?"

"I shot him."

"Shot him?"

"Yes."

"You mean, *shot* him?"

"Yes, yes, yes! I shot him with George's air gun."

A whistling sigh escaped Lord Emsworth. He leaned back in his chair, and the library seemed to be dancing old country dances before his eyes. To say that he felt weak with relief would be to understate the effect of this extraordinary communication. His relief was so intense that he felt absolutely boneless. Not once but many times during the past quarter of an hour he had said to himself that only a miracle could save him from the consequences of his sins, and now the miracle had happened. No one was more alive than he to the fact that women are abundantly possessed of crust, but after this surely even Connie could not have the crust to reproach him for what he had done.

"Shot him?" he said, recovering speech.

A fleeting touch of the old imperiousness returned to Lady Constance.

"Do stop saying 'shot him?' Clarence! Isn't it bad enough to have done a perfectly mad thing, without having to listen to you talking like a parrot? Oh dear! Oh dear!"

"But what did you do it for?"

"I don't know. I tell you I don't know. Something seemed suddenly to come over me. It was as if I had been bewitched. After you went out, I thought I would take the gun to Beach——"

"Why?"

"I . . . I . . . Well, I thought it would be safer with him than lying about in the library. So I took it down to his pantry. And all the way there I kept remembering what a wonderful shot I had been as a child——"

"What?" Lord Emsworth could not let this pass. "What do you mean, you were a wonderful shot as a child? You've never shot in your life."

"I have. Clarence, you were talking about Julia shooting Miss Mapleton. It wasn't Julia—it was I. She had made me stay in and do my rivers of Europe over again, so I shot her. I was a splendid shot in those days."

"I bet you weren't as good as me," said Lord Emsworth, piqued. "I used to shoot rats."

"So used I to shoot rats."

"How many rats did you ever shoot?"

"Oh, Clarence, Clarence! Never mind about the rats."

"No," said Lord Emsworth, called to order. "No, dash it. Never mind about the rats. Tell me about this Beach business."

"Well, when I got to the pantry it was empty, and

I saw Beach outside by the laurel bush, reading in a deck chair——"

"How far away?"

"I don't know. What does it matter? About six feet, I suppose."

"Six feet? Ha!"

"And I shot him. I couldn't resist it. It was like some horrible obsession. There was a sort of hideous picture in my mind of how he would jump. So I shot him."

"How do you know you did? I expect you missed him."

"No. Because he sprang up. And then he saw me at the window and came in, and I said, 'Oh, Beach, I want you to take this air gun and keep it,' and he said, 'Very good, m'lady.' "

"He didn't say anything about your shooting him?"

"No. And I have been hoping and hoping that he had not realized what had happened. I have been in an agony of suspense. But now you tell me that he has given his notice, so he must have done. Clarence," cried Lady Constance, clasping her hands like a persecuted heroine, "you see the awful position, don't you? If he leaves us, he will spread the story all over the county and people will think I'm mad. I shall never be able to live it down. You must persuade him to withdraw his notice. Offer him double wages. Offer him anything. He must not be allowed to leave. If he does, I shall never . . . Sh!"

"What do you mean, sh . . . Oh, ah," said Lord Emsworth, at last observing that the door was opening.

It was his niece Jane who entered.

"Oh, hullo, Aunt Constance," she said. "I was wondering if you were in here. Mr Baxter's looking for you."

Lady Constance was distrait.

"Mr Baxter?"

"Yes. I heard him asking Beach where you were. I think he wants to see you about something," said Jane.

She directed Lord Emsworth a swift glance, accompanied by a fleeting wink. "Remember!" said the glance. "Categorically!" said the wink.

Footsteps sounded outside. Rupert Baxter strode into the room.

At an earlier point in this chronicle, we have compared the aspect of Rupert Baxter, when burning with resentment, to a thundercloud, and it is possible that the reader may have formed a mental picture of just an ordinary thundercloud, the kind that rumbles a bit but does not really amount to anything very much. It was not this kind of cloud that the secretary resembled now, but one of those which bursts over cities in the tropics, inundating countrysides while thousands flee. He moved darkly towards Lady Constance, his hand outstretched. Lord Emsworth he ignored.

"I have come to say good-bye, Lady Constance," he said.

There were not many statements that could have roused Lady Constance from her preoccupation, but this one did. She ceased to be the sportswoman brooding on memories of shikari, and stared aghast.

"Good-bye?"

"Good-bye."

"But, Mr Baxter, you are not leaving us?"

"Precisely."

For the first time, Rupert Baxter deigned to recognise that the ninth Earl was present.

"I am not prepared," he said bitterly, "to remain in a house where my chief duty appears to be to act as a target for Lord Emsworth and his air gun."

"What!"

"Exactly."

In the silence which followed these words, Jane once more gave her uncle that glance of encouragement and stimulation—that glance which said "Be firm!" To her astonishment, she perceived that it was not needed. Lord Emsworth was firm already. His face was calm, his eye steady, and his pince-nez were not even quivering.

"The fellow's potty," said Lord Emsworth in a clear, resonant voice. "Absolutely potty. Always told you he was. Target for my air gun? Pooh! Pah! What's he talking about?"

Rupert Baxter quivered. His spectacles flashed fire.

"Do you deny that you shot me, Lord Emsworth?"

"Certainly I do."

"Perhaps you will deny admitting to this lady here in the writing room that you shot me?"

"Certainly I do."

"Did you tell me that you had shot Mr Baxter, Uncle Clarence?" said Jane. "I didn't hear you."

"Of course I didn't."

"I thought you hadn't. I should have remembered it."

Rupert Baxter's hands shot ceilingwards, as if he were calling upon heaven to see justice done.

"You admitted it to me personally. You begged me not to tell anyone. You tried to put matters right by engaging me as your secretary, and I accepted the position. At that time I was perfectly willing to forget the entire affair. But when, not half an hour later . . ."

Lord Emsworth raised his eyebrows. Jane raised hers.

"How very extraordinary," said Jane.

"Most," said Lord Emsworth.

He removed his pince-nez and began to polish them, speaking soothingly the while. But his manner, though soothing, was very resolute.

"Baxter, my dear fellow," he said, "there's only one explanation for all this. It's just what I was telling you. You've been having these hallucinations of yours again. I never said a word to you about shooting you. I never said a word to my niece about shooting you. Why should I, when I hadn't? And, as for what you say about engaging you as my secretary, the absurdity of the thing is manifest on the very face of it. There is nothing on earth that would induce me to have you as my secretary. I don't want to hurt your feelings, but I'd rather be dead in a ditch. Now, listen, my dear Baxter, I'll tell you what to do. You just jump on that motor bicycle of yours and go on touring England where you left off. And soon you will find that the fresh air will do wonders for that pottiness of yours. In a day or two you won't know . . ."

Rupert Baxter turned and stalked from the room.

"Mr Baxter!" cried Lady Constance.

Her intention of going after the fellow and pleading with him to continue inflicting his beastly presence on the quiet home life of Blandings Castle was so plain that Lord Emsworth did not hesitate.

"Connie!"

"But, Clarence!"

"Constance, you will remain where you are. You will not stir a step."

"But, Clarence!"

"Not a dashed step. You hear me? Let him scram!"

Lady Constance halted, irresolute. Then suddenly she met the full force of the pince-nez and it was as if she—like Rupert Baxter—had been struck by a bullet. She collapsed into a chair and sat there twisting her rings forlornly.

"Oh, and by the way, Connie," said Lord Emsworth, "I've been meaning to tell you. I've given that fellow Abercrombie that job he was asking for. I thought it all over carefully, and decided to drop him a line saying that pursuant on our recent conversation I was offering him Simmons' place. I've been making inquiries, and I find he's a capital fellow."

"He's a baa-lamb," said Jane.

"You hear? Jane says he's a baa-lamb. Just the sort of chap we want about the place."

"So now we're going to get married."

"So now they're going to get married. An excellent match, don't you think, Connie?"

Lady Constance did not speak. Lord Emsworth raised his voice a little.

"Don't you, Connie?"

Lady Constance leaped in her seat as if she had heard the last trump.

"Very," she said. "Oh, very."

"Right," said Lord Emsworth. "And now I'll go and talk to Beach."

In the pantry, gazing sadly out on the stableyard, Beach, the butler, sat sipping a glass of port. In moments of mental stress, port was to Beach what Whiffle was to his employer, or, as we must now ruefully put it, his late employer. He flew to it when Life had got him down, and never before had Life got him down as it had now.

Sitting there in his pantry, that pantry which so soon would know him no more, Beach was in the depths. He mourned like some fallen monarch about to say goodbye to all his greatness and pass into exile. The die was cast. The end had come. Eighteen years, eighteen happy years, he had been in service at Blandings Castle, and now he must go forth, never to return. Little wonder that he sipped port. A weaker man would have swigged brandy.

Something tempestuous burst open the door, and he perceived that his privacy had been invaded by Lord Emsworth. He rose, and stood staring. In all the eighteen years during which he had held office, his employer had never before paid a visit to the pantry.

But it was not simply the other's presence that caused his gooseberry eyes to dilate to their full width, remarkable though that was. The mystery went deeper than that. For this was a strange, unfamiliar Lord Emsworth, a Lord Emsworth who glared where once he had blinked, who spurned the floor like a mettlesome charger, who banged tables and spilled port.

"Beach," thundered this changeling, "what the deuce is all this dashed nonsense?"

"M'lord?"

"You know what I mean. About leaving me. Have you gone off your head?"

A sigh shook the butler's massive frame.

"I fear that in the circumstances it is inevitable, m'lord."

"Why? What are you talking about? Don't be an ass, Beach. Inevitable, indeed! Never heard such nonsense in my life. Why is it inevitable? Look me in the face and answer me that."

"I feel it is better to tender my resignation than to be dismissed, m'lord."

It was Lord Emsworth's turn to stare.

"Dismissed?"

"Yes, m'lord."

"Beach, you're tight."

"No, m'lord. Has not Mr Baxter spoken to you, m'lord?"

"Of course he's spoken to me. He's been gassing away half the afternoon. What's that got to do with it?"

Another sigh, seeming to start at the soles of his flat feet, set the butler's waistcoat rippling like corn in the wind.

"I see that Mr Baxter has not yet informed you, m'lord. I assumed that he would have done so before this. But it is a mere matter of time, I fear, before he makes his report."

"Informed me of what?"

"I regret to say, m'lord, that in a moment of uncontrollable impulse I shot Mr Baxter."

Lord Emsworth's pince-nez flew from his nose. Without them he could see only indistinctly, but he continued to stare at the butler, and in his eyes there appeared an expression which was a blend of several emotions. Amazement would have been the chief of these, had it not been exceeded by affection. He did not speak, but his eyes said, "My brother!"

"With Master George's air gun, m'lord, which her ladyship left in my custody. I regret to say, m'lord, that upon receipt of the weapon I went out into the grounds and came upon Mr Baxter walking near the shrubbery. I tried to resist the temptation, m'lord, but it was too keen. I was seized with an urge which I have not experienced since I was a small lad, and, in short, I——"

"Plugged him?"

"Yes, m'lord."

Lord Emsworth could put two and two together.

"So that's what he was talking about in the library. That's what made him change his mind and send me that note. . . . How far was he away when you shot him?"

"A matter of a few feet, m'lord. I endeavoured to conceal myself behind a tree, but he turned very sharply, and I was so convinced that he had detected me that I felt I had no alternative but to resign my situation before he could make his report to you, m'lord."

"And I thought you were leaving because my sister Connie shot you!"

"Her ladyship did not shoot me, m'lord. It is true that the weapon exploded accidentally in her ladyship's hand, but the bullet passed me harmlessly."

Lord Emsworth snorted.

"And she said she was a good shot! Can't even hit a sitting butler at six feet. Listen to me, Beach. I want no more of this nonsense of you resigning. Bless my soul, how do you suppose I could get on without you? How long have you been here?"

"Eighteen years, m'lord."

"Eighteen years! And you talk of resigning! Of all the dashed, absurd ideas!"

"But I fear, m'lord, when her ladyship learns——"

"Her ladyship won't learn. Baxter won't tell her. Baxter's gone."

"Gone, m'lord?"

"Gone forever."

"But I understood, m'lord——"

"Never mind what you understood. He's gone. A few feet away, did you say?"

"M'lord?"

"Did you say Baxter was only a few feet away when you got him?"

"Yes, m'lord."

"Ah!" said Lord Emsworth.

He took the gun absently from the table and absently slipped a slug into the breach. He was feeling pleased and proud, as champions do whose pre-eminence is undisputed. Connie had missed a mark like Beach—practically a haystack—at six feet. Beach had plugged Baxter, true, and so had young George—but only with the muzzle of the gun almost touching the fellow. It had been left for him, Clarence, ninth Earl of Emsworth, to do the real shooting. . . .

A damping thought came to diminish his complacency. It was as if a voice had whispered in his ear the word "Fluke!" His jaw dropped a little, and he stood for a while, brooding. He felt flattened and discouraged.

Had it been merely a fluke, that superb shot from the library window? Had he been mistaken in supposing that the ancient skill still lingered? Would he—which was what the voice was hinting—under similar conditions miss nine times out of ten?

A stuttering, sputtering noise broke in upon his reverie. He raised his eyes to the window. Out in the stableyard, Rupert Baxter was starting up his motor bicycle.

"Mr Baxter, m'lord."

"I see him."

An overwhelming desire came upon Lord Emsworth to put this thing to the test, to silence forever that taunting voice.

"How far away would you say he was, Beach?"

"Fully twenty yards, m'lord."

"Watch!" said Lord Emsworth.

Into the sputtering of the bicycle there cut a soft pop. It was followed by a sharp howl. Rupert Baxter, who had been leaning on the handle bars, rose six inches with his hand to his thigh.

"There!" said Lord Emsworth.

Baxter had ceased to rub his thigh. He was a man of intelligence, and he realised that anyone on the premises of Blandings Castle who wasted time hanging about and rubbing thighs was simply asking for it. To one trapped in this inferno of a Blandings Castle instant flight was the only way of winning to safety. The sputtering rose to a crescendo, diminished, died away altogether. Rupert Baxter had gone on, touring England.

Lord Emsworth was still gazing out of the window, raptly, as if looking at the X which marked the spot. For a long moment Beach stood staring reverently at his turned back. Then, as if performing some symbolic rite in keeping with the dignity of the scene, he reached for his glass of port and raised it in a silent toast.

Peace reigned in the butler's pantry. The sweet air of the summer evening poured in through the open window. It was as if Nature had blown the All Clear.

Blandings Castle was itself again.

THE MEDICINE GIRL

THE eighteenth hole at Bingley-on-Sea, that golfers' mecca on the south coast of England, is one of those freak holes—a very short mashie shot up a very steep hill off a tee screened from the clubhouse by a belt of trees. From the terrace, where the stout man in the vivid plus fours stood waiting for his partner to arrive for the morning round, only the green was visible.

On this green, falling from the sky in a perfect arc, there suddenly descended a white ball. It struck the ground, took a backspin, and rolled to within a foot of the hole.

The stout man congealed like one who has seen a vision. So might a knight of the Middle Ages have looked, on beholding the Holy Grail. He had been at Bingley only two days, and so had played this hole only six times; but he knew that if he played it for the rest of his life he would never get a two on it, as this unseen expert was so obviously about to do. Four was Sir Hugo Drake's best—his worst twenty-seven, on the occasion when he overran the green and got imbedded in a sort of Sahara which lay beyond it.

A player like this, he decided, demanded inspection

at close range. Possibly it was the pro, taking a little practice; but even the pro might reasonably expect homage after such a shot. Sir Hugo toddled over to the green; and, having reached it and peered into the depths, stood stunned with amazement.

It was not the pro. It was not a man at all. It was a girl—and a small girl, at that. That she was also extremely pretty seemed of slight importance to Sir Hugo. He was not a man who paid much attention to a woman's looks. What mattered to him was that he stood in the presence of a female who could handle a mashie like that. And being a man who liked to give credit where credit was due, he said so.

"My dear young lady," puffed Sir Hugo, "that was an extraordinarily fine stroke."

"Thank you."

"Where on earth did you learn to play like that?" asked Sir Hugo reverently.

"At Garden City, mostly."

The name was new to Sir Hugo.

"Garden City?"

"It's outside New York."

"Oh?" Sir Hugo was enlightened. He had a deep respect for transatlantic golf. "You come from America?"

"Yes. I've been in London about two years. I'm surprised my game hasn't gone off more. I don't get much time for playing."

Sir Hugo sighed.

"Nor do I," he replied sadly. "A busy specialist, you know . . . They keep one's nose pretty tightly to the grindstone."

"A specialist?" The girl seemed suddenly interested. "What sort of specialist?"

"Nerves."

"Really?"

"Drake's my name. Sir Hugo Drake."

The girl's interest was now unmistakable. She beamed.

"Fancy!" she said. "I thought your last book was wonderful. This is a proud moment for a mere general practitioner, Sir Hugo."

"A what?"

"A general practitioner. I'm one."

Sir Hugo gaped.

"Good God! You're not a doctor?"

"Yes, I am. Smith. Sally Smith. Doctor Sally Smith."

"Good God!" exclaimed Sir Hugo again.

The suspicion of a shadow passed over the girl's face. She was always meeting men who exclaimed "Good God!" or its equivalent when informed of her profession, and she disliked it. It seemed to her that they said it in the voice a small boy would use on being introduced to a circus freak. The male mind did not appear to be able to grasp immediately the fact that a woman doctor need not of necessity be a gargoyle with steel-rimmed spectacles and a wash-leather complexion.

However, this was a nice old man, so she decided not to bite his head off.

"I suppose it does seem funny," she said. "But there it is."

"Funny?" said Sir Hugo, recovering. "Not at all. Certainly not. Quite the contrary."

"I like being a doctor, and it doesn't do anybody any harm—at least, I've never killed a patient yet—so what I say to myself is, why not?"

"Quite," said Sir Hugo. "Why not? Precisely. Very sensible."

The girl tapped her ball into the hole and picked it up.

"Nice course, this," she said.

"Very," said Sir Hugo. "Are you making a long stay?"

"Just a two weeks' vacation. Are you here for long?"

Sir Hugo Drake had now come to look upon this girl as a soul mate. A member of his own profession and a golfer capable of a two on the eighteenth, she deserved, he felt, his full confidence. He was not a man who, as a rule, discussed his private affairs with strangers, but he could not bring himself to regard as a stranger a girl so outstanding at the short mashie shot.

"I don't know how long I'm going to be here," he confided. "The fact is, I'm looking for my nephew."

"Have you lost him?" Sally asked, surprised.

"He's given me the slip," said Sir Hugo, turning a deeper mauve, for the affair had caused him much annoyance. "He was living quietly in the country, down in Hampshire, and he came up to London, and suddenly he disappeared from London, and I met a man who said he had seen him down here—in company," said Sir Hugo, lowering his voice to a portentous whisper, "with a female of flashy appearance."

Sally smiled.

"Not me," she said.

"I wish it had been you," said Sir Hugo devoutly.

"If he would only have the sense to fall in love with a nice girl like you, I could be easier in my mind."

"You shouldn't worry."

"But I do worry," said Sir Hugo vehemently. "His poor mother was my sister, and since her death I have regarded myself as *in loco parentis* to the boy. Causes me a great deal of anxiety. Too much money, that's what he's got, and too much time on his hands. When he was at Cambridge, he came within an ace," said Sir Hugo, fixing his companion with a gaze calculated to make the flesh creep, "of marrying a girl in a tobacco shop!"

"Boys will be boys."

"Not while I'm *in loco parentis* to them, they won't," said Sir Hugo stoutly. "The trouble with William is that he's impulsive. Got a habit of falling in love at first sight. I don't know who this flashy female is, but I've come down here to break the thing up and take him back to Woollam Chersey, where he belongs."

"Is that the name of his place in the country?"

"Yes."

"I should have thought he would be safe, living in the country."

"He is. He is safe, while living in the country. But he keeps dashing away from the country and losing his head. Oh well, I mustn't bother you with my troubles. I see my partner looking for me."

He whooped and waved his hand at the terrace. A long, thin man, clad like himself in plus fours of a regrettable pattern, whooped and waved back.

"Hope we shall meet again," he said.

"I hope so," said Sally.

"Give me a lesson, perhaps?"

"I should be delighted."

"Good!" said Sir Hugo, and strode off to the first tee.

On the front—or esplanade—of Bingley-on-Sea stands the Hotel Superba; and at twenty minutes past four the thin mist which had been hanging over the resort since lunchtime disappeared, and there filtered through the windows of Suite Number Seven on the second floor that curious, faint gamboge light which passes for sunshine in England. Its mild rays shone deprecatingly on one of those many-colored carpets peculiar to suites at south-coast hotels; on the engraving of "The Stag at Bay" over the mantelpiece; on the table set for tea; and on Marie, maid to Mrs. Higginbotham, who had just deposited on the table a plate of sandwiches.

In addition to the sunshine, there entered also the strains of a jazz band, presumably from the winter garden below, where Swiss waiters prowled among potted palms, and such of the Superba's guests as wished to do so were encouraged to dance. Carried away by the melody Marie went so far as to dance a step or two herself. And so absorbed was she in this pursuit that a knocking on the outer door did not penetrate to her consciousness.

It got through, however, to Mrs Higginbotham in the bedroom, and she gave tongue.

"Marie!"

The maid ceased to pirouette. Her employer's voice

was one of those which impress themselves on the most preoccupied.

"Yes, moddom?"

"Are you deaf, you poor fish? Somebody at the door."

"Very good, moddom."

Marie opened the door. There was nothing much to reward her for the effort. Merely a man in spats.

"Mrs Higginbotham in?" asked this individual.

"Yes sir."

The visitor crossed the threshold. He was an immaculate and yet somehow subtly battered person in the early thirties. He wore a suit of gray material and unimpeachable cut and—until he removed it—a white derby hat. In his right eye there was a monocle, and through this he inspected the tea table. With a slight diminution of what appeared to be a constitutional gloom, he moved towards it and picked up a sandwich.

Mrs Higginbotham, still a disembodied voice, continued to interest herself in the proceedings.

"Is that you, Bill?"

"It is not Mr Bannister, moddom. It is——"

Marie looked at the feaster inquiringly. He was now well into his second sandwich, but he could still speak, and did so.

"Lord Tidmouth."

"It is Lord Tidmouth, moddom."

"Who the dickens is Lord Tidmouth?"

The newcomer seemed to feel that he ought to enter into the spirit of this long-distance conversation. He approached the bedroom door.

"What ho within there! Is that Lottie?"

"Who are you?"

"Tidmouth's the name at the present. It was Bixby till I hooked the old title. I don't know if you remember me. We used to be married once."

Evidently Mrs Higginbotham possessed one of those highly trained memories from which no fact, however trivial, escapes. She uttered a pleased screech.

"Squiffy!"

"That's right."

"Well, I'm blowed! Where did you spring from?"

"Oh, various parts. I've been traveling a lot. Not been in England for some years. I happened to blow down here and saw you going up in the lift—yesterday, that was—and I asked your name and they told me you were staying here. So at the earliest opportunity up I popped."

"Splendid! I'll be out in a minute."

"Right ho. I say, when did you acquire the Higginbotham?"

"About two years ago."

"Is he here?"

"No. Kensal Green Cemetery."

"Oh? Well, see you soon."

Lord Tidmouth wandered back to the table and started on another sandwich.

"I shan't be long now," Mrs Higginbotham assured him. "I'm just shaving."

"What!"

"My neck, you silly ass."

"Oh!"

"Have a sandwich."

"I am."

"You're what?"

"A sandwich. I mean, I'm having one. And most extraordinarily good they are. Sardine, or my trained senses deceive me."

He tested this theory by taking another, and all doubts were removed.

"Yes," he continued. "Absolutely sardine. Lottie!"

"Hullo?"

"I read an interesting thing in the paper the other day," said Lord Tidmouth. "It appears that the sardine's worst enemy is the halibut, and I give you my word that until I read it I didn't know the sardine *had* an enemy. And I don't mind telling you that my opinion of the halibut has gone down considerably. Very considerably. Fancy anything wanting to bully a sardine. I mean to say . . ."

He would have proceeded further, but at this moment there was a flash of light in the doorway of the bedroom, and he found himself blinking at one of the most vivid suits of pajamas ever conceived by the diseased mind of a fashionable haberdasher.

"Holy smoke!" he exclaimed. "I mean—well, well, well!"

"Well, well, well!" said Lottie.

"Well, well, well, *well!*" said Lord Tidmouth.

He took her hand in a sort of trance. He was visibly affected. The thought that he had been married to this and had allowed it to get away from him was evidently moving him powerfully. His monocle slipped from his eye and danced madly on the end of its string.

"My gosh!" he said. "Is that how you look?"

"That's how."

"Well, well, well, well, well, *well!*" said Lord Tidmouth.

Lottie moved to the mirror and scrutinised herself in it. She was pleased that her very considerable beauty had won this striking tribute.

"Sit down," she said.

Lord Tidmouth sat down.

"Tell me all," he said.

"All what?"

"All about yourself. Who was the recent Higginbotham?"

"Oh, a man. Very rich, from up north. I met him when I was in 'Follow the Girl.' I went back to the stage after you and I parted brass rags. He passed on last July."

"Marry again?"

"Ass! If I had, would my name still be Higginbotham?"

"Something in that," agreed his lordship.

"I mean, a girl doesn't call herself Higginbotham unless she has to."

"Absolutely not."

"Still, I *am* sort of engaged."

"Oh?"

"To a man named Bannister. Bill Bannister. Country squire sort of chap. Has a big place in Hampshire. Woollam Chersey it's called."

"What!" Lord Tidmouth's manner became almost animated. "Bill Bannister? One of my oldest pals. I'd like to see old Bill again."

"Well, you will, if you stick around. He's calling soon to take me to dance. Tell me about yourself."

"Oh, I've just been mooching round."

"Did *you* marry again?"

"Oh yes, here and there. My second wife ran away with a Frenchman."

"Did you get a divorce?"

"Yes, and married again. My third wife ran away with a Spaniard."

"Too bad."

"When I married my fourth wife . . ."

"Who did she run away with?"

"A Brazilian."

"Your home during the last few years seems to have been a sort of meeting place of the nations."

"Yes."

"How many wives have you got now?"

"None at the moment. The supply has sort of petered out. By the way, talking of wives, how do you feel on the subject of rocking horses?"

"What on earth are you talking about?"

"You see, tomorrow is my second wife's first son's third birthday, and I've just bought him a rocking horse."

"You still keep up with them, then?"

"Oh, a fellow has to be civil. Anyway, I've just bought this rocking horse, and I told the man to send it round here till my train went. You don't mind?"

"Of course not."

"Thanks."

There was a pause. The jazz band below had now begun to play a waltz of a singularly glutinous nature. Its effect on the pair in the sitting room seemed to be to induce a certain sentimentality.

"Odd," said Lord Tidmouth.

"What's odd?"

"Meeting again like this after all these years."

"Yes."

There was another pause.

"Dancing much these days?" asked Lord Tidmouth.

"Quite a lot."

"Why not a spot now? Music and everything."

"That's an idea."

They started to dance, and Lord Tidmouth's emotion appeared to deepen. He sighed once or twice.

"Good tune."

"Topping."

Into the rather fishlike eyes of Lord Tidmouth there had begun to creep a strange light, indicative of a brain at work. He was not a man who often thought, but he was thinking now. And what he was thinking was that, conditions having placed such an action within the sphere of practical politics, it would be silly not to kiss this girl. Here she was, he meant to say, within range, as it were, and . . . well, to put it in a nutshell, how about it?

He kissed her.

And, as he did so, the door opened and there appeared on the threshold a large young man in a flannel suit. His agreeable face, at the moment of his entry, had been wearing a rather preoccupied look. This, as he observed the entwined couple before him, changed to one of disapproval. He eyed them in silence for a space, then in a cold voice he said:

"Good afternoon!"

The effect of these words on the tender scene was

immediate. It broke it up like a bomb. Lord Tidmouth released his erstwhile helpmeet and straightened his tie. Lottie bit her tongue.

There was one of those embarrassing pauses.

"I didn't hear you come in," said Lottie.

"So I imagined," said Bill Bannister.

Silence fell again. It was not one of those episodes about which there is much to be said. It impeded rather than inspired conversation.

"Well, I'll go and get dressed," said Lottie.

"I should," said Bill.

Lord Tidmouth, during these exchanges, had been directing at his long-lost friend a look in which remorse and brotherly love were nicely blended. Remorse now faded, and brotherly love had the field to itself. Bill, turning to deal with this cuckoo in the nest, was surprised to observe him advancing with outstretched hand.

"Bill, old man!" said Lord Tidmouth emotionally.

"Eh?" said Bill, at a loss.

Lord Tidmouth sighed.

"Have you really forgotten me, Bill?" he said sadly. "Your ancient pal? Well, well, well! Name of Tidmouth. Used to be Bixby."

Bill stared.

"It isn't Squiffy?"

"It *is* Squiffy."

"For heaven's sake!"

Complete amiability appeared to reign in young Mr Bannister's bosom once more. He gripped the outstretched hand warmly.

"Well, I'm dashed!"

"Me, too, old boy."

"I haven't seen you for years."

"I haven't seen *you* for years."

They talked for a while of the dear old days, as friends reunited will do.

"I hear you're still living at the old address, Bill," said Lord Tidmouth. "If I hadn't run into you like this, I was going to drop you a line."

"Why not come down there for a bit?" said Bill hospitably.

Lord Tidmouth looked doubtful.

"Well, I'd love to, Bill, old man," he said, "but the fact is—been having domestic troubles of late, and all that—left me a bit on the moody side. I'm more or less of a broken man these days, and don't feel quite up to country-house parties."

"It won't be a country-house party. Just you and me and my uncle."

"Which uncle is that?"

"I've only one. Sir Hugo Drake, the nerve specialist."

"I never met him. Nice chap?"

"Oh, not so bad. He'd be all right if he could get it into his head that I'm a grown-up man and not still a kid in knickerbockers. He will fuss over me like a hen, and it drives me crazy. He has a fit every time I look at a girl. He'd die if he ever saw Lottie."

Lord Tidmouth's manner betrayed a certain embarrassment.

"I say, Bill, old man."

"Hullo?"

Lord Tidmouth coughed.

"Touching on that little contretemps, if I may so express it, which occurred just now, I should like to offer a few simple, manly explanations."

"Oh, don't apologise."

"Carried away, don't you know. What with the music and the sardine sandwiches . . ."

"That's all right."

"Furthermore, Lottie and I used to be married once, and that forms a sort of bond, if you follow me."

Bill's eyebrows shot up.

"Married?"

"Absolutely married. Long time ago, of course, but somehow the taste still lingered. And when I found her supple form nestling in my arms . . ."

"Squiffy," said Bill earnestly, "kindly stop apologising. Nothing could have been more fortunate. It gives me a decent excuse for getting out of an entanglement which has been getting on my nerves for weeks. Lottie's a good sort, but she's too—what's the word?"

"Jumpy?"

"Jumpy is right. When you were married to her, Squiffy, did she ever give you the devil?"

"Frequently."

"For no reason?"

"For no reason whatever."

Bill sighed.

"You know how it is, Squiffy."

"How what is, old boy?"

"Well, you meet a girl like Lottie and she sweeps you off your feet. And then . . . well, then you begin to think a bit."

"I see what you mean."

"Besides . . ."

Bill paused. He, like Squiffy a short while before, seemed embarrassed. He went to the table and drank cold tea.

"Squiffy . . ."

"Hullo?"

Bill mused for a moment.

"Squiffy . . ."

"Yes, old man?"

"Squiffy, have you ever felt a sort of strange emptiness in the heart? A sort of aching void of the soul?"

"Oh, rather."

"What do you do about it?"

"I generally take a couple of cocktails."

Bill shook his head.

"Cocktails aren't any good. Nothing's any good. I've read books, gone in for sport, tried work. No use whatever."

"What sort of work?"

"Stock farming. And what's the result? I have a thousand pigs, and my heart is empty."

"What you want is a tonic."

"No. I know what I want, Squiffy. I want love." Lord Tidmouth, that expert, viewed his friend with concern.

"Don't you believe it! Love? Listen, old boy. The amount of love I've had in the last few years, if placed end to end, would reach from London to Paris. And look at me! Besides, I thought you said you had decided to edge away from Lottie."

"Lottie isn't the right girl for me. A good sort, yes. But not the right girl for me. Now, this other girl . . ."

"What other girl?"

"This girl I'm telling you about."

"You've haven't been telling me about any girl. You haven't so much as mentioned a girl. Do you mean to say . . ."

Bill nodded.

"Yes, I've found the real thing at last."

Lord Tidmouth was interested. He went to the table and selected a sardine sandwich with quivering fingers.

"Who is she?" he asked.

"I don't know. I've only seen her out on the links. She's a poem, Squiffy—all health and fresh air and wholesomeness."

"Ever spoken to her?"

"No. I hadn't the nerve. She's so far above me."

"Tall girl, eh?"

"Spiritually, you ass."

"Oh, I see."

There was a pause.

"I'm going to get to know her somehow," said Bill at length.

"How?"

"I don't know. But I shall."

"And then?"

"I shall marry her."

Lord Tidmouth breathed reflectively.

"Shortly after my arrival in this room," he said, "Lottie gave me to understand that you were practically engaged to marry *her*."

"Yes," said Bill unhappily.

"Then, obviously, what you want to do first," said Lord Tidmouth, "is to get it well into Lottie's mind that it's all off."

"I know. But how?"

"It should be done tactfully."

"Of course."

"Gracefully . . . kindly . . . leaving no hard feelings. But, nevertheless, quite definitely."

"Yes."

Lord Tidmouth pondered.

"Your best plan, old boy," he said, "is to leave the whole thing to me. I understand women. I know exactly the right things to say. Leave the whole thing absolutely and entirely to me, contenting yourself with just murmuring the necessary responses."

Bill brightened.

"You're sure you can manage it?"

"My dear chap!"

"You'll be tactful?"

"Tactful as dammit. All my wives always raved about my tact. They legged it away from me like rabbits, one after the other, but they always admitted that in the matter of tact I stood alone."

"Well, I'm trusting you."

"And so you may, old boy."

The bedroom door opened, and Lottie appeared, dressed for the dance.

Bill Bannister looked at Lord Tidmouth. He looked appealingly, as a young soldier in a tight place might have looked at Napoleon. Lord Tidmouth returned the gaze with a reassuring nod and a leave-it-to-me wave of the hand.

"I'm ready," said Lottie.

Lord Tidmouth eyed her owlishly.

"Ready for what, old thing?"

"To dance."

"With Bill?"

"With Bill."

Tact gleamed from Lord Tidmouth's monocle.

"Bill isn't going to dance."

"But he said he would."

"He's made up his mind to stay in."

"Well, I've made up my face to go out."

"Shall I tell you something, Lottie?" said Lord Tidmouth.

"Go ahead."

"Bill's never going to dance with you again. Never, never again. He's going home. Back to Happy Hampshire."

A dangerous gleam appeared in Lottie's beautiful, but formidable eyes. She directed it at her shrinking playmate.

"Is this true, Bill?"

Bill Bannister er-yessed in a small voice. It was not for him to question the methods of a master of tact like Tidmouth, but he could not restrain a feeling that the news might have been broken a little more gently.

"You see," said Bill, "I simply must go home. There's the estate to look after and . . . Well, that's all there is to it, I think it's time I went home."

"A thousand pigs are pining for him," said Tidmouth.

"Let me get this straight," said Lottie in a strange, tense voice, not unlike that of a tigress from whom some practical joker is endeavouring to steal the daily ration of meat. "Are you leaving me flat?"

Lord Tidmouth was delighted at his former helpmeet's ready intelligence. Of all his wives, he reflected, Lottie had always been quickest at the uptake.

"That's right," he said. "You've put the thing in a nutshell. It's all off, and so is he."

Ignoring a sharp, whistling, sighing noise which proceeded from the lips which had once promised to love, honor and obey him, he resumed his discourse.

"You see, Bill's a country gentleman, old girl . . . lives in the wilds, half-a-dozen miles from anywhere . . . and he doesn't think you would quite fit into the picture."

"Oh? I'm not fit to associate with his beastly vicars and plowboys, eh?" asked Lottie with ominous calm.

"He doesn't say that," urged Lord Tidmouth. "What he means is that you wouldn't be happy in a small village. He's doing you a kindness, really. Why, dash it, if you got fed up with me in the middle of London, how much fedder-up you would be in a place like Woollam Chersey with a bird like Bill. Good heavens, there's nothing offensive in the man's attitude. He admires and respects you, but he feels that Woollam Chersey is not for you. Lots of the world's most wonderful women would be out of place in Woollam Chersey. Queen Elizabeth . . . Catherine of Russia . . . Cleopatra . . . dozens of them."

He paused, with the complacency of an orator who is conscious of having struck the right note.

"Besides," said Bill, who was not so sure that his collaborator was putting this thing across so well as he thought he was, "if I can't come in without finding you kissing . . ."

"Old boy!" murmured Lord Tidmouth reproachfully. "Bygones be bygones. 'Let the dead past bury its dead.' "

Lottie sniffed.

"So that's the trouble? You know as well as I do that Squiffy means nothing to me any longer. There's no need for you to be jealous."

"I'm not jealous."

"Oh?" said Lottie sharply. "And *why* aren't you, may I ask? I see it all now. There's somebody else."

"No, no," said Lord Tidmouth. "Quite wrong. Absolutely not so."

"There is! Some woman is stealing him away from me." Her voice rose. "Who is she? What's her name? Tell me her name? Who is she?"

She rested her hands on her hips, and from beneath lowering eyebrows glared militantly. Her manner interested Lord Tidmouth, and caused him to advance a theory to explain it.

"I say, Lottie, old girl," asked his lordship, "have you any Spanish blood in you?"

"Now listen, Lottie . . ."

This from Bill, who was not enjoying the glare.

"I won't listen!"

"My second wife was half Spanish," proceeded Lord Tidmouth chattily. "How well I remember . . ."

"Shut up!"

"Oh, rather," said his lordship. "I merely spoke."

Lottie turned to Bill again.

"So," she said, "you want to get rid of me, do you? You want to throw me aside like a—like a——"

"Worn-out glove," prompted Lord Tidmouth.

"Like a worn-out glove. You think you're going to abandon me like an——"

"Old tube of tooth paste."

"Shut up!"

"Oh, rather."

Lottie's eyes flashed.

"Let me tell you, you're mistaken if you think you can get rid of *me* so easily."

"Lottie," said Bill, "please!"

"Lottie, please!" said Lord Tidmouth.

"Lottie, please! Lottie, please! Lottie, please!" cried the injured woman in the tones which had intimidated a hundred theatrical dressing rooms and which, when heard during the course of their brief married life by the late Mr Higginbotham, had always been enough to send that pusillanimous cotton magnate shooting off to his club for refuge.

She ran to the tea table and snatched up a cup.

"There!"

She hurled the cup down with a crash.

"Did you ring, sir?"

It was a bellboy who spoke. He had appeared in the doorway with a smooth promptness which spoke well for the efficiency of the service at the Superba. This was due partly to long training and partly to the fact that for some moments back he had been standing with his ear glued to the keyhole.

"And there!" cried Lottie, demolishing a second cup.

This one produced Marie.

"Did you call, moddom?"

"And there!" said Lottie. "And there! And there!"

Another cup, saucer and the teapot joined the ruins on the floor.

"Lottie," said Bill urgently, "pull yourself together."

"Absolutely," agreed Lord Tidmouth. "Cups cost money, what?"

A piercing scream from the sufferer nearly broke the remaining cup on the table. Marie, advancing solicitously, was just in time to catch her employer as she fell. There was general consternation. All those present were disturbed and distressed, except the bellboy, who had not had such an enjoyable time since the day, six months ago, when the couple in Suite Ten had settled a lovers' tiff in his presence with chairs, the leg of a table, and a series of small china ornaments from the mantelpiece.

As always on occasions such as this, the air became full of a babble of words.

"Water," cried Marie.

"Vinegar!" recommended the bellboy.

"Eau de cologne!" said Bill.

"Pepper!" said Lord Tidmouth.

Marie had another suggestion.

"Give her air!"

So had the bellboy.

"Slap her hands!"

Lord Tidmouth went further.

"Sit on her head!" he advised.

The clamour was affecting Bill Bannister's nervous system.

"Will you be quiet!" he roared.

The noise subsided.

"Now, then," said Bill, taking command. He turned to the bellboy. "Go for a doctor."

"Yes sir."

"And you," continued Bill, addressing Marie, "take her into the bedroom."

"Yes sir."

The mob scene diminished. Bill, mopping his forehead, was aware of his old friend, Lord Tidmouth, hovering to and fro. He eyed him sourly.

"What are you hanging about for?" he demanded.

Lord Tidmouth reflected.

"Well, honestly, old chap, I don't quite know. Just lending sympathy and moral support, as it were."

"Get a doctor."

"But the boy's getting one."

"Well, get another. Get a dozen."

Lord Tidmouth patted his shoulder with infinite gentleness and understanding.

"I know just how you're feeling, old boy," he said. "You've never seen Lottie in quite this frame of mind before, and you find it upsetting. To me, of course, all this is old stuff. How well I remember," said Lord Tidmouth, beginning to dictate his autobiography, "how clearly it all comes back—that second week of our honeymoon when, in a spirit of kindly criticism, I told her that her new hat looked like nothing on earth. People talk about the San Francisco earthquake . . ."

"Get *out!*"

"Just as you say, old boy."

"And don't come back without a doctor."

"I won't," Lord Tidmouth assured him. "I'll get

one if I have to rob a hospital. For the moment, then, laddie, tinkerty-tonk!"

The room now empty, Bill felt more composed. He called sharply to Marie, who popped out of the bedroom like a cuckoo from a clock.

"Marie!"

"Sir?"

"How is she?"

"Still unconscious, sir. And I don't like her breathing. If you ask me, it's storterous."

" 'Storterous'?"

"Sort of puffy. Like this."

Taking in a supply of air, Marie emitted it in a series of moaning gasps. It was not an inartistic performance, but Bill did not like it.

"Marie!" he said.

"Sir?"

"When I want any farmyard imitations, I'll ask for them."

"Very good, sir."

Hurt by destructive criticism, the maid withdrew into the bedroom. The door had scarcely closed behind her when the bellboy appeared. He had the unmistakable look of a bellboy who is about to deliver the goods.

"The doctor, sir," he announced with modest pride.

Bill heaved a relieved sigh.

"Send him in," he said.

And, having said it, he stood gaping. Framed in the doorway was a young and becomingly dressed girl. She carried a small black bag, and at the sight of her Bill Bannister's eyes widened to an incredulous stare and his jaw drooped like a lily. Then there swept over him so tumultuous a rush of ecstasy that his vocal cords seemed tangled in a knot.

He swallowed convulsively, and realised despairingly that speech for the moment was entirely beyond him.

Sally eyed him composedly. She had been going out for a walk when the bellboy found her, and she was anxious to finish the task before her and resume that walk as quickly as possible. Of the emotions surging in Bill's soul she had no inkling. And certainly she did not share them. Bill meant nothing to her. She had never seen him before in her life, and was not excited by the sight of him now. She had set him down at a glance as one of those typical, pleasant, idle young men whose charm made so slight an impression on her. Only workers interested Sally Smith.

She was on the point of coming briskly to business, when the extraordinary popeyed nature of his stare forced itself on her attention. A moment later, he advanced a step towards her, still looking like a prawn, and in an odd, strangled voice emitted the single word, "Guk!"

That, at least, was how it sounded to Sally. She raised her eyebrows.

"I beg your pardon?" she said.

Bill Bannister, with a supreme effort, had now got his Adam's apple back into position and regained control of his vocal cords. But even now the sight of this girl rendered speaking difficult. At close range, he found himself observing things about her which had escaped him at a distance. Her nose, which he had supposed straight, turned up at the tip. He had never seen her teeth before. He liked them.

"It can't be!" he said.

"I don't quite understand," said Sally.

"I—er—mean," said Bill. "What I mean is . . . I've seen you before."

"Really? Where?"

"Out on the links."

"Yes? I've been playing quite a lot."

"Yes," said Bill. "I saw you there . . . Out on the links . . . I saw you several times out on the links."

He paused a moment, wishing to make his meaning clearer.

"You were out on the links," he said, "and I saw you."

"I see," said Sally. "And now, where is my patient?"

"Patient?"

"I was told that someone here wanted a doctor."

"Yes. A—sort of a friend of mine has had a kind of nervous breakdown."

"A female friend, I suppose?"

"Er—yes."

"Well, hadn't I better see her?"

A bright light shone upon Bill.

"You don't mean to say you're a doctor?"

"I do."

"Gosh! I mean . . . I say, *do* sit down, won't you?"

"I really can't waste time like this," said Sally coldly. "If you don't want me to attend the patient, I'll go."

"But . . . she can't see a doctor now."

"Why not?"

"She isn't well."

Sally's momentary pique faded. This extraordinary young man amused her.

"My dear good man," she said, "are you always like this, or have I just struck one of your bad days?"

Bill writhed.

"I know I'm an idiot . . ."

"Ah! A lucid moment."

"It's the shock of seeing you walk in like this."

"Why shouldn't I walk in? You sent for me."

"Yes, but you don't understand. I mean, I've seen you out on the golf links."

"So you said before."

"You see—Mrs . . ."

"Miss."

"Thank God!"

"I beg your pardon?"

"Nothing, nothing. I—er—that is to say—or, putting it rather differently . . . Oh, my goodness!"

"What's the matter?"

"You take my breath away."

"For shortness of breath try a jujube. And now, please, my patient."

"Oh yes . . ."

Bill went to the door of the bedroom and called softly:

"Marie!"

Marie appeared in the doorway.

"Yes sir?"

"How is she?"

"Asleep, sir."

"Fine!" said Bill, brightening. "See that she doesn't

wake up." He came back to Sally. "The maid says the patient has fallen asleep."

Sally nodded.

"Quite natural. Sleep often follows violent hysteria."

"But, I say, how do you know it was hysteria?"

"By the broken china. Long-distance diagnosis. Well, let her have her sleep-out."

"I will."

There was a pause.

"Tea," said Bill, at length desperately. "Won't you have some tea?"

"Where is it?"

Bill looked about him.

"Well, on the floor, mostly," he admitted. "But I could ring for some more."

"Don't bother. I don't like tea much, anyway."

"You're American, aren't you?"

"I am."

"It's a rummy thing, Americans never seem very keen on tea."

"No."

There was another pause.

"I say," said Bill, "I didn't get your name."

"Doctor Sally Smith. What's yours?"

"Bannister. William Bannister."

"You live here?"

"Certainly not," said Bill, shocked. "I'm staying at the Majestic. I live down in Hampshire."

"One of those big country houses, I suppose?"

"Pretty big."

"I thought so. You look opulent," said Sally, pleased that her original opinion had been confirmed. A rich idler, this man, she felt. Not unpleasant, it was true—she liked his face and was amused by him—but nevertheless idle and rich.

Bill, by this time, had gradually become something more nearly resembling a sentient being. Indeed, he was now quite at his ease again and feeling extraordinarily happy. That this girl and he should be sitting chatting together like this was so wonderful that it put him right on top of his form. He straightened his tie and threw his whole soul into one devoted gaze.

Sally got the gaze and did not like it. For some moments now she had been wishing that this perfect stranger would either make his eyes rather less soulful or else refrain from directing them at her. She was a liberal-minded girl and did not disapprove of admiration from the other sex—indeed, she had grown accustomed to exciting it—but something seemed to whisper to her that this William Bannister could do with a little womanly quelling.

"Would you mind not looking at me like that?" she said coolly.

The soulful look faded out of Bill's eyes as if he had been hit between them with a brick. He felt disconcerted and annoyed. He disliked being snubbed, even by a girl for whom his whole being yearned.

"I'm *not* looking at you like that," he replied with spirit. "At least, I'm not trying to."

Sally nodded tolerantly.

"I see," she said. "Automatic, eh? Very interesting, from a medical point of view. Unconscious reaction of the facial and labial muscles at sight of a pretty woman."

Bill's pique increased. He resented this calm treating of himself as something odd on a microscopic slide.

"I am sorry," he said haughtily, "if I embarrassed you."

Sally laughed.

"You didn't embarrass me," she said "Did I seem to you to show embarrassment? I thought I had my vascular motors under much better control."

"Your—— What did you say?"

"Vascular motors. They regulate the paling and flushing of the skin. In other words, I didn't blush."

"Oh, ah! I see."

The conversation flagged again.

"Do you know," said Bill, hoisting it to its legs again, "I was most awfully surprised when you said you were a doctor."

"Most men seem to be."

"I mean, you don't look like a doctor."

"How ought a doctor to look?"

Bill reflected.

"Well, most of them seem sort of fagged and overworked. Haggard chaps. I mean, it must be an awful strain."

Sally laughed.

"Oh, it's not so bad. You needn't waste your pity on me, Mr Bannister. I'm as fit as a fiddle, thank heaven, and enjoy every minute of my life. I have a good practice and quite enough money. I go to theatres and concerts. I play games. I spend my vacations travelling. I love my work. I love my recreations. I love life."

"You're wonderful!"

"And why shouldn't I? I earn every bit of pleasure

that I get. I like nice clothes, nice shoes, nice stockings—because I buy them myself. I'm like the Village Blacksmith—I owe not any man. I wonder if you've the remotest idea how happy it can make a woman feel just to be a worker and *alive*—with good nerves, good circulation and good muscles. Feel my arm. Like iron."

"Wonderful!"

"And my legs. Hard as a rock. Prod 'em."

"No, really!"

"Go on."

She looked at him with amusement.

"You're blushing!"

Bill was unable to deny the charge.

"Yes," he said. "I'm afraid my vascular motors aren't as well controlled as yours."

"Can't you admire a well-rounded, highly perfected leg in a purely detached spirit as a noble work of nature?"

"Sorry—no. I'm afraid I've never quite managed to do that."

"Why, in some countries the women go swimming with nothing on."

"And the men buy telescopes."

"Don't snigger."

"Forgive me," said Bill. "I laugh, like Figaro, that I may not weep."

She regarded him curiously.

"What do you want to weep about?"

Bill sighed.

"I'm feeling a little depressed," he said. "In the life you have outlined—this hard, tense, independent, self-sufficing life with its good nerves and good circulation and muscles of the brawny arm as strong as iron bands —don't you think—it's just a suggestion—don't you think there's something a little *bleak?*"

" 'Bleak'?"

Bill nodded.

"Well, frankly . . ."

"Always be frank."

"Frankly, then," said Bill, "it reminds me of the sort of nightmare H. G. Wells would have after cold pork. It seems to leave out the one thing that makes life worth living."

"You mean love?"

"Exactly. I grant you one hundred per cent on nerves and circulation and general fitness; I admire your biceps; I'm sure your leg muscle is all it should be; and I take off my hat to your vascular motors . . . but doesn't it strike you that you're just the merest trifle lacking in *sentiment?*"

She frowned.

"Nothing of the kind. All I'm lacking in is sentimentality. I don't droop and blush and giggle . . ."

"No, I noticed that."

". . . But naturally I don't intend to exclude love from my life. I'm not such a fool."

"Ah!"

"Why do you say 'Ah'?"

A touch of dignity came into Bill's manner.

"Listen!" he said. "You're the loveliest girl I ever met, but you've got to stop bullying me. I shall say 'Ah' just as often as I please."

"I merely asked because most people, when they

stand in front of me and say 'Ah', expect me to examine their throats."

She paused.

"Why are you so interested in my views on love, Mr Bannister?" she asked casually.

Even Bill, quick worker though he had been from boyhood, would have shrunk—had the conditions been other than they were—from laying bare his soul at this extremely early point in his association with this girl. Emotion might have urged him to do so, but Prudence would have plucked at his sleeve. So intense, however, was his desire to shatter his companion's maddening aloofness . . . at least, was aloofness exactly the word? . . . dispassionate friendliness described it better . . . no, *detached* . . . that was the word he wanted . . . she was so cool and detached and seemed so utterly oblivious to the importance of a Bannister's yearning that he let Emotion have its way. And if Prudence did any plucking, he failed to notice it.

"I'll tell you why," he said explosively. "Because, the moment I saw you out there on the links, I knew you were the one girl . . ."

"You mean you've fallen in love with me?"

"I have. . . . The news doesn't seem to surprise you," said Bill resentfully.

Sally laughed.

"Oh, it's not such a terrible shock."

"You've heard the same sort of thing before, from other men, I suppose?"

"Dozens of times."

"I might have known it," said Bill gloomily. "Just my luck. And I suppose——"

"No. You're wrong."

Bill became animated again.

"You mean there's nobody else?"

"Nobody."

Bill's animation approached fever point.

"Then do you think . . . do you suppose . . . might it happen . . . would it be . . . or, putting it another way, is it possible . . ."

"Crisper, crisper. And simpler. What you're trying to suggest now is that perhaps I might one day love you. Am I right?"

"You take the words out of my mouth."

"I had to, or they would never have emerged at all. Well, if I ever love a man, I shall inform him of the fact, simply and naturally, as if I were saying, 'Good morning.' "

Bill hesitated.

"Tell me," he said, "have you ever—er—wished a man good morning?"

"No. That experience has yet to come."

"Wonderful!"

"Not so very wonderful. It simply means I haven't met the right man."

Bill could not allow a totally false statement like this to pass uncorrected.

"Yes, you have," he assured her. "You don't know it yet, but you have." He advanced towards her, full of his theme. "You have, really."

"Oh?"

"Yes," said Bill. He drew a deep breath. "Gosh!" he exclaimed. "I feel as if a great weight had rolled off me. I had always hoped in my heart that women like you existed, and now it's all come true. Don't laugh at me. It's come upon me like a whirlwind. I never expected it. I never guessed. I never . . ."

"Excuse me, sir," said Marie, appearing at the bedroom door.

Bill regarded her with marked displeasure. In the past, Marie had always seemed to him rather a nice girl, but now he felt he had seldom encountered a more pronounced pest.

"Well," he said irritably, "what is it?"

"If you please, sir, she's awake now."

Bill could make nothing of this. The girl appeared to him to be babbling. Sheer gossip from the padded cell.

"Awake?" he said. "What on earth are you talking about? Who's awake?"

"Why, moddom, sir."

Bill blinked like an awakened somnambulist.

"Moddom?"

Sally laughed.

"I think you had forgotten our patient, hadn't you?"

She turned briskly to Marie.

"Ask her to come in, please. I will examine her at once."

It was a calmer and more subdued Lottie who emerged from the bedroom. But it was plain that the volcano was not altogether extinct. In her manner, as she suddenly beheld a charming and attractive girl in Bill's society in her sitting room, there were obvious indications that something of the old fire still lingered. She stiffened. She glared in hostile fashion. Bill, watching, was disturbed to see her hands go to her hips in a well-remembered gesture.

"Oh?" said Lottie. "And who may this be?"

"I'm the doctor," said Sally.

"You think I'm going to swallow that?"

Sally sighed resignedly.

"Can you read?"

"Of course I can read."

"Then read that," said Sally, producing a card.

Lottie scrutinised it doubtfully. Then her manner changed.

"Doctor Sally Smith," she said. "Well, I suppose that's all right. Still, it looks funny to me. And let me tell you that if there is any funny business going on between you two, I'll very soon . . ."

"Quiet, please," said Sally.

She spoke calmly, but the speaker stopped as if she had run into a brick wall.

"I want to make an examination," said Sally.

"Perhaps I'd better leave you?" said Bill.

"Just as you like."

"I'll go for a stroll on the front."

"All right," said Sally. "I shan't be long."

She put her stethoscope together as the door closed. Lottie, having recovered, felt disposed for conversation.

"You'll forgive me, I'm sure, Doctor . . ." She paused. "Isn't that too silly of me, I've forgotten your damned name."

"It's quite an easy one to remember," said Sally, busy with her stethoscope. "Smith."

Lottie beamed.

"Oh, thank you. I was saying, Doctor, that I was sure you'd forgive me for flying off the handle a little just now. The fact is, I've just been having a bit of a row with Mr Bannister, and coming in and finding you two together like that, naturally I said to myself . . ."

"Take off that bathrobe."

"Eh? Oh, all right. Let me see, where was I? What started it all was him saying to me—or, rather, Squiffy did, and he didn't contradict it—that he wasn't ever going to take me dancing again. 'Oh,' I said, 'and why not, may I ask?' 'I'm going home,' he said. 'Going home?' I said. 'Yes,' he said, 'going home.' So naturally I said, 'I know what the trouble with *you* is,' I said, 'you want to cast me off like a worn-out glove. But if you think for one moment that I'm going to stand anything like that . . .' "

"The lungs appear sound," said Sally.

" 'You're mistaken,' I said . . ."

"Take a deep breath. Well, the heart seems all right. Now for the reflexes. Cross your legs . . . Nothing the matter with them. All right, that's all."

"Examination over?"

"Yes."

Lottie became interested.

"What's wrong with me?"

"Nothing much. You need a rest."

"Aren't you going to look at my tongue?"

"I can tell, without looking at it, that that needs a rest, too. What you want is a few weeks in a nice quiet sanitarium."

"You're going to send me to a sanitarium?"

"Well, I'm advising you to go. You need a place

where there are cold baths and plain food and no cigarettes and no cocktails."

Lottie shuddered.

"It sounds like hell," she said. She frowned. "I believe it's a trick."

"A trick?"

"I believe you're just trying to get me out of the way so that you can have him to yourself."

"Him?" Sally stared. "You can't mean—— Do you really imagine for one moment that I'm in love with Mr Bannister?"

"You aren't?"

"Of course not."

"And you want me to go to a sanitarium?"

"I think you ought to."

"Well," said Lottie, "it all looks funny to *me!*"

The door opened and Lord Tidmouth appeared. He seemed pleased with himself.

"Hullo!" said Lord Tidmouth. "I say, I've snaffled a medicine man." His eye rested on Sally. He stared. "Hullo!"

Sally returned his gaze composedly.

"I have already examined the patient," she said.

"*You* have?" said Lord Tidmouth, perplexed.

"Yes. My name is Doctor Smith."

"*Doctor* Smith?"

"Doctor Smith."

Lord Tidmouth's was not a very agile brain, but it was capable of flashes of intuition.

"You mean *you're* a doctor?" he said, brightly.

"Yes."

"I see. Of course," said Lord Tidmouth, with the

air of a man who is always prepared to listen to reason, "there *are* lady doctors."

"Yes. I'm one of them."

"Absolutely. Yes, I see your point. I say," said Lord Tidmouth, "this is rather awkward. Old Bill sent me to get a doctor, and I grabbed one in the lobby."

"I'm afraid there's nothing for him to do here."

"Not a thing," agreed Lottie. "What do you think I'm doing here, Squiffy, you poor nut—holding a medical convention?"

Lord Tidmouth rubbed his chin.

"But he's apt to be a bit shirty, isn't he, if he finds I've lugged him up here for nothing? He wasn't any too pleased at having to come at all. He was on his way to the links."

"Oh well," said Sally, sympathizing with his concern, "as you've called him in, we can have a consultation, if he likes. Where is he?"

"Navigating the stairs. Stout old boy, not very quick on his pins." He went to the door. "This way, Doc," he called.

A puffing noise without announced that the medicine man was nearing journey's end. The next moment he had entered, and Sally, turning to the door, was surprised to find that this was no stranger in their midst but an old acquaintance.

"Why, Sir Hugo!" she said.

Sir Hugo Drake had just enough breath left to say, "God bless my soul! You here?" After that, he resumed his puffing.

Lord Tidmouth became apologetic.

"I'm awfully sorry," he said, addressing his panting

captive, "I'm afraid there's been a misunderstanding."

"Lord Tidmouth," explained Sally, "didn't know that I was here."

"No," said his lordship. "The whole trouble was, you see, old Bill got the wind up and sent the entire strength of the company out scouring the town for medicos. It begins to look like a full house."

Sir Hugo realised the position.

"No need for me at all, eh? Well, I'm just as pleased. I've an appointment on the links. Of course, if you'd like a consultation . . ."

"Could you spare the time?" asked Sally.

"Certainly, if you wish it. Mustn't take too long, though."

"Oh, of course not. Only a few minutes."

"Very well, then. This young lady the patient?"

"Yes."

"Well, step into the bedroom, young lady, and we'll go into your case."

Lottie rose obediently. She was feeling a little flattered at this inrush of doctors on her behalf.

"She says I ought to go into a sanitarium," she said, indicating Sally.

"Subject to Sir Hugo's opinion," said Sally.

Sir Hugo nodded.

"Oh, we'll thresh the whole thing out, never fear. We'll go into your case minutely. Run along, my dear."

"Well, I ought to be all right between the two of you," said Lottie, and closed the bedroom door behind her.

Lord Tidmouth seemed relieved that matters had reached such an amicable settlement. He had had visions of this red-faced bird setting about him with a niblick.

"Then I'll leave you to it, what? I've often wondered," he said meditatively, "what you doctors talk about when you hold consultations. Lots of deep stuff, I expect."

For a moment after the departure of Lord Tidmouth there was silence in the room. Sir Hugo was still engaged in recovering his full supply of breath. This done, he looked at Sally inquiringly.

"What's the trouble?"

"Oh, nothing," said Sally. "Just a little nerves."

Sir Hugo cocked an eye at the débris on the floor.

"Seems to have been violent."

"Yes. That type. Too many cocktails and cigarettes, and no self-restraint. I thought she ought to have a few weeks' rest."

Sir Hugo snorted.

"I imagined from the way that young fellow snatched me up and carried me off that it was a matter of life and death. Silly idiot! Now I shall be late for my golf match."

"How did you get on this morning after you left me?" asked Sally.

Sir Hugo sighed, as Napoleon might have sighed if somebody had met him after the battle of Waterloo and asked, "Well, how did it all come out?"

"He beat me four and three."

"What a shame!"

"I didn't seem able to do anything right," said Sir Hugo, wallowing in this womanly sympathy. "If I didn't hook, I sliced. And if I didn't slice, I topped."

"That's too bad."

"I only needed a nine to win the fourteenth, and I ought to have got it easily. But I blew up on the green."

"That's often the way, isn't it?"

"Mark you," said Sir Hugo, "I wasn't so bad off the tee. Some of my drives were extremely good. It was the short shots that beat me. Just the ones you are so wonderful at. If I could play my mashie as you do, my handicap would be down below twenty before I knew where I was."

"What do you find is the trouble? Shanking?"

"No, topping, principally."

"You oughtn't to look up."

"I know I oughtn't, but I do."

"Do you think you are gripping right?" asked Sally.

"Well, I'm *gripping,"* said Sir Hugo. "I don't know if I'm doing it right."

"Would you like me to show you?"

"My dear young lady, I should like it above all things!"

A monocled head appeared round the edge of the door. Curiosity had been too much for Lord Tidmouth.

"How are you getting on?" he inquired.

"Kindly leave us alone, young man," said Sir Hugo testily. "We are at a very difficult point in the diagnosis."

"Oh, right ho. Poo-boop-a-doop," said Lord Tidmouth amiably, and vanished again.

Sir Hugo turned to Sally.

"You were saying you would show me . . ."

Sally stretched out a hand towards the golf bag.

"May I borrow one of your clubs?" she said. "Now,

then. So much depends on the right grip. Do you use the Vardon?"

"I used to, but lately I've gone back to the double-V."

"Well, the great thing is not to grip too tight. Grip firmly but lightly."

"Firmly but lightly. I see."

"The hands should be kept low, and, above all, should finish low. So many people finish their iron shots with the hands up as if they were driving."

"True," said Sir Hugo. "True."

"At the finish of the chip shot the club should be very little above the horizontal. Not like in the drive."

Sir Hugo nodded.

"I see. Talking of driving, it may interest you to hear of a little experience I had the other day. I had made my drive . . ."

"A rather similar thing once happened to me," said Sally. "It was this way . . ."

"I went to play my second," proceeded Sir Hugo, who may not have been much good as a golfer, but stood almost alone as a golf bore. A man who had outtalked tough, forceful men in clubs, he was not going to let himself be silenced by a mere girl. "I went to play my second, and, believe me or believe me not . . ."

"What do you think?" said Sally. "I found . . ."

"I just . . ."

"I simply . . ."

The bedroom door opened abruptly.

"Haven't you two finished yet?" asked Lottie peevishly.

Sir Hugo started like one awakened from a beautiful dream.

"Oh, quite, quite," he said, embarrassed. "We were just about to call you. We've examined your case from every angle . . ."

"And Sir Hugo agrees with me . . ." said Sally.

"Exactly. That your trouble . . ."

". . . Is a slight matter of nerves . . ."

". . . Nothing of any consequence, though disagreeable . . ."

"And you must be kept in a sanitarium . . ."

"Firmly but lightly," said Sir Hugo. "I mean—ah—just so."

Lord Tidmouth manifested himself again.

"Hullo," he said. "Consultation over?"

"Yes," said Lottie. "They say I ought to go to a sanitarium."

"I can recommend this one," said Sir Hugo. "I will write down the address."

"Oh, all right," said Lottie. "Leave it on the table. I'm going out."

"To find Bill?" said Lord Tidmouth. "He's probably on the front somewhere."

Lottie laughed a bitter laugh.

"Bill? I don't want Bill. I've nothing to say to Mr Bannister. If I'm to be dumped in a sanitarium, I'm going to get in a bit of dancing first. Come along and shake them up, Squiffy?"

"Absolutely," agreed Lord Tidmouth. "Just what the old system needs. Well, toodle-oo, everybody."

Sir Hugo was staring openmouthed at the closed door. He had the air of a man who has received an unpleasant shock.

"*Bannister,* did she say?"

"Yes. Mr Bannister was here when I came. He went out."

Sir Hugo snorted powerfully.

"So this is the woman he's been fooling around! I might have guessed it would be some peroxide blonde."

Sally saw daylight.

"Is Mr Bannister the nephew you were telling me about?"

"He is. And that is the woman! Of all the maddening, worthless nephews a man was ever cursed with . . ." He paused, and seemed to ponder. "Just show me that grip once more, will you?" he said, coming out of his reverie.

"All right," said Sally agreeably. "But don't you want to worry about your nephew?"

"He can wait," said Sir Hugo grimly.

"I see. Well, give me your hands——" She took his hands and clasped them round the club. And it was in this attitude that Bill, returning for the latest bulletin, found them.

Bill's first emotion was one of excusable wrath at the spectacle. Here was the only girl he had ever really loved, and he had no sooner left her than she started holding hands with a man of advanced years in a suit of plus fours of the kind that makes horses shy. He cleared his throat austerely, and was about to speak when the plus-foured one turned:

"William!" he said, and Bill wilted.

If one of the more austere of the minor prophets had worn plus fours, he would have looked just as Sir Hugo Drake was looking now. The great specialist had drawn himself up, and he could not have regarded Bill more sternly if the latter had been a germ.

"So I've found you, have I!"

"Oh—hullo, Uncle!" said Bill.

"Don't say 'Hullo, Uncle!' to me," boomed Sir Hugo. "This is a pleasant surprise for a man who stands *in loco parentis*, is it not! I come down here to this place, to this Bingley-on-Sea, and before I've hardly had time to put a ball down on the first tee, I am called in to attend to your female associates!"

"Uncle, please!"

Sir Hugo strode to the door.

"I am returning to Woollam Chersey tonight, William," he said. "I shall expect you to accompany me."

"I can't!"

"Why not?"

Bill looked helplessly at Sally.

"I'll be back in a day or two," he said.

"Then I shall remain till you leave," said Sir Hugo. "And let me tell you I shall watch this suite like a hawk."

"There's no *need* for you to watch this suite . . ."

"There is every need for me to watch this suite. Good God, boy! I've seen the female! If you imagine that I'm going to stand idly by and see you get yourself inextricably entangled with a woman who dyes her hair and throws teacups about hotels, you are vastly mistaken." He looked at his watch. "Great heavens! Is that the time? I must fly. I'll remember what you told me about that grip. Firmly but lightly. Hands not too much over. William, I shall be seeing you again. We will discuss this affair then."

Although his uncle—corporeally considered—had now left him, his aura or influence seemed still to oppress William Bannister. He gulped once or twice before speaking.

"How on earth did he get here?" he gasped.

"Lord Tidmouth found him in the lobby and dragged him up," said Sally. "Poor Mr Bannister, you don't have much luck with your medical advisers, do you?" She moved towards the door. "Well, good-bye."

Bill quivered.

"You're not going?"

"Yes, I am. Will you give me your address?"

"Woollam Chersey, Hampshire, finds me." He drew a deep breath. "How wonderful! You want to write to me?"

"No. I just want to know where to send my bill."

"Good heavens!"

"What's the matter?"

Bill walked across to the sofa and kicked it violently.

"It's enough to drive a man mad," he said. "Whenever I say anything—anything with any sentiment in it—you immediately become the doctor again."

"What do you expect me to do—swoon in your arms?"

"You haven't an atom of feeling in you."

"Oh yes, I have. And someday the right man will bring it out. Cheer up, Mr Bannister. You look like a sulky baby that's been refused its bottle." She laughed. "I think your uncle's quite right, and you're still a small boy."

Bill scowled.

"Oh? I'll prove to you someday that I'm grown up."

Sally laughed again.

"Oh, I'm not saying you may not grow up someday. But at present you're just a child."

"I'm not."

"You are."

"I'm not."

"Yes, you are."

There was a knock at the door. The bellboy entered.

"Please, sir," said the bellboy, "your rocking horse has arrived."

"What!" cried Bill.

"There!" cried Sally.

Bill passed a hand through his disordered hair.

"My rocking horse? What do you mean, my rocking horse?"

"Well, all I know is, there's a rocking horse outside. Shall they bring it in?"

"No!" cried Bill.

"Yes," said Sally. "Good-bye, Mr Bannister. Naturally you will want to be alone. You don't want grown-ups around at a moment like this. Good-bye."

"Come back!" shouted Bill. But Sally had gone.

If there was a thought in the mind of Lord Tidmouth, as he sat, some two weeks after his visit to Bingley-on-Sea, playing solitaire in the living hall of his friend Bill Bannister's country seat at Woollam Chersey, in the county of Hampshire, it was a vaguely formulated feeling that life was extremely pleasant and that there was no getting away from it that these all-male parties were the best. He had had an excellent dinner, the lamps were lighted, and it seemed to him that there was nothing whatever to worry about in the world.

Lord Tidmouth liked peace and quiet. Women, in his experience, militated against an atmosphere of quiet peace. Look at his second wife, for instance. For the matter of that, look at his third and fourth. He was placidly content that the Manor, Woollam Chersey, harboured, besides himself, only William, his host, inert now in a neighbouring armchair, and William's uncle, Sir Hugo Drake, at present occupied in the passage without, practising putts into a tumbler.

The room in which Bill and Lord Tidmouth sat was old and panelled. Its furniture was masculine and solid. From the walls portraits of dead and gone Bannisters gazed down, and in one corner there was a suit of armour, which it was Lord Tidmouth's practice to tap smartly whenever he passed it. He liked the ringing sound it gave out. What with an occasional tap on this suit of armour, plenty to eat and drink, and sufficient opportunities for playing solitaire, Lord Tidmouth found life at Woollam Chersey satisfactory.

A kindly soul, he wished he could have thought that his host was in a similar frame of mind. As far as he allowed himself to worry about anything, he was a little worried about good old Bill. The man seemed on edge. Very far from his merry self he had been since that afternoon at Bingley. This troubled Lord Tidmouth at times.

It did not, however, trouble him to the extent of spoiling his enjoyment in his game of solitaire. With pursed lips he uncovered a card, held it in air, put it on one of the piles, removed a second card from another pile and put it on a third pile—in fact, went through all the movements peculiar to those addicted to this strange game.

It is almost inevitable that a man who is playing solitaire will sooner or later sing. Lord Tidmouth, who had for some little time been humming in an undertone, now came boldly into the open and committed himself to the rendition of a popular ballad.

"I fee-ar naw faw in shee-ining arr-mour,
Though his lance be swift and—er—keen . . ."

In his armchair Bill stirred uneasily.

"But I fee-ar, I fee-ar the glarr-moor
Ther-oo thy der-ooping larr-shes seen,
I fee-ar, I fee-ar the GLAR-moor . . ."

"Oh, shut up!" said Bill.

Lord Tidmouth, ceasing to sing, turned amiably.

"Sorry, old top," he said. "I thought you were dead."

"What are you doing?"

"Playing solitaire, laddie." He fiddled with the cards, and absently burst into song once more. "Just playing SOL-i-taire . . ."

"Stop it!"

"Stop playing?"

"Stop yowling."

"Oh, right ho."

Bill rose and surveyed the card-strewn table with an unfriendly eye.

"Do you mean to say you really get any pleasure out of that rotten game?"

"Darned good game," protested Lord Tidmouth. He manipulated the cards. "Did you ever hear the story of the ventriloquist who played solitaire? He used to annoy his wife by holding long conversations with himself in his sleep. It became such a trial to the poor woman that she had serious thoughts of getting a divorce. And then one evening, by the greatest good luck, he caught himself cheating at solitaire and never spoke to himself again."

"Silly idiot!"

"Harsh words, old man, from host to guest. Nice place you've got here, Bill."

"Glad you like it."

"Been in the family quite a time, I take it?"

"A few centuries."

Bill's manner became furtive. He glanced to and fro in a conspiratorial fashion. It seemed that whatever had been on his mind all the evening was coming to a head.

"Squiffy!"

"Hullo?"

"Where's my uncle?"

"Out in the corridor putting vigorously. What a man!"

"Thank God that 'll keep him occupied for awhile. Squiffy, there's something I want to tell you."

"Carry on, old boy."

"Tonight I . . ."

He broke off. A stout figure, swathed in a mauve smoking jacket and carrying a putter, had entered.

"It's coming!" said Sir Hugo Drake joyfully. "The knack is coming. I'm getting it. Four out of my last seven shots straight into the glass."

"I think I'll take a shot in a glass myself," said Lord

Tidmouth, rising and making for the table where the decanter and siphon so invitingly stood.

"I fancy I have at last found out what has been wrong with my putting . . . William!"

"Hullo?"

"I say I think I have at last found out what has been wrong with my putting."

"Oh?"

"I've been gripping too tight. How right that girl was. Grip firmly but lightly, she said, that's the secret. It stands to reason . . ."

"Excuse me," said Bill, and removed himself with the smooth swiftness of a family ghost.

Sir Hugo stood staring after him. This was not the first time activity of this sort had suddenly descended upon his nephew in the middle of a conversation. He did not like it. Apart from the incivility of it, it seemed to him ominous. He confided this fear to Lord Tidmouth, who was still occupied with his spot.

"Lord Tidmouth!"

His companion lowered his glass courteously.

"Present!" he said. "Here in person."

Sir Hugo jerked a thumb towards the door.

"Did you see that?"

"What?"

"Did you see the curious, sudden way that boy left the room?"

"He did move fairly nippily," agreed Lord Tidmouth. "Now you saw him and now you didn't, as it were."

"He has been like that ever since he got home—nervous, rude, jumpy, abrupt."

"Yes, I've noticed he's been a bit jumpy."

"What do you suppose is the matter with him?"

"Not been eating enough yeast," said Lord Tidmouth confidently.

"No! He's in love."

"You think so?"

"I'm sure of it. I noticed it the day I arrived here. I had begun to tell him about the long brassie shot I made at the sixteenth hole, and he gave a sort of hollow gasp and walked away."

"Walked away?"

"Walked away in the middle of a sentence. The boy's in love. There can be no other explanation."

Lord Tidmouth considered.

"Now I come to remember it, he did say something to me down at that seaside place about being in love."

"I was sure of it. William is pining for that peroxide woman."

"You mean Lottie?"

"The flashy young person I sent to the sanitarium."

Lord Tidmouth shook his head.

"I don't think so. I have an idea he told me he was in love with someone else."

Sir Hugo was not a man who took kindly to having his diagnoses questioned.

"Absurd! Nothing of the kind. Do you think I don't know what I'm talking about? He was infatuated with that young woman then, and he's still infatuated with her. Possibly we ought not to be surprised. After all, they parted only a mere two weeks ago. But I confess I am much disturbed."

"What are you going to do about it?"

A senile cunning gleamed from Sir Hugo's eyes.

"Rather ask what *have* I done about it."

"All right. What *have* you done about it?"

"Never mind."

"Then why did you tell me to ask?" said Lord Tidmouth, justly aggrieved.

He went to the table and mixed himself another whisky and soda with an injured air. Sir Hugo was far too occupied to observe it.

"Young man," he said, "have you ever studied psychology?"

"Psy——"

"—chology."

Lord Tidmouth shook his head.

"Well, no," he said, "not to any great extent. They didn't teach me much at school except the difference between right and wrong. There *is* some difference, but I've forgotten what."

"Have you ever asked yourself what is the secret of the glamour which this young woman exercises over William?"

"I suppose it's the same she used to exercise over *me*. Used to be married to her once, don't you know."

"What!"

"Oh yes. But it blew over."

Sir Hugo considered this unforeseen piece of information. He seemed to be turning it over in his mind.

"I cannot decide whether that is good or bad."

"Bit of both, I found it."

"I mean, whether it helps my plan or not."

"What plan?"

"It is based on psychology. I ask myself, What is

this young person's attraction for William based on?"

"Psychology?" asked Lord Tidmouth, who was becoming fogged.

"It is due to the fact that he has encountered her so far only in the gaudy atmosphere of hotels and dance halls—her natural setting. But suppose he should see her in the home of his ancestors, where every stick and stone breathes of family traditions, beneath the eyes of the family portraits? What then?"

"I'll bite. What?"

"She would disgust him. His self-respect would awaken. The scales would fall from his eyes, and his infatuation would wither and decay. Whatever his faults, William is a Bannister."

"In that case, it might be a sound scheme to invite her down here for a visit."

Sir Hugo chuckled.

"Ha, ha! Young man, can you keep a secret?"

"I don't know. I've never tried."

"Well, let me tell you this, Lord Tidmouth. I have the situation well in hand. Youth," said Sir Hugo, "may fancy it can control its own destiny, but Age, with its riper wisdom, is generally able, should the occasion arise, to lay it a stymie. Excuse me, I must go and putt."

Lord Tidmouth resumed his solitaire. He was glad Sir Hugo had left him. He had nothing specific against the old buster, but it was pleasanter to be alone. Presently he was deep in his game once more, and singing like a nightingale.

"My strength's something—something . . ." sang

Lord Tidmouth. And then, more confidently, as one feeling himself on secure ground:

"And a right good shield of hides untanned . . ."

He put a red five on a black six.

"And a right good shield of hides untanned . . ."

A four of clubs went on the red five.

"Which on my arm I ber-huckle . . ."

A slight but definite sound as of one in pain, coming from his immediate rear, aroused him, and he turned. He perceived his friend William Bannister.

"Hullo, Bill, old man. You back?"

Bill was looking cautiously about him.

"Where's my uncle?"

"Just oozed off. Want me to call him?"

"Good heavens, no. Squiffy . . ."

"Hullo?"

Bill did not reply for a few moments. These moments he occupied in wandering in a rather feverish manner about the room, fiddling with various objects that came in his path. He halted at the mantelpiece, gazed for a while at the portrait of his great-grandfather which hung above it, quickly wearied of the spectacle and resumed his prowling. Lord Tidmouth watched him with growing disapproval. Between Sir Hugo Drake and this William, his quiet, peaceful evening was being entirely disorganised.

"Squiffy!" said Bill, halting suddenly.

"Still here," replied Lord Tidmouth plaintively. "What's the idea? Training for a marathon?"

"Squiffy," said Bill, "listen to me. We're pals, aren't we?"

"Absolutely. Bosom is the way I should put it."

"Very well, then. I want you to do me a great service."

"What?"

"Get my uncle out of the way tonight."

"Murder him?"

"If you like. Anyway, go to his room with him and see that he gets to sleep. Tonight I want to be alone."

Lord Tidmouth had listened so far, but he refused to listen any further without lodging a definite protest. It was not so much the fact that, having been invited down to this place for a restful visit, he found himself requested by his host to go and tell his uncle bedtime stories. What was jarring his sensitive soul was the sinister atmosphere his old friend had begun to create.

"Bill, old man," he said, "you're being very mysterious this P. M. You shimmer about and dash in and out of rooms and make dark, significant speeches. All you need is a mask and false whiskers and you could step into any mystery play and no questions asked. What's up?"

"I'll tell you."

"You forgot to say 'Hist'!"

Bill drew up a chair and sank his voice to a whisper.

"I've got a big thing on tonight and I must not be interrupted."

The pained look on Lord Tidmouth's face deepened. Of course, he supposed, it didn't really matter, seeing that they were alone, but he did wish that Bill could conduct a chat with an old crony without converting it into something that suggested an executive session of the Black Hand or a conference between apaches in some underground den in Montmartre.

"Old egg," he said, "do stop being mysterious. A big thing, you say? Well, tell me in a frank, manly way what it is. Get it right off the chest, and we'll both feel easier."

Bill mused, as if seeking words.

"Well, if you want the thing in a nutshell, tonight, Squiffy, I put my fate to the test—to win or lose it all, as the poet says."

"What poet?"

"What the devil does it matter what poet?"

"I merely asked."

"Montrose, if you really want to know."

"I don't."

Bill rose and resumed his pacing.

"Squiffy, do you know what it is to be in love?"

"Do I!" Lord Tidmouth spoke with a specialist's briskness. "My dear chap, except for an occasional rainy Monday, I don't suppose I've been out of love in the last six years. If you think a man can accumulate four wives without knowing what it is to be in love, try it and see."

"Well, I'm in love. So much in love that I could howl like a dog." He broke off and regarded his companion sharply. "I suppose," he said, "you're going to ask 'What dog?' "

"No, no," Lord Tidmouth assured him. He knew—no man better—that there were all sorts of dogs. Mastiffs, Pekes, Alsatians, Aberdeen terriers . . . scores of them. He had had no intention of saying "What dog?"

Bill clenched his hands.

"It's awful. It's killing me."

Lord Tidmouth was impressed.

"Bill, old man," he said, "this is serious news. We all thought you had got over it. So your old uncle was actually right! Well, well!"

"What do you mean?"

"I felt all along," proceeded Lord Tidmouth, "that something like this would happen. I wanted to warn you at the time. You see, having been married to her myself, I know her fascination. Yes, I nearly warned you at the time. 'Bill, old bird,' I came within a toucher of saying, 'pause before it is too late!' And now she's in a sanitarium, and you're pining for her. 'Oh, for the touch of a vanished hand . . .' "

Bill stared an unfriendly stare.

"What on earth are you talking about? Who's in a sanitarium?"

"Lottie, of course."

"Lottie? Are you really idiot enough to suppose I'm in love with Lottie?"

His tone stung Lord Tidmouth.

"Better men than you have been, Bill," he said. "Myself, for one. The recent Higginbotham, presumably, for another. Let me tell you that there are many more difficult things in this world than falling in love with Lottie. Whom are you in love with, then?"

Bill breathed rapturously.

"Sally!"

"Who's Sally?"

"Sally Smith."

Lord Tidmouth made a great mental effort.

"You don't mean the lady doctor down at Bingley?"

"Yes, I do."

"And you're in love with her?"

"Yes."

"Well," said Lord Tidmouth, bewildered, "this is all new stuff to me." He reflected. "But, if you miss her so much, why did you come down here, miles away from her?"

"I couldn't stay near her. It was driving me mad."

"Why?"

"She wouldn't let me tell her how much I loved her."

"I see."

Bill sprang up.

"Shall I tell you something, Squiffy?"

"By all means, old boy. I'm here to listen."

"I went to see her just before I left Bingley. I was absolutely determined that this time I would ask her to marry me. And do you know what happened?"

"What?"

A bitter laugh escaped Bill Bannister. At least, Lord Tidmouth presumed that it was a bitter laugh. It had sounded more like a death rattle.

"The moment I appeared—before I could even speak—she said: 'Put out your tongue!' "

"What did you do?"

"I put it out. 'Coated,' she said, and prescribed a mild tonic. Now, could I have followed that up by asking her to be my wife?"

"It wasn't what you would call a good cue," admitted Lord Tidmouth.

"I left," said Bill. "I came away, cursing. Cursing everything—myself, my luck and the fate that ever brought us together. I came down here, hoping that I would get over it. Not a chance. I'm worse than ever. But today, thank heaven, I got an idea."

"What was that?"

Bill looked about the room warily, as if suspecting the presence of Hugo Drakes in every nook and cranny. Relieved to see not even one, he resumed.

"I said to myself—she's a doctor. If I were ill, she would fly to my side. I looked her up in the telephone book. I found her name. I sat staring at that telephone book most of the afternoon, and it stared back at me. At five o'clock I gave in and . . ."

"Good Lord! Telephoned?"

"Yes. I pretended to be my man. I said that Mr Bannister was seriously ill. We were sending the car and would she come at once."

Lord Tidmouth whistled.

"You certainly don't mind taking a chance."

"Not when there's something worth taking a chance for. It's a two hours' ride in the car. The chauffeur left at half-past six. He should have reached her between half-past eight and nine. She ought to get here just about eleven."

"It's nearly eleven now."

"Yes. So can you wonder I'm a little jumpy?"

"Do you think she'll come?"

Bill quivered.

"She *must* come. She must. And I shall have it out with her, fairly and squarely. No more dodging and evasion. She shan't put me off this time. . . . So now perhaps you understand why you've got to keep my infernal, snooping, blundering, fussing busybody of an uncle out of the way."

"But he'll hear her drive up in the car."

"Why? The car's almost noiseless."

Lord Tidmouth pondered.

"Well," he said at length, "I'm glad I'm not you."

"Why?"

"Because it is my firm and settled belief, old top, that, when she gets here and finds it was all a put-up job, this female is going to cut up rough."

"Don't call her a female."

"Well, she *is*, isn't she? I mean, that's rather what you might call the idea, I should have thought."

"She won't suspect. I shall convince her that I'm a sick man."

"By the time she has done with you you probably will be. Hell hath no fury like a woman who's come eighty miles to be made a fool of."

"Don't be such a pessimist."

"Oh, all right. Have it your own way. All I can say is, may the Lord have mercy on your soul. I mean . . ."

"Sh!" whispered Bill sharply. He turned to the door. "Hullo, Uncle, how's the putting coming along?"

Sir Hugo Drake was in spacious mood. He beamed cordially.

"A very marked and sustained improvement."

"That's good. Off to bed now?"

"Yes. Off to bed now. Early to bed, early to rise, nothing like it for keeping the eye clear and the hand steady."

"Tidmouth wants to come up with you and have a chat."

"Delighted."

"Tell him that excellent story of yours about the caddie and the indiarubber tee."

"Certainly. Well, come along, my boy. You coming, William?"

"No, I think I'll sit up a little longer."

"Good night, then. See you in the morning."

He wandered out. Lord Tidmouth lingered. He seemed a little anxious.

"Is that a long story, Bill?"

"Longish," admitted Bill. "But to help a pal, Squiffy . . ."

"Oh, all right," said Lord Tidmouth resignedly. "We Tidmouths never desert a friend. Well, honk honk!"

He smiled bravely, and followed Sir Hugo.

The summons to William Bannister's sickbed had come to Sally, oddly enough, at a moment when she had just been thinking of that sufferer. For it is a curious fact that, busy woman though she was, she had found herself thinking quite a good deal about Bill in these last two weeks. And, if excuses must be made for her, let these meditations be set down to the quality in him that made him different from other men—his naïve directness.

Sally, both in her native America and during her stay in England, had been called upon at fairly frequent intervals to reject the proffered hands and hearts of many men. These had conducted the negotiations in a variety of ways, but none, not even the most forceful, had affected her quite like William Bannister. There was a childlike earnestness about his wooing which she found engaging.

It seemed a pity to her that with the admirable quality of directness he should combine that other quality which above all others in this world she despised and disliked—the quality of being content to sit down and loaf his life away on inherited money. She had seen so many of these good-looking, amiable, feckless Englishmen of private means, and all her instincts rose against them. Except as a joke, they were impossible. With so much to be done in life, they did nothing.

And Bill Bannister was one of them. She liked his looks and that easy, athletic swing of his body. She found him pleasant and agreeable. But he was also bone-idle, a well-bred waster, a drone who had nothing better to do with his time than hang about seashore resorts, dangling after perfumed and peroxided females of doubtful character.

For Sally's verdict on Lottie, pieced together from a brief acquaintance and a review of the dubious circumstances in which he had found her, was not a flattering one. She ignored the "Higginbotham" which should have been such a hallmark of respectability. She thoroughly disbelieved in the Higginbotham. Her views on the late Mr Higginbotham were identical with those of Betsy Prigg on her friend Sairey Gamp's friend Mrs Harris. Firmly and decisively, Sally had set Lottie down in the ranks of those who are so well described as "no better than they should be."

Sometimes Sally wondered a little why it was that

she should feel this odd indignation against a woman who was virtually a complete stranger. It could not be because the other had ensnared William Bannister. William Bannister and his affairs were, of course, nothing to her. So what might have seemed to a superficial investigator a straight case of jealousy was nothing of the kind. It did not matter to her a row of pins who entrapped William Bannister.

Nevertheless, every time she thought of Lottie, an odd thrill of indignation passed through Sally.

And every time she thought of William Bannister wasting his time on such a woman, she felt another thrill of indignation.

The whole thing was perplexing.

Her feelings, as she bowled along the Hampshire roads in Bill's car tonight, were mixed. She was sorry he was not feeling well, though she much doubted whether his ailment were as severe as she had been given to understand. Men were all alike—men of Bill Bannister's kind especially so. A pain in the toe and they thought they were dying.

Of the chance of visiting the home of Bill's ancestors she was glad. With her American love of the practical she combined that other American love for old houses and historic associations. She had read up The Manor, Woollam Chersey, in *Stately Homes of England,* and was intrigued to find that parts of it dated back to the thirteenth century, while even the more modern portions were at least Elizabethan. She looked forward to seeing on the morrow its park, its messuages, its pleasances and the record-breaking oak planted by the actual hand of King Charles the First.

Tonight, as she passed through the great gateway and bowled up the drive, there was little to be seen. Dark trees and banks of shrubs blocked what little would have been visible in the darkness. It was only when the car stopped that she realised that she had reached the house.

Sally got out and dismissed the chauffeur. She could find her way in. There was an open french window at the end of the lawn on her left, from which light proceeded. She made her way thither, and on the threshold stopped. A rather remarkable sight had met her eyes. Inside, walking with the brisk step of a man in perfect health up and down a cosily furnished room, was her patient. Anyone less wasted with sickness she had never seen.

Up and down the floor paced Bill. He was smoking a cigarette. A thrill of honest indignation shot through Sally. She saw all. And in the darkness her teeth came together with a little click.

Somewhere in the room a telephone tinkled. Bill moved beyond her range of vision. But his voice came to her clearly.

"Hullo? . . . Grosvenor 7525? . . . Doctor Smith's house? . . . This is Mr Bannister's valet speaking. Can you tell me if the doctor has left? . . . Just before nine? . . . Thank you . . . Hullo . . . The doctor will not be returning tonight . . . Yes, very serious. She will have to sit up with the patient . . . Yes . . . Good night."

There came the click of the receiver being replaced, and then for some moments silence. But a few moments later there was something for Sally to see again. Her patient had apparently left the room during this interval, for he now reappeared wearing a dark silk dressing gown. He then proceeded to arrange a pillow and lie down on the sofa. And after that he seemed to be of the opinion that the stage was adequately set, for he remained there without moving.

Sally waited no longer. Outwardly calm, but seething within with what Lord Tidmouth had called the fury of a woman who has driven eighty miles to be made a fool of, she walked briskly into the room.

"Good evening!" she said suddenly and sharply, and Bill Bannister shot up from the sofa as though propelled by an explosive.

Bill stood staring. His nervous system, in its highly strung condition, was not proof against this entirely unexpected greeting. The Manor was not haunted, but if it had been and if the family spectre had suddenly presented itself at his elbow and barked at him, he would have reacted in a very similar way. He gulped, and fingered his collar.

"You made me jump!" he said plaintively.

Sally was cool and hostile.

"Weren't you expecting me?"

"Er—yes. Yes. Of course."

"Well, here I am."

This was undeniable, and Bill should have accepted it as such. He should also have sunk back on the sofa, thus indicating that the effort he had just made had been too much for his frail strength. Instead, he became gushingly hospitable.

"I say, do sit down, won't you? Won't you have something to eat—something to drink?"

Sally raised her eyebrows.

"I must say," she observed, "that for a man who has brought a doctor a night journey of eighty miles you look surprisingly well."

Bill rejected the idea passionately.

"I'm not," he cried. "I'm desperately ill."

"Oh?" said Sally.

Bill's manner became defiant, almost sullen.

"You can't tell how a man's feeling just by looking at him," he said.

"I don't intend to. We'll have a thorough examination."

A devout look came into Bill's eyes.

"It's like a dream," he said.

"What is?"

"Your being here . . . in my home . . ."

"Tell me your symptoms," said Sally.

Bill blinked.

"Did you say symptoms?"

"I did."

"Well . . . I say, do let me help you off with your coat."

"I can manage," said Sally. She removed her wraps and threw them on a chair. "Now, then . . . Hello! You're shivering!"

"Am I?" said Bill.

"Do you feel chilly?"

"No. Hot all over."

"Let me feel your pulse . . . H'm! A hundred and ten. Very interesting. And yet you haven't a temperature. A pulse of a hundred and ten without fever. Quite remarkable. Do you feel dizzy?"

"Yes," said Bill truthfully.

"Then sit down."

"Thanks," said Bill, doing so. "Won't you?"

Sally opened her bag, and from it removed an odd something, at which her patient gazed with unconcealed apprehension.

"What's that?" he asked.

"Stethoscope," said Sally briefly. "Now we can get on."

"Yes," said Bill doubtfully. He had heard of stethoscopes and knew them to be comparatively harmless, but he was still uneasy. In his visions of this moment, he had always seen this girl bending over him with a divine sympathy in her lovely eyes—trembling a little, perhaps—possibly passing a cool hand over his forehead. Up to the present, she had done none of these things. Instead, she seemed to him—though this, he forced himself to feel, was merely due to his guilty conscience—annoyed about something.

A simple solution of the mystery came to him. In spite of the fact that she had ignored his previous offer of refreshment, she really needed some. She had had a tiring journey, and tiring journeys always affected women like this. He recalled an aunt of his, who, until you shot a cup of tea into her, always became—even after the simplest trip—a menace to man and beast.

"I say, do have something to eat and drink," he urged.

Sally frowned.

"Later," she said. "Now, then—the symptoms, please."

Bill made a last effort to stem the tide.

"Must we talk about my symptoms?" he asked plaintively.

"Might I mention," retorted Sally, "that I've driven eighty miles simply in order to talk about them."

"But surely there's not such a desperate hurry as all that? I mean, can't we have just five minutes' conversation. . . ." Her eye was not encouraging, but he persevered. "You don't seem to understand how tremendously happy it makes me—to see you sitting there . . ."

Sally cut into his rambling discourse like an east wind.

"It may seem eccentric to you, Mr Bannister," she said frigidly, "but when I get an urgent call to visit an invalid I find my thoughts sort of straying in the direction of his health. It's a foolish habit we doctors have. So may I repeat—the symptoms?" She fixed him with a compelling glance. "When," she asked, "did you first notice that there was anything wrong with you?"

Bill could answer that.

"Three weeks ago."

"About the time you first met me."

"Yes."

"An odd coincidence. What happened?"

"My heart stood still."

"It couldn't."

"It did."

"Hearts don't stand still."

"Mine did," insisted Bill stoutly. "It then had strong palpitations. They've been getting worse ever since. Sometimes," he proceeded, beginning to get into his stride, "I feel as if I were going to suffocate. It is as if I were being choked inside by an iron hand."

"Probably dyspepia. Go on."

"My hands tremble. My head aches. My feet feel like lead. I have floating spots before the eyes and I can't sleep."

"No?"

"Not a wink. I toss on my pillow. I turn feverishly from side to side. But it's all no good. Dawn comes and finds me still awake. I stare before me hopelessly. Another night," concluded Bill with fine pathos, "has passed, and in the garden outside the roosters are crowing."

"Anything connected with roosters," said Sally, "you had better tell to a vet."

A man in a sitting position finds it difficult to draw himself up indignantly, but Bill did his best.

"Is that all you can do to a patient—laugh at him?"

"If you think I am finding this a laughing matter," said Sally grimly, "you're wrong. Undress, please."

Bill started violently.

"What . . . what did you say?" he quavered.

"Undress," Sally repeated.

"But . . . but I can't."

"Would you like me to help you?"

"I mean—is it necessary?"

"Quite."

"But . . ."

Sally surveyed him coolly.

"I notice the vascular motors are still under poor control," she said. "Why do you blush?"

"What do you expect me to do—cheer?" Bill's voice

shook. The prude in him had been deeply stirred. "Look here," he demanded, "do you mean to tell me this is the first time any of your male patients has jibbed at undressing in front of you?"

"Oh no. I had a case last week."

"I'm glad," said Bill primly, "that somebody has a little delicacy besides myself."

"It wasn't delicacy. He didn't want me to see that he was wearing detachable cuffs. You know the kind? They fasten on with a clip, and are generally made of celluloid. Like motion-picture films."

"Er—do you go much to the pictures?" asked Bill.

Sally refused to allow the conversation to be diverted.

"Never mind whether I go to the pictures," she said. "Please undress."

Bill gave up the struggle. He threw off his dressing gown.

"That 'll do for the present," said Sally. "I can't think what you were making such a fuss about. Your cuffs aren't detachable. . . . Now, please."

She placed the stethoscope against his chest, and applied her ear to it. Bill gazed down upon the top of her head emotionally.

"I wonder," he said, "if you realise what this means to me—to see you here—in my home—to feel that we two are alone together at last . . ."

"Did you ever have any children's diseases?"

"No. . . . Alone together at last . . ."

"Mumps?" said Sally.

Bill gulped.

"No!"

"Measles?"

"No!" shouted Bill.

Sally looked up.

"I merely asked," she said.

Bill was quivering with self-pity.

"It's too bad," he said. "Here I am, trying to pour out my soul to you, and you keep interrupting with questions about mumps and measles."

"My dear Mr Bannister," said Sally, "I'm not interested in your soul. My job has to do with what the hymnbook calls your 'vile body.' "

There was a pause. She put her ear to the stethoscope again.

"Can't you understand," cried Bill, breaking into eloquence once more, "that the mere sight of you sets every nerve in my body tingling? When you came in I felt like a traveller in the desert who is dying of thirst and suddenly comes upon an oasis. I felt . . ."

"Any retching or nausea?"

"Oh, my God!"

"Now tell me about your sex life," said Sally.

Bill recoiled.

"Stand still."

"I won't stand still," said Bill explosively.

"Then move about," said Sally equably. "But give me the information I asked for."

Bill eyed her austerely.

"Don't you know the meaning of the word 'reticence'?" he asked.

"Of course not. I'm a doctor."

Bill took a turn up and down the room.

"Well, naturally," he said with dignity, halting once more, "I have had—er—experiences—like other men."

Sally was at the stethoscope again.

"Um-hum?" she said.

"I admit it. There *have* been women in my life."

"Say ninety-nine."

"Not half as many as that!"

"Say ninety-nine, please."

"Oh?" Bill became calmer. "I didn't . . . I thought . . . I imagined that you were referring . . . Well, in short, ninety-nine."

Sally straightened herself. She put the stethoscope away.

"Thank you," she said. "Your lungs appear to be all right. Remove the rest of your clothes, please."

"What!"

"You heard."

"I won't do it," cried Bill pinkly.

Sally shrugged her shoulders.

"Just as you like," she said. "Then the examination is finished." She paused. "Tell me, Mr Bannister," she asked, "just to satisfy my curiosity, what sort of a fool did you think I was?"

Bill gaped.

"I beg your pardon?"

"I'm glad you have the grace to. Did you imagine that this was the first time I had ever been called out into the country?"

"I . . ."

"Let me tell you it is not. And do you know what usually happens when I am called to the country? I see you don't," she said, as Bill choked wordlessly. "Well, when I am sent for to visit a patient in the country, Mr Bannister, the road is lined with anxious relatives, waiting for the car. They help me out and bustle me into the house. They run around like chickens with their heads cut off—and everybody who isn't having hysterics on the stairs is in the kitchen brewing camomile tea."

"Camomile tea?"

"People who get sick in the country are always given camomile tea."

"I never knew that before."

"You'll learn a lot of things," said Sally, "if you stick around with me. And one of them, Mr Bannister, is that I'm not a complete idiot. You'll excuse my slight warmth. I've driven eighty miles on a fool's errand, and somehow I find it a little irritating."

Bill waved his hands agitatedly.

"But I tell you you're wrong."

"What! Have you the nerve to pretend there's anything whatever the matter with you?"

"Certainly there is. I—I'm not myself."

"I congratulate you."

"I'm a very sick man."

"And I'm a very angry woman."

Bill coughed an injured cough.

"Of course, if you don't believe me, there's nothing more to say."

"Oh, isn't there?" said Sally. "I'll find plenty more to say, trust *me*. I may as well tell you, Mr Bannister, that when I arrived I looked in at the window and saw you striding about, the picture of health. A moment later, the telephone rang and you went to it and said you were your valet . . ."

Bill flushed darkly. He moved to the window and stood there, looking out with his back turned. Sally watched him with satisfaction. Her outburst had left her feeling more amiable.

Bill wheeled round. His face was set. He spoke through clenched teeth.

"I see," he said. "So you knew all along, and you've been amusing yourself at my expense?"

"You might say—getting a little of my own back."

"You've had a lot of fun with me, haven't you?"

"Quite a good deal, since you mention it."

"And now, I suppose, you're going?"

"Going?" said Sally. "Of course I'm not. I shall sleep here. You don't expect me to drive all night, do you?"

"I beg your pardon," said Bill. He pointed to the gallery that ran round two sides of the room. "You'll be up there."

"Thank you."

Bill laughed shortly.

"Well, it's something, I suppose, that you have consented to sleep under my roof."

"You could hardly have expected me to go to the garage."

"No. I suppose you would like to be turning in, then?"

"Yes, please."

"I'll show you your room."

"You have already."

"Well . . . good night," said Bill.

"Good night," said Sally.

He stood without moving, watching her as she went up the stairs. She reached the door, opened it, and was gone. Bill turned sharply and flung himself into a chair.

He had been sitting for some minutes, with only his thoughts for unpleasant company, when there was the sound of a footstep on the stairs, and he sprang up as though electrified.

But it was not Sally. It was only Lord Tidmouth. That ill-used gentleman was looking rather weary, and his eyes, as he reached the foot of the stairs, were fixed purposefully on the decanter on the table. He moved towards it with a stealthy rapidity, like a leopard; and only when he had poured into a glass a generous measure of the life-restoring fluid did he turn to his host.

"Hullo, Bill, old man," said his lordship.

Bill regarded him sourly.

"Oh, it's you, is it?" he said.

Lord Tidmouth sighed.

"What's left of me after an hour's tête-à-tête with the old relative," he said. "Bill, that uncle of yours waggles a wicked jawbone!"

"Does he?"

"He talked and talked and talked. And then he talked some more. Mostly about his mashie shots. I got him off to bye-bye at last, and I've tottered down to restore the tissues with a spot of alcohol. They say," continued Lord Tidmouth earnestly, "that strong drink biteth like a serpent and—if I remember correctly—stingeth like a jolly old adder. Well, all I have to say is—let it! That's what I say, Bill—*let* it! It's what it's there for. Excuse me for a moment, old man, while I mix myself a stiffish serpent and soda."

He turned to the table again.

"So you got him off to sleep?" said Bill.

Lord Tidmouth's fingers had been closing about the siphon, but he courteously suspended operations in order to reply to his host's question.

"Yes," he said, "I got him off to sleep. But at infinite cost to life and limb. I feel a perfect wreck. However, I've left him slumbering like a little child, one hand still clutching James Braid's *Advanced Golf*. So that's that."

"Much obliged. Well, I'll be turning in."

"Half a moment," said Lord Tidmouth. "Isn't it about time that lady doctor of yours rolled up? Allowing two hours for the journey—that is, assuming she had no puncture or blowout or engine trouble or lost the way or . . . "

"Oh, go to blazes!" said Bill.

Lord Tidmouth watched his disappearing back with rather an aggrieved air.

"Not one of our good listeners!" he murmured.

Then, having sterner work before him than the consideration of a host's brusqueness, he addressed himself once more to the siphon.

Lord Tidmouth was a careful man with siphons. Experience had taught him that a too vehement pressing of the trigger led to disaster. Strong drink might bite like an adder, but soda water could spout like a geyser. He knew the perils perfectly, and it was, therefore, all the more annoying that a moment later a hissing stream should have shot up between his cuff and his skin.

This happened because, as he was in the very act of working the trigger arrangement, a loud and breezy voice in his immediate rear spoke.

"Hullo!" it said.

Voices speaking to Lord Tidmouth where no voice should have been always affected him powerfully. He became involved in a Niagara of seltzer, from which he emerged to gaze censoriously at the intruder.

"If you know me a thousand years," he was beginning, as he turned, "never do that again!" Then he saw the newcomer steadily and saw her whole. For it was a she. It was, as a matter of fact, none other than the first of his battalion of wives—the exuberant Lottie Higginbotham. And he stared at her as at a vision.

"Great God of Battles!" said Lord Tidmouth. "You!"

Lottie was completely at her ease. She placed on the floor the suitcase which she was carrying, and with a dexterous hand removed the whisky and soda from her companion's grasp. She drank deeply and, having done so, sighed with satisfaction.

"You always did know how to mix them, Squiffy," she said.

It was a handsome compliment—and rather touching, in its way, as giving evidence that the memory of the dear old days still lingered. But Lord Tidmouth paid no attention to it. He was still goggling.

"What on earth are you doing here?" he asked blankly.

"Who, me?" said Lottie.

"Yes, you."

"I was sent for."

"How do you mean, sent for?"

"I got a telegram from Bill's uncle asking me to come."

A blinding flash of light illuminated Lord Tidmouth's darkness. He recalled the veiled hints the old boy had dropped earlier in the evening. So this was what he had been hinting at!

"Did he specify that you were to come beetling in at midnight?" he inquired.

"I came directly I got the telegram. It sounded interesting."

"Oh?" Lord Tidmouth pondered for awhile. "Well, welcome to the manor and all that sort of rot," he said.

Lottie was very bright and animated. She flitted about the room like a hummingbird.

"This looks a pretty good sort of place," she said. "I can see myself in a place like this. Who are all these?" she asked, indicating the portraits.

"Just ancestors," said Lord Tidmouth. "Bill's. Bill's ancestors."

"No beauty chorus," was Lottie's comment, after she had made her round of inspection. "Talking of Bill, is he expecting me?"

"No, he's not!"

"Oh? Then I shall come on him as a surprise."

"Surprise," said Lord Tidmouth, with feeling, "is *right!*"

"Listen," said Lottie. "Do you know why Sir Hugo wanted me to come here?"

Lord Tidmouth was embarrassed. He did know, but he could hardly impart the information.

"I couldn't tell you."

"I'm telling *you,*" said Lottie brightly. "I thought it all out on the train. Bill has discovered that he can't get on without me. I knew it would happen. He's pining for me. Yessir, that's what that boy's doing—pining for me."

"Well . . ."

"It stands to reason," argued Lottie, "he must be pretty crazy about me to make his old uncle wire for me in such a hurry."

Lord Tidmouth closed his eyes. He seemed to be praying.

"Full information," he said, "will no doubt be supplied tomorrow by the aged relative. But, if you'll take a pal's advice—if you'll be guided by one to whom you once stood in a sacred and tender relationship, viz., marriage," explained Lord Tidmouth, "you will biff off at the earliest opportunity."

"What!"

"At the very earliest opp."

"What are you talking about?"

Lord Tidmouth groaned in spirit. He was feeling unequal to the situation. At any moment now, he told himself, that lady doctor of old Bill's would be breezing in, and naturally the last thing the dear old boy would wish was to have the place congested with extraneous females. Sir Hugo Drake, the pre-eminent dodderer, had made a proper mess of things.

"You just tuck yourself away somewhere till tomorrow morning," he urged, "and then we'll smuggle you off."

Lottie stared. She had never had a very high opinion of her former husband's intelligence, but she had never known him to descend into such abysses of lunacy as this.

"I think you're cuckoo," she said. "What do I want

to go away for? Bill's in love with me and can't live without me."

"Absolutely," said Lord Tidmouth. "Of course. Quite so. Yes. Beyond a question. Indubitably. Only . . ."

"Well?"

"Nothing, nothing. You see that room on top of the stairs? Technically, it's mine, but you can have it for tonight. Not the one to the right. That's Bill's. The one to the left. Accept it with my hearty good wishes."

"What 'll you do?"

"Oh, I'll doss somewhere. And in the morning . . ."

Lottie eyed him sharply.

"Listen!" she said.

"Hullo?"

"Is anything the matter?"

"The matter?"

"You're acting sort of mysterious, it seems to me, and I'm wondering if there's any funny business going on. Are you trying to keep Bill and me apart?"

"No, no."

"Well, you better hadn't, that's all," said Lottie decidedly. "If I find you're pulling any smooth stuff, I'll murder you. Nothing could be fairer than that, could it?"

"Absolutely not."

"Well, good night, then."

"Good night!" said Lord Tidmouth.

Alone at last, he found in the confused welter of his thoughts one thing clear—that he had not yet had that drink and that he wanted it now more than ever. He moved to the table, and began the ritual again. He had barely completed it when once more a voice spoke behind him.

"You still up?" It was his old friend, Bill Bannister. There was surprise in Bill's voice. Also irritation and peevishness. "Why the devil don't you go to bed?"

"Why don't *you?*" rejoined Lord Tidmouth, not unreasonably.

"I'm restless," said Bill. "I can't sleep."

Lord Tidmouth eyed him pityingly. The nonsleeping his old friend had done so far would, he felt, be a mere nothing compared to the nonsleeping he would do when he heard the latest.

"Bill," he said, and his tone was the unmistakable tone of a man who is going to break something gently. "I've a piece of information to impart."

"Keep it for the morning."

"But it's serious. Bill, we have a little visitor!"

"I know. I know."

Lord Tidmouth was relieved.

"Oh, you *know?* I thought you didn't. But how do you know?" he went on, puzzled. "She only just . . ."

"Stop babbling and go to bed."

"Yes, but, Bill . . ."

"Shut up."

"Lottie . . ."

"Don't talk to me about Lottie."

"I was only saying that Lottie . . ."

"Stop it."

"I just wanted to mention that Lottie . . ."

"Will you get out!"

Lord Tidmouth gave it up.

"Oh, all right," he said resignedly. "I think I'll take

a stroll in the garden. Well, bung-oh! And I came down here for a rest cure!"

Bill ran quickly up the stairs and knocked at Sally's door. The conclusion of their recent conversation had left him in a nervous and disordered frame of mind. Though she had plainly shown herself of the opinion that all had been said that needed to be said, he was unable to adopt this view. He was full of talk, and considered that in their late interview he had but scratched the surface.

"Sally!" he said in a choking voice.

A voice from within answered.

"What is it? Who's there?"

"Come out. I want to talk to you."

Sally emerged. She was wearing a pale green wrap.

"Well?" she said.

Bill did not answer immediately. The sight of the wrap had had a stunning effect. He had not supposed that it was possible that this girl could look prettier than when he had seen her last, but she had accomplished this stupendous feat with ease. His legs shook, and he leaned against the banisters.

"Have you got everything you want?" he managed to ask at length.

"Yes, thank you. I find that you have given me your room."

"Yes."

"Where are you going to sleep?"

"I shall manage."

"Oh? Well, it's very kind of you." She paused. "Was that all you wanted to say to me?"

"No," said Bill urgently.

"Well?"

"Don't stand in that doorway. Come out here."

"Just as you like. Well?"

Bill gulped.

"I've been walking about in the garden," he said.

"Yes?"

"Thinking."

"Yes?"

"Trying to get a grip on myself."

"I hope you were successful," said Sally politely.

"I wasn't."

Sally smiled indulgently.

"Too bad," she said. "Well, good night."

"Come back."

"Sorry," said Sally, returning. "I thought you had finished."

"I haven't begun." He moved to the head of the stairs. "Come on down. We can't talk here."

"Do we want to talk?"

"I do."

"Oh, very well."

She followed him down the stairs.

"Now," said Bill, "we can begin."

Sally had perched herself on the arm of a chair. She eyed him coolly.

"Don't you country folk ever go to bed?" she asked. "I had no idea you wandered about the house all night, knocking at people's doors and dragging them out for cosy talks."

Bill scowled.

"You seem amused."

"I am," said Sally.

"Oh? Well, let me tell you," said Bill, "that we have now finished with the amusing part of this business. I now propose to call your attention to the fact that this little farce, which seems to entertain you so much, has a serious side. I'm going to have it out with you here and now."

"Proceed. You interest me strangely."

"Don't laugh at me!"

"What else do you expect me to do?"

Bill ground his heel into the carpet.

"In the first place," he said, "I admit that I did get you down here by a trick."

"A contemptible trick."

"That's as it may be. Anyway, you're here, and you've got to listen to me."

Sally yawned.

"And to cut a long story short . . ."

"I'll make it short enough. Three words will be sufficient. I love you."

"This is wonderful news."

"That's right. Laugh! Listen. You think you can play the fool with a man as much as you please—hold him off with a raised eyebrow when he becomes too pressing—keep him under control with a laugh . . . "

"Why, this is eloquence! The Boy Orator!"

"Oh, you may sneer, but you know in your heart you're afraid."

Sally stiffened. The smile faded from her lips. She froze.

"Afraid? You flatter yourself."

"I may not be your match at fencing," said Bill,

"but the bludgeon is quite as handy a weapon as the rapier."

"From the insight you have given me into your character tonight," said Sally, "I should have thought your favourite weapon would have been the blackjack."

"You and I are going to settle things tonight. You have known right from the start that I loved you, and from our first meeting you have fought me. All right! Tonight shall decide which of us two is the strongest."

"*Stronger*. Didn't they teach you that at school? Even when insulting a woman, always be grammatical."

Bill glowered.

"So I'm insulting you? By offering you my love?"

"No," said Sally. "By suggesting that, if I refuse it, you will employ force. For that is what you are suggesting, is it not?"

"Yes. It is."

"Good," said Sally. "Then excuse me for a moment."

She got up.

"What are you doing?"

"I was merely going to fetch my bag and prepare a soothing injection. I should think two centigrams of morphia would be sufficient."

Bill seized her wrist.

"Stop fooling!"

"Oh!" Sally could not restrain a gasp. "You're very strong."

"I'm glad you're beginning to realise it."

"Let me go."

"I won't!" said Bill. "Never again. Well?" he said. "Here you are, in my arms. How do you like it? Now try to be aloof and superior. Now try to hold me off with your matter-of-factness."

"You beast!"

"Beast, eh?" Bill laughed. "I'm improving. Just now I was only a poor fool—just something to laugh at. Laugh at me now—if you can."

Sally suddenly ceased to struggle.

"Oh well!" she said. "They always warned me it was dangerous to be a doctor. Do you know, the last man who treated me like this was a lunatic. In the violent ward of an asylum. But he was more decent than you. He merely wanted to murder me."

She felt the arms that were holding her unclasp. She sank onto the sofa. Bill was looking away from her, out of the window. After a moment, he spoke.

"All right," he said. "You win. I beg your pardon," he said formally.

Sally was herself again.

"Don't mention it," she said. "You might just as well apologise for having rheumatism."

"What!"

"It wasn't your fault. The thing was purely pathological. But I shall have to cure you . . . I'll write you a little prescription."

Bill started.

"For God's sake!"

Sally went to the desk, and took up a pencil.

"Kalii bromati . . . " he heard her murmur. "Natrii bromati . . . Grammata quinque . . . " She got up. "Here you are," she said amiably. "One powder three times a day after meals. Any druggist will make that up for you."

"You're very kind!"

"In addition there will be hygienic regulation of your mode of living. Avoid excitement and mental strain."

"Thanks," said Bill. "That's a great help."

"Take plenty of fresh air, do physical jerks every morning, and eat plenty of vegetables. Good night!"

She stroked his face softly, and he quivered. He looked up amazed.

"Sally!"

"What's the matter?"

"You stroked my face."

"Yes."

"Gently."

"Yes."

"Almost—lovingly."

"Yes."

Bill blinked.

"Then . . ."

"Oh, don't jump to conclusions," said Sally. "The gesture was purely automatic. We doctors often stroke our patients' faces when they have passed the crisis."

"Oh? So you think I have passed the crisis?"

"I think so. You see, you had the sense to call in a good doctor. Good night."

She walked composedly up the stairs. And, as she did so, the door of Lottie's room opened, and its occupant came yawning into view.

"Squiffy!" called Lottie, who, thinking things over in bed, had decided that what was needed to induce sleep was another of her erstwhile mate's scientifically blended glassfuls.

Her eye fell on Bill, gaping below, and she gave tongue cheerily.

"Hullo, Bill!"

She perceived Sally.

"Hul-*lo!*" she said.

Sally said nothing. She walked into her room, and Bill, standing as in a trance, heard the key click in the lock.

Bill came to life. Dashing past Lottie, he rushed at the door. He shook the handle.

"Sally!" he cried. "Sally!"

There was no answer.

Sir Hugo Drake had passed a restful night, undisturbed by dreams of foozled mashie shots. Morning found him sleeping like the little child of Lord Tidmouth's description. Waking as the sun crept over his pillow, he yawned, sat up, and perceived that another day, with all its possibilities for improving a man's putting, had arrived. He donned his favourite suit of plus fours, and, taking putter and ball, went down to the hall.

He had just grounded the ball and was taking careful aim at the leg of the sofa when from the recesses of that sofa two clenched fists suddenly rose in air and an unseen someone uttered the gasping sigh of the newly awakened.

"God bless my soul!" said Sir Hugo.

It was his nephew William. That much was plain from the tousled head which now appeared. Sir Hugo drew nearer to observe this strange phenomenon.

"Oh, hullo, Uncle," said Bill drowsily.

Sir Hugo was a man who always went to the root of a problem.

"William!" he cried. "What are you doing there?"

"Eugh!" replied Bill, stretching. He blinked. "What?" he asked sleepily.

Sir Hugo was not to be diverted from his theme.

"That's what *I* said—'What?' "

"What?"

"Yes, what?"

Bill rubbed his eyes.

"What what?" he asked.

Sir Hugo became impatient.

"Good God, boy, wake up!"

Bill rose to his feet. He inspected his uncle uncertainly.

"What did you ask me?" he said.

"Have you been sleeping there all night?"

"Yes," said Bill. "Oo, I'm stiff!"

"But why?"

"Well, wouldn't *you* be stiff if you had slept all night on a hardish sofa?"

"I'm not asking you why you're stiff. I'm asking you why you slept on that sofa."

Bill was awake now.

"I gave up my room to a lady."

"You gave up your room to a lady?"

"Yes. I . . . Oh, heavens!" said Bill peevishly. "Need we do this vaudeville cross-talk stuff so early in the morning?"

"But I don't understand. Did a lady arrive last night?"

"Yes. Soon after eleven."

"Good God!" Like Lord Tidmouth, he felt that Lottie had not wasted time. "Did you see her?"

"Of course I saw her."

"I mean—you spoke to her? You had a talk—a conversation—an interview with her?"

"Yes."

Sir Hugo probed delicately for information.

"What occurred?"

"How do you mean, what occurred?"

"Well—er—did you come to an understanding?"

"No!" said Bill.

"Did you—ah—how shall I put it?—did you shower her face with kisses?"

"No, I did not!"

Sir Hugo looked like a minor prophet receiving good news about the latest battle with the Philistines.

"Capital! Excellent! Precisely as I foresaw. When the test came, you found you were a Bannister, after all. I knew it. I knew it."

Bill regarded his rejoicing relative sourly.

"Uncle," he said, "you're gibbering."

He spoke with feeling. The one thing a man does not want to meet, when he has slept all night on a sofa and has not had breakfast, is a gibbering uncle.

"I'm not gibbering," said Sir Hugo. "I repeat that you have proved yourself a true Bannister. You have come nobly out of the ordeal. I foresaw the whole thing. Directly you saw this woman in the home of your ancestors, beneath the gaze of the family portraits, the scales fell from your eyes, and your infatuation withered and died."

Bill would have none of this.

"It did not wither," he said emphatically.

Sir Hugo stared.

"It did not wither?"

"It did not wither."

"You say it did not wither?"

Bill gave him a nasty look.

"Damn it, Uncle, you're back to the cross-talk stuff again."

"You mean to tell me," cried Sir Hugo, "that, even after you have seen this woman in your ancestral home, you are still infatuated with her?"

"More than ever."

"Good God!"

"And I'm not going to rest," said Bill, "till I have made her my wife."

"Your wife?"

"My wife."

"Your——"

Bill held up a warning hand.

"Uncle!"

"You want to *marry* her?"

"Yes."

"But . . . Good heavens, boy! Have you reflected?"

"Yes."

"Have you considered?"

"Yes."

"Have you gone off your head?"

"Yes. No," said Bill quickly. "What do you mean?"

"You—a Bannister—want to marry this woman?"

"Yes. And I'm going to find her now and tell her so."

Sir Hugo gazed after him blankly. He mopped his forehead and stared gloomily into the future. He was feeling that this was going to put him right off his game. He doubted if he would break a hundred today—after this.

He was still brooding bleakly on this lamentable state of affairs when the door of the room to the left of the stairs opened and Lottie came out, all brightness and camaraderie. Her air of sparkling-eyed cheerfulness smote Sir Hugo like a blow, even before she had come within speaking range.

"Hello, Doc," said Lottie amiably.

"Good morning," said Sir Hugo.

"You don't seem surprised to see me."

"No. I heard that you had arrived. I have just been talking to William, and he has told me the appalling news."

Lottie was puzzled.

"What news?"

"He is resolved to marry you."

A slight but distinct cloud marred Lottie's shining morning face. She looked at her companion narrowly, and her hands began to steal towards her hips.

"Just what," she asked, "do you mean by 'appalling news'?"

"It is appalling," said Sir Hugo stoutly.

Lottie breathed softly through her nose.

"You think I'm not good enough for him?"

"Precisely."

"Listen," said Lottie, in a spirit of enquiry, "what's the earliest in the morning you ever got a sock right on the side of the head?"

For the first time Sir Hugo became aware that something he had said—he could not think what—had apparently disturbed and annoyed this woman before him. He did not like the way she was advancing upon him. He had seen tigresses in the zoo walk just like that.

A swift thinker, he took refuge behind a chair and held up a deprecating hand.

"Now, now, my good girl . . ."

"Don't you call me a good girl!"

"No, no," said Sir Hugo hastily. "You're not, you're not. But, my dear Miss . . ."

"Mrs."

"My dear Mrs . . ."

"Higginbotham is the name."

"My dear Mrs Higginbotham, cannot you see for yourself how impossible this match is?"

Lottie drew in her breath sharply.

"Honest," she said, "I owe it to my womanly feelings to paste you one."

"No, no, be reasonable."

"How do you mean it's impossible?" demanded Lottie warmly. "If Bill's so crazy about me . . ."

"But William is a Bannister."

"What of it?"

"And you . . ." Sir Hugo paused carefully. He realised that infinite tact was required. "After all—in the kindliest spirit of academic enquiry—who *are* you?"

"Née Burke. Relict of the late Edward Higginbotham," said Lottie briefly.

"I mean, what is your family?"

"If anybody's been telling you I've a family, it's not true."

"You misunderstand me. But the whole thing is impossible, quite impossible."

"How do you mean?"

Sir Hugo drew a deep breath, and eyed Mr Higginbotham's widow severely.

"My dear young lady," said Sir Hugo, "have you really reflected what marriage to William would be like? My nephew, you must remember, my dear Mrs Higginbotham, is a Bannister. And without meaning to be in any way offensive, I think you will admit that your social position is scarcely equal to that of a Bannister. I fear the county would resent it bitterly if William should be considered to have married beneath him. Cannot you see how unpleasant it would be for you, received by nobody, ignored by all? Your proud, generous spirit would never endure it. And, believe me," said Sir Hugo feelingly, "this damned out-of-the-way place is quite dull enough even when you have got a neighbour or two to talk to. My dear girl, you would be bored stiff in a week."

Lottie frowned thoughtfully. Hers was a mind that could face facts, and she had to admit that she had never considered this aspect of the matter before.

"I never thought of that," she said.

"Think of it now," urged Sir Hugo. "Think of it very carefully. In fact, in order to enable you to think the better, I will leave you. Just sit quietly in one of these chairs, and try to picture to yourself what it would be like for you here during—say—the months of January and February, with no amusements, no friends—in short, nothing to entertain you but William. Think it over, Mrs Higginbotham," said Sir Hugo. "And, if you wish to secure me for a further consultation, you will find me walking in the raspberry bushes."

He bustled out, and Lottie, taking his advice, sat down in a chair and began to think. He had opened up a new line of thought.

Presently, there was a sound behind her, the sound of one meditatively singing, "I fear no foe in shining armour," and she was aware that she had been joined by Lord Tidmouth.

"Hullo, old egg," said Lord Tidmouth.

"Hullo, Squiffy," said Lottie.

She was pleased to see him. Although, some years earlier, she had been compelled to sever the matrimonial bond that linked them, she had always thought kindly of dear old Squiffy. He was her sort. He liked dancing and noisy parties and going to the races and breezing to and fro about London. Theirs, in short, was a spiritual affinity.

"Squiffy," she said, "I've just been having a talk with old what's-his-name."

"Sir Hugo?"

"Yes. Do you know what he said?"

"I can tell you *verbatim,*" replied Lord Tidmouth confidently. "He said that, while fair off the tee, he had a lot of trouble with his mashie shots, and this he attributed to . . ."

"No. He was talking about Bill."

"What about Bill?"

"Well, what would happen if I married Bill."

"What did the old boy predict?"

"He said I would be bored stiff."

Lord Tidmouth considered.

"Well," he said, "I'm not saying he wasn't right. Bill is a stout fellow, one of the best, but you can't get away from the fact that he insists on spending most of his life in this rather mouldy spot."

"Is it mouldy?"

"Pretty mouldy, from what I have seen of it. All right if you care for being buried in the country . . ."

"It's a pretty place. As far as I've seen—from my window."

"It *is* pretty," agreed Lord Tidmouth. "Very pretty. You might call it picturesque. Have you seen the river?"

"No."

"It lies at the bottom of the garden. Except during the winter months, when—they tell me—the garden lies at the bottom of the river."

Lottie shivered.

"It wouldn't be a very lively place in winter, would it?"

"Not compared with some such spot as London."

"Are you living in London now, Squiffy?"

Lord Tidmouth nodded.

"Yes," he said, "I've come back to lay my old bones in the metrop, when I've done with them, that's to say. I've got a rather sweetish little flat in the Albany."

"The Albany!" breathed Lottie wistfully.

"Right in the centre of things and handy for the theatres, opera houses and places of amusement. All the liveliest joints within a mere biscuit throw."

"Yes."

"Wasted on me, of course, because I never throw biscuits," said Lord Tidmouth. "You must come and see my little nest."

"I will."

"Do."

"Have you plenty of room there?"

"Eh? Oh yes, lots of room."

Lottie paused.

"Room for me?"

"Oh yes."

"I mean—what's the word I want?"

"I don't know, old thing. Where did you see it last?"

"Permanently," said Lottie. "That's it." She came to him and grasped the lapels of his coat. She looked up at him invitingly. "How would you like to have me running round the place, Squiffy?"

Lord Tidmouth wrinkled his forehead.

"I don't think I'm quite getting this," he said. "It seems to be sort of floating past me. If it wasn't for the fact that you're so keen on Bill, I should say you were . . ."

"I'm going to give Bill up."

"No, really?"

"Yes. I couldn't stick it here. The old boy was quite right. It would give me the willies in a week."

"Something in that."

"And the thought crossed my mind . . ."

"Well?"

"It just occurred to me as a passing idea . . ."

"What?"

"Well, you and me . . ."

"What about us?"

Lottie pulled at his coat.

"We always suited each other, Squiffy," she said. "I'm not denying we had our rows, but we're older now, and I think we should hit it off. We both like the same things. I think we should be awfully happy if we had another try at it."

Lord Tidmouth stared at her, impressed.

"Perfectly amazing you should say that," he said. "The very same thought occurred to me the moment I saw you at Bingley. I remember saying to myself, 'Squiffy, old man,' I said, 'haven't you rather, as it were, let a dashed good thing slip from your grasp?' And I replied to myself, 'Yes, old man, I have.' "

Lottie beamed at this twin soul.

"I'm awfully fond of you, Squiffy."

"Awfully nice of you to say so."

"After all, what are brains?"

"Quite."

"Or looks?"

"Exactly."

"Kiss me."

"Right ho."

"Nice?"

"Fine."

"Have another."

"Thanks."

"Once again?"

"In one moment, old thing," said Lord Tidmouth. "We will go into this matter later, when we have a spot more privacy. I observe our genial host approaching."

He waved his hand at the Last of the Bannisters, who was coming in through the french windows from the lawn.

Bill was peevish.

"Oh, there you are!" he said, sighting Lottie.

"Yes, here I am."

" 'Morning, Bill," said Lord Tidmouth agreeably.

"Go to hell!" said Bill.

"Right ho," said his lordship.

Bill turned to Lottie.

"Are you proposing to stay here long?" he asked.

"No," said Lottie. "I'm going off to London with my future husband."

"Your—who?"

"Me," said Lord Tidmouth.

Bill digested the news. It did not seem to relieve his gloom.

"Oh?" he said. "Well, a fat lot of use that is—now."

Lottie looked hurt.

"Bill! I believe you're cross with me."

"Cross!"

"Isn't he cross?" asked Lottie, turning to her betrothed for support.

Lord Tidmouth adjusted his monocle and surveyed Bill keenly.

"Yes," he said, having completed the inspection, "I think he's cross."

Bill quivered with righteous wrath.

"You've only ruined my life, that's all."

"Oh, don't say that, old top."

"I just met her in the garden." Bill's face twisted. "She wouldn't look at me."

"Who wouldn't?" asked Lord Tidmouth.

Bill brooded a moment. Then he turned to Lottie.

"Breakfast is ready in the morning room," he said. "I should be much obliged if you would get yours quick—and go."

"Well, I must say you're a darned fine host!"

"Oh, get along."

"All right," said Lottie proudly. "I'm going."

"Save the brown egg for me," said Lord Tidmouth. "I must remain here awhile and reason with this bird. Bill," he said reproachfully, as Lottie left the room, "you're very hard on that poor little girl, Bill. You show a nasty, domineering, sheik-y spirit which I don't like to see."

"I could wring her neck. What did she want to come here for—and last night of all nights?"

"But be fair, old man. She was sent for. Telegrams were dispatched."

"Sent for?"

"Yes. By the aged relative. He wired to her to come."

Bill stared.

"My uncle did?"

"Yes."

"Why on earth?"

"Well, it was like this . . ."

Bill blazed into fury.

"I'd like to wring *his* neck. Where is he? I'll go and have a heart-to-heart talk with the old fool. What the devil does he mean by it? *I'll* talk to him."

Lord Tidmouth followed him to the door.

"Steady, old man. Be judicious. Exercise discretion."

He realised that his audience had walked out on him and was now beyond earshot. He came back into the room, and was debating within himself whether it were best to breakfast now, or to postpone that feast till after one or two of the murders which seemed imminent had taken place, when Sally came in from the garden.

"Oh, hullo," he said. "So you got here?"

"Yes," said Sally shortly.

"Well—er—good morning and so forth."

"Good morning."

Lord Tidmouth may not have been one of the world's great thinkers, but he could put two and two together. This female, he reasoned, had turned up, after all, last night, and had presumably seen instantly through poor old Bill's pretence of illness. This would account, in his opinion, for her air of pronounced shirtiness.

"Nice day," he said, for want of a better remark.

"Is it?"

"If you're looking for Bill," said Lord Tidmouth perseveringly, "he's gone out to murder his uncle."

"I am not looking for Mr Bannister."

"Oh?" said Lord Tidmouth. "Oh? Well, in that case, right ho. Coming in to breakfast?"

"No."

"Oh?"

There was a silence. Lord Tidmouth was not equal to breaking it. Conversationally, he had shot his bolt.

It was Sally who finally spoke.

"Lord Tidmouth."

"On the spot."

Sally choked.

"That woman . . . that—that woman . . . how long has she been here?"

"Lottie?" said Lord Tidmouth.

"I don't know her name."

"Well, it's Lottie," he assured her. "Short for Charlotte, I believe. Though you never know."

"Has she been living here?"

"Absolutely not. She arrived last night, round about midnight."

"What! Is that true?"

"Oh, rather. The old uncle sent for her."

"Sir Hugo? Sir *Hugo* sent for her?"

"That's right."

"But why?"

"Well, as far as I could follow him, it was something to do with psychology and all that sort of rot."

"I don't understand you."

"Well, it was this way: I gather that he thought old Bill was pining for her, and he fancied it would cure him if he saw her in the old ancestral home. Old Bill had nothing to do with it. He got the shock of his life when he saw her."

Sally drew a deep breath.

"Oh! Well, that's a relief."

"Glad you're pleased," said Lord Tidmouth politely.

"I thought my patient had had a relapse. Which, after I had been working on him for three weeks, would have been too bad."

Lord Tidmouth was seeing deeper and deeper into this business every moment.

"Old Bill's potty about you," he said.

"Indeed?"

"Absolutely potty. Many's the time he's raved about you to me. He says he could howl like a dog."

"Really?"

"And, as for Lottie, if that's the trouble, don't give her another thought. If it's of any interest, she's going to marry *me*."

Sally was surprised.

"You? But that's very rapid, isn't it?"

"Rapid?"

"I mean, you've only seen her about twice, haven't you?"

Lord Tidmouth laughed indulgently.

"My dear old soul," he said, "the above and self were man and wife for years and years . . . Well, at least eighteen months. I am speaking now of some time ago, when I was in my prime."

"You mean, you used to be married to—her?"

"Absolutely. And we've decided to give it another try. You never know but what these things will take better a second time. I think we'll be like the paper on the wall. Great Lovers of History, if you know what I mean. I can honestly say I've never married a woman I felt more pally towards than Lottie."

Sally held out her hand.

"I hope you'll be very happy, Lord Tidmouth," she said.

"Thanks," said his lordship. "Thanks frightfully. And you?"

"What do you mean?"

"Well, my dear old thing . . . I mean, now that you know that Bill's relations with Lottie were strictly on the up-and-up, and realising, as you must do, that he's perfectly goofy about you, what I'm driving at is, why don't you marry the poor old blighter and put him out of his misery?"

"Lord Tidmouth, mind your own business!"

Lord Tidmouth winced beneath the harsh words.

"I say," he said plaintively, "you needn't bite a fellow's head off like that."

Sally laughed.

"Poor Lord Tidmouth! I oughtn't to have snubbed you, ought I?"

"Don't apologise. I'm used to it. My third wife was a great snubber."

"I was only annoyed for a moment that you should think I could possibly be in love with Mr Bannister."

Lord Tidmouth could not follow this.

"Don't see why you shouldn't be," he said. "Bill's an excellent chap."

"A rich waster."

"Handsome . . ."

"Mere conventional good looks."

"Kind to animals."

"Well, I'm not an animal. If ever I fall in love, Lord Tidmouth, it will be with someone who is some use in the world. Mr Bannister is not my sort. If he had ever done one decent stroke of work in his life . . ."

"You're pretty strong on work, aren't you?"

"It's my gospel. A man who doesn't work is simply an excrescence on the social fabric."

Lord Tidmouth's monocle fell from its resting place.

"Pardon me while I wince once more," he said. "That one found a chink in the Tidmouth armour."

"Oh, you!" said Sally, smiling. "One doesn't expect you to work. You're a mere butterfly."

"Pardon me. I may be a butterfly, but I am not mere."

"You're not a bad sort, anyway."

"Dear lady, your words are as music to my years. Exit rapidly before you change your mind. Teuf-teuf!" said Lord Tidmouth, disappearing in the direction of the breakfast room.

Sir Hugo came bustling in from the garden. A recent glance at his watch, taken in conjunction with a sense of emptiness, had told him that it was time he breakfasted.

At the sight of Sally, he stopped, astonished.

He peered at her, blinking. He seemed to be wondering whether much anxiety of mind had affected his eyesight.

"Doctor Smith!"

"Good morning, Sir Hugo."

"I had no notion you were here."

"I was sent for—last night—professionally."

"Somebody ill?"

"Not now."

"Are you making a long stay?"

"No. I shall leave almost immediately. I have to be in London for my hospital rounds."

"Oh? Have you seen my nephew William?"

"Not since last night. Lord Tidmouth says he went out to look for you."

"I am most anxious to find him. I have something of the most vital importance to say to him."

"Yes?" said Sally indifferently.

"I am endeavouring to save him from making a ghastly blunder and ruining his whole life. He is on the very verge of taking a step which can only result in the most terrible disaster . . . By the way, I knew there was something I wanted to ask you. When you putt, which leg do you rest the weight on?"

"I always putt off the left leg."

"Indeed? Now, that's most interesting. The left, eh?"

"Yes."

"Some people say the right."

"Yes. J. H. Taylor says the right."

"Still, Walter Hagen prefers the left."

"He ought to know."

"Yes. I remember seeing Walter Hagen hole a most remarkable putt. He was fully thirty feet from the hole on an undulating green. He . . ." Sir Hugo broke off. Something with the general aspect of a thundercloud had loomed through the french windows. "Ah, William," he said, "I was looking for you."

Bill gazed at him blackly.

"Oh, you were?" he said. "Well, I was looking for *you*. What's all this that Tidmouth tells me?"

"Tidmouth tells you?"

"Yes, Tidmouth tells me."

"Tidmouth tells you?"

A spasm shook Bill.

"Will you stop that cross-talk stuff!" he cried. "What Tidmouth told me was that you had got hold of some asinine idea that I'm in love with Lottie Higginbotham."

"Quite correct. And what I say, William—and I say this very seriously——"

Bill cut in on his oration.

"There's only one woman in the world that I love or ever shall love," he said, "and that's Sally."

"Sally?" said Sir Hugo, blinking.

"I'm Sally," said Sally.

Sir Hugo looked from one to the other. He seemed stunned.

"You love this girl?" he gasped at length.

"Yes."

Sir Hugo raised both hands, like a minor prophet blessing the people. His mauve face was lit up with a happiness which, as a rule, was only to be found there on the rare occasions when he laid an approach putt dead.

"My dear boy!" he boomed. "My dear young lady! This is the most wonderful news I have ever had. Bless you, bless you. My dear Doctor, take him! Take him, I say, and may he be as happy as I should be in his place. I'll leave you. Naturally you wish to be alone. Dear me, this is splendid news. William, you have made me a very happy man. What did you say your handicap was, my dear?"

"Six—at Garden City."

"Six at Garden City! Wonderful! What the Bannisters need," said Sir Hugo, "is a golfer like you in the family."

He toddled off, rejoicing, to his breakfast.

Bill laughed nervously.

"I'm afraid," he said, "Uncle was a little premature."

"A little, perhaps."

"But don't you think . . ."

"No, I'm afraid not."

"I had nothing to do with Lottie's being here last night."

"I know that."

"And doesn't it make any difference?"

"No."

"But, Sally . . ."

"No. I'm afraid you're not my sort of man."

"I love you."

"Is love everything?"

"Yes."

"No," said Sally. "Respect matters, too."

"I see. You despise me?"

"Not despise. But I can't take you seriously."

"I see."

She thought that he was going to say more, but he stopped there. He walked to the desk and sat down.

"I'm sorry," said Sally.

"Don't mention it," said Bill coldly. "Have you had breakfast?"

"Not yet."

"You'd better go along and have it, then. It's in the morning room."

"Aren't you having any?"

"I had a cup of coffee just now in the kitchen. I don't want any more."

"Have I spoiled your appetite?" asked Sally demurely.

"Not at all," said Bill with dignity. "I very seldom eat much breakfast."

"Nor do I. A very healthful plan."

Bill had opened the drawer of the desk, and was pulling papers out of it. He spoke without looking up, and his tone was frigid.

"You will excuse me, won't you?" he said formally.

Sally was curious.

"What are you doing?"

"I thought of doing a little work."

Sally gasped.

"Work?" she cried, astounded.

She drew a step nearer, her eyes round.

"Yes," said Bill aloofly. "Business connected with the estate. I've been neglecting it."

"Work!" said Sally, in a whisper.

Bill regarded her coldly.

"You won't think me rude? I've got rather behindhand. I've been a little worried lately."

"I didn't know you ever did any work!"

"Oh? Well, I do. A considerable amount of work. Do you suppose a place like this runs itself?"

"But I never dreamed of this," said Sally, still in the same hushed voice. "Do you mind if I sit here? I won't disturb you."

"Please do," said Bill indifferently.

She settled herself in a chair, and sat watching him. Ostentatiously ignoring her presence, he started to busy himself with the papers.

Some moments passed.

"How are you getting on?" she asked.

"All right, thanks."

"I won't disturb you."

"That's all right."

There was another silence.

"You don't mind my sitting here?" said Sally.

"Not at all."

"Just go on as if I were not here."

"Very well."

"I would hate to feel I was disturbing you."

"Kind of you."

"So I won't say another word."

"All right."

There was a brief interval of silence. Then Sally got up and stood behind him.

"What are you working at?" she asked.

Bill looked up and answered distantly.

"Well, if the information conveys anything to you, I am writing out an order for some new Alpha separators."

"Alpha . . . what?"

"Separators. They are machines you use to separate the cream from the milk."

"How interesting!" She came closer. "Why do you want Alpha separators?"

"Because I happen to own a dairy farm."

"You do? Tell me more."

"More what?"

"More about your dairy farm."

Bill raised his eyebrows.

"Why? Does it interest you?"

"Tremendously," said Sally. "Anything to do with work interests me. . . . An Alpha separator—it sounds complicated."

"Why?"

"Well, it does."

"It isn't. If you're really interested . . ."

"Oh, I am."

Bill's manner lost something of its frigidity. His dairy farm was very near to his heart. He had fussed over it for years, as if it had been a baby sister, and he welcomed the chance of holding forth on the subject. So few people ever allowed him to do so.

"It's based on centrifugal force," he said.

"Yes?"

"Here's a diagram." An ardent note came into his voice. "That thing there is the reservoir."

"I see."

"Below it," proceeded Bill emotionally, "is the regulator with a float valve . . ."

"Go on," said Sally, thrilled.

All the coldness had now left Bill Bannister's demeanour and speech. An almost fanatical note had replaced it. He spoke with a loving warmth which would have excited the respectful envy of the author of the Song of Solomon.

"As soon as the regulator is full," he said, his eyes shining with a strange light, "the float valve shuts off the influx."

Sally was all enthusiasm.

"How frightfully clever of it!"

"Shall I tell you something?" said Bill, growing still more ardent.

"Do!"

"That machine," said Bill devoutly, "can separate two thousand seven hundred and twenty-four quarts of milk in an hour!"

Sally closed her eyes ecstatically.

"Two thousand . . ."

". . . seven hundred and twenty-four."

They looked at each other in silence.

"It's the most wonderful thing I ever heard," whispered Sally.

Bill beamed.

"I thought you'd be pleased."

"Oh, I *am!*" She pointed. "And what's that little ninctobinkus?"

"That?" Bill paused, the better to prepare her for the big news. "That," he said passionately, "is the Holstein butter churner."

"O-o-oh!" breathed Sally.

He looked at her anxiously.

"Is anything the matter?"

"No, no. Go on talking."

"About milk?"

Sally nodded.

"Yes," she said. "I never knew it could be so exciting. Do you get your milk from contented cows?"

"They've never complained to me yet," said Bill. He placed his finger on the paper. "See that thing? The sterilizer!"

"Wonderful!" said Sally.

"That's the boiler there. At seventy degrees centigrade the obligatory and optional bacteria are destroyed."

"Serve them right!" said Sally. She looked at him with almost uncontrollable excitement. "Do you mean seriously to tell me," she asked, "that you are familiar with the bacteria of milk?"

"Of course I am."

Sally's eyes danced delightedly.

"But this is extraordinary!" she cried. "The cavillus acidi lactici . . ."

"The bacillus lactis acidi . . ."

"The bactorium koli . . ."

"The bacillus erogenes . . ."

"The proteus vulgaris . . ."

"The streptococci . . ."

"The colosiridium butiricum . . ."

"The bacillus butiricus," cried Bill, rolling the words round his tongue in an ecstasy. "The bacillus sluorovenus. *And* the penicilium glaucum!"

Sally leaned on the desk. She felt weak.

"Great heavens!"

"What's the matter?"

"It can't be possible!"

"What?"

"That you actually do know something about something, after all," said Sally, staring at him. "You really do do work—decent, honest, respectable work!"

The fanatic milk gleam died out of Bill's eyes. Her words had reminded him that this was no congenial crony who stood before him, but the girl who had flouted his deepest feelings; who had laughed and mocked at his protestations of love; who had told him in so many words that he was not a person to be taken seriously.

He stiffened. His manner took on a cold hostility once more.

"I do," he said. "And from now on I'm going to work harder than ever. Don't you imagine," he went on, his eyes stony and forbidding, "that, just because you've turned me down, I'm going to sit moaning and fussing over my broken heart. I'm going to *work*, and not think about you any more."

Sally beamed.

"That's the stuff!"

"I shall forget you."

"Fine!"

"Completely."

"Splendid!"

"Put you right out of my mind forever."

"Magnificent!"

Bill thumped the desk with a hamlike fist.

"As soon as you have left this house," he said, "I shall order new tractors."

"Yes, do," said Sally.

"New harrows," said Bill remorselessly.

"Bravo!"

"And fertilizers."

Sally's eyes were shining.

"Fertilizers, too!"

"Also," thundered Bill, "Chili saltpetre and Thomas tap cinders."

"*Not* Thomas tap cinders?"

"Yes. Thomas tap cinders," said Bill uncompromisingly.

"I never heard anything so absolutely glorious in my life," said Sally.

The telephone rang sharply. Bill took up the receiver.

"Hullo? This is Mr Bannister . . . For you," he said, handing her the instrument.

Sally sat on the desk.

"Hello?" she said. "Yes, speaking . . . Now? . . . Quite impossible, I'm afraid . . . You might try Doctor Borstal. He substitutes for me . . . I can't possibly leave here now. The case I am attending is very serious. Much more serious than I thought . . . Good-bye."

The interruption had caused another radical alteration in Bill Bannister's feelings. Forgotten were the stouthearted words of a moment ago. Looking hungrily at Sally, as she sat swinging her feet from the desk, he melted again. Forget her? Put her right out of his mind? He couldn't do it in a million years.

"Sally . . ." he cried.

She had jumped off the desk and was fumbling in her bag.

"One moment," she said. "I'm looking for my thermometer."

"Are you feverish?"

"That's just what I want to find out."

"Sally . . ."

"Go on," she said. "I'm listening."

She put the thermometer in her mouth. Bill stood over her, though every instinct urged him to grovel on the floor. He was desperate now. The thought that soon she would be gone—right out of his life—lent him an unusual eloquence. Words poured from him like ashes from a Thomas tap cinder.

"Sally . . . Sally . . . Sally . . . I love you. I know you're sick of hearing me say it, but I can't help myself. I love you. I love you."

Sally nodded encouragingly.

"M'hm," she said.

"I never knew how much I loved you till I saw you here—among my things—sitting on my desk—— Won't you marry me, Sally? Think of all the fun we'd have. You would love this place. We would ride every morning through the fields, with the clean, fresh wind blowing in our faces."

"M'hm."

"And all around us there would be life and movement . . . things growing . . . human beings like carved statues against the morning sky . . . The good smell of the earth . . . animals . . . benzine and crude oil . . . benzine and crude oil, Sally!"

"M'hm!"

"It's summer. The fields would be like gold in the morning. Sparkling in the sun. Harvest time. Ripe wheat. Do you hear, Sally? Ripe wheat shining in the summer sun, and you and I riding together . . . oh, Sally!"

She drew the thermometer from her mouth.

"I have no fever," she said.

"Sally . . ."

"But I'm trembling, and my pulse is a hundred and ten. And—do you know——"

"What?"

"I've lost control of my vascular motors."

"Sally!"

"One moment. I am faced with the most difficult diagnosis of my career. I ascertain the following: The organs are intact. I have no pain. No fever. But the pulse is a hundred and ten. The reflexes are heightened. On the periphery of the skin I note a strong radiation of warmth. A slight twitching in the nape of the neck. The hands tremble. The heart action is quickened. Every symptom points to something serious . . . something very serious indeed."

"You're ill!"

"I'm not ill. I'm in love. Yes, that is what I diagnose —acute love!"

She looked at him.

"Do you remember what I said to you that day we met? If ever I found a man I could love I would tell him so as frankly as if I were saying good morning."

She came towards him, holding out her hands.

"Good morning, Bill!"

"I say," said Lord Tidmouth, manifesting himself suddenly in the doorway, "do you two know that breakfast . . ." He broke off. His educated eye, trained by years of marrying one woman after another with scarcely a breathing space in between, had taken in the situation at a glance. "Sorry!" he said. "Excuse it, please!"

The door closed. From the passage beyond they heard his voice announcing that he feared no foe in shining armour.

BURIED TREASURE

THE SITUATION in Germany had come up for discussion in the bar parlour of the Angler's Rest, and it was generally agreed that Hitler was standing at the crossroads and would soon be compelled to do something definite. His present policy, said a Whisky and Splash, was mere shilly-shallying.

"He'll have to let it grow or shave it off," said the Whisky and Splash. "He can't go on sitting on the fence like this. Either a man has a moustache or he has not. There can be no middle course."

The thoughtful pause which followed these words was broken by a Small Bass.

"Talking of moustaches," he said, "you don't seem to see any nowadays, not what I call moustaches. What's become of them?"

"I've often asked myself the same question," said a Gin and Italian Vermouth. "Where, I've often asked myself, are the great sweeping moustaches of our boyhood? I've got a photograph of my grandfather as a young man in the album at home, and he's just a pair of eyes staring over a sort of quickset hedge."

"Special cups they used to have," said the Small

Bass, "to keep the vegetation out of their coffee. Ah well, those days are gone forever."

Mr Mulliner shook his head.

"Not entirely," he said, stirring his hot scotch and lemon. "I admit that they are rarer than they used to be, but in the remoter rural districts you will still find these curious growths flourishing. What causes them to survive is partly boredom and partly the good, clean spirit of amateur sport which has made us Englishmen what we are."

The Small Bass said he did not quite get that.

"What I mean," said Mr Mulliner, "is that life has not much to offer in the way of excitement to men who are buried in the country all the year round, so for want of anything better to do they grow moustaches at one another."

"Sort of competitively, as it were?"

"Exactly. One landowner will start to try to surpass his neighbour in luxuriance of moustache, and the neighbour, inflamed, fights right back at him. There is often a great deal of very intense feeling about these contests, with not a little wagering on the side. So, at least, my nephew Brancepeth, the artist, tells me. And he should know, for his present affluence and happiness are directly due to one of them."

"Did he grow a moustache?"

"No. He was merely caught up in the whirlwind of the struggle for supremacy between Lord Bromborough, of Rumpling Hall, Lower Rumpling, Norfolk, and Sir Preston Potter, Bart., of Wapleigh Towers in the same county. Most of the vintage moustaches nowadays are to be found in Norfolk and Suffolk. I suppose the keen, moist sea air brings them on. Certainly it, or some equally stimulating agency, had brought on those of Lord Bromborough and Sir Preston Potter, for in the whole of England at that time there were probably no two finer specimens than the former's Joyeuse and the latter's Love in Idleness.

It was Lord Bromborough's daughter Muriel (since Mrs Mulliner) who had entitled these two moustaches in this manner. A poetic, imaginative girl, much addicted to reading old sagas and romances, she had adapted to modern conditions the practice of the ancient heroes of bestowing names on their favourite swords. King Arthur, you will remember, had his Excalibur, Charlemagne his Flamberge, Doolin of Mayence the famous Merveilleuse: and Muriel saw no reason why this custom should be allowed to die out. A pretty idea, she thought, and I thought it a pretty idea when my nephew Brancepeth told me of it, and he thought it a pretty idea when told of it by Muriel.

For Muriel and Brancepeth had made one another's acquaintance some time before this story opens. The girl, unlike her father, who never left the ancestral acres, came often to London, and on one of these visits my nephew was introduced to her.

With Brancepeth it seems to have been a case of love at first sight, and it was not long before Muriel admitted to returning his passion. She had been favourably attracted to him from the moment when she found that their dance steps fitted, and when some little while later he offered to paint her portrait for nothing there was a look in her eyes which it was impossible to mistake. As early as the middle of the first sitting he folded her in his arms, and she nestled against his waistcoat with a low, cooing gurgle. Both knew that in the other they had found a soul mate.

Such, then, was the relationship of the young couple when one summer morning Brancepeth's telephone rang and, removing the receiver, he heard the voice of the girl he loved.

"Hey, cocky," she was saying.

"What ho, reptile," responded Brancepeth. "Where are you speaking from?"

"Rumpling. Listen, I've got a job for you."

"What sort of job?"

"A commission. Father wants his portrait painted."

"Oh yes?"

"Yes. His sinister design is to present it to the local Men's Club. I don't know what he's got against them. A nasty jar it'll be for the poor fellows when they learn of it."

"Why, is the old dad a bit of a gargoyle?"

"You never spoke a truer word. All moustache and eyebrows. The former has to be seen to be believed."

"Pretty septic?"

"My dear! Suppurating. Well, are you on? I've told Father you're the coming man."

"So I am," said Brancepeth. "I'm coming this afternoon."

He was as good as his word. He caught the 3:15 train from Liverpool Street and at 7:20 alighted at the little station of Lower Rumpling, arriving at the Hall just in time to dress for dinner.

Always a rapid dresser, tonight Brancepeth excelled himself, for he yearned to see Muriel once more after their extended separation. Racing down to the drawing room, however, tying his tie as he went, he found that his impetuosity had brought him there too early. The only occupant of the room at the moment of his entrance was a portly man whom, from the evidence submitted, he took to be his host. Except for a few outlying ears and the tip of a nose, the fellow was entirely moustache, and until he set eyes upon it, Brancepeth tells me, he had never really appreciated the full significance of those opening words of Longfellow's Evangeline, "This is the forest primeval."

He introduced himself courteously.

"How do you do, Lord Bromborough? My name is Mulliner."

The other regarded him over the zareba—with displeasure, it seemed to Brancepeth.

"What do you mean—Lord Bromborough?" he snapped curtly.

Brancepeth said he had meant Lord Bromborough.

"I'm not Lord Bromborough," said the man.

Brancepeth was taken aback.

"Oh, aren't you?" he said. "I'm sorry."

"I'm glad," said the man. "Whatever gave you the silly idea that I was Lord Bromborough?"

"I was told that he had a very fine moustache."

"Who told you that?"

"His daughter."

The other snorted.

"You can't go by what a man's daughter says. She's biased. Prejudiced. Blinded by filial love, and all that sort of thing. If I wanted an opinion on a moustache, I wouldn't go to a man's daughter. I'd go to somebody who knew about moustaches. 'Mr Walkinshaw,' I'd say, or whatever the name might be . . . Bromborough's moustache a very fine moustache, indeed! Pshaw! Bromborough *has* a moustache—of a sort. He is not clean shaven—I concede that—but fine? Pooh. Absurd. Ridiculous. Preposterous. Never heard such nonsense in my life."

He turned pettishly away, and so hurt and offended was his manner that Brancepeth had no heart to continue the conversation. Muttering something about having forgotten his handkerchief, he sidled from the room and hung about on the landing outside. And presently Muriel came tripping down the stairs, looking more beautiful than ever.

She seemed delighted to see him.

"Hullo, Brancepeth, you old bounder," she said cordially. "So you got here? What are you doing parked on the stairs? Why aren't you in the drawing room?"

Brancepeth shot a glance at the closed door and lowered his voice.

"There's a hairy bird in there who wasn't any too matey. I thought it must be your father and accosted him as such, and he got extraordinarily peevish. He seemed to resent my saying that I had heard your father had a fine moustache."

The girl laughed.

"Golly! You put your foot in it properly. Old Potter's madly jealous of Father's moustache. That was Sir Preston Potter, of Wapleigh Towers, one of our better-known local Barts. He and his son are staying here." She broke off to address the butler, a kindly, silver-haired old man who at this moment mounted the stairs. "Hullo, Phipps, are you ambling up to announce the tea and shrimps? You're a bit early. I don't think Father and Mr Potter are down yet. Ah, here's Father," she said, as a brilliantly moustached man of middle age appeared. "Father, this is Mr Mulliner."

Brancepeth eyed his host keenly as he shook hands, and his heart sank a little. He saw that the task of committing this man to canvas was going to be a difficult one. The recent slurs of Sir Preston Potter had been entirely without justification. Lord Bromborough's moustache was an extraordinarily fine one, fully as lush as that which barred the public from getting a square view of the baronet. It seemed to Brancepeth, indeed, that the job before him was more one for a landscape artist than a portrait painter.

Sir Preston Potter, however, who now emerged from the drawing room, clung stoutly to his opinion. He looked sneeringly at his rival.

"You been clipping your moustache, Bromborough?"

"Of course I have not been clipping my moustache," replied Lord Bromborough shortly. It was only too plain that there was bad blood between the two men. "What the deuce would I clip my moustache for? What makes you think I've been clipping my moustache?"

"I thought it had shrunk," said Sir Preston Potter. "It looks very small to me, very small. Perhaps the moth's been at it."

Lord Bromborough quivered beneath the coarse insult, but his patrician breeding checked the hot reply which rose to his lips. He was a host. Controlling himself with a strong effort, he turned the conversation to the subject of early mangel-wurzels; and it was while he was speaking of these with eloquence and even fire that a young man with butter-coloured hair came hurrying down the stairs.

"Buck up, Edwin," said Muriel impatiently. "What's the idea of keeping us all waiting like this?"

"Oh, sorry," said the young man.

"So you ought to be. Well, now you're here, I'd like to introduce you to Mr Mulliner. He's come to paint Father's portrait. Mr Mulliner . . . Mr Edwin Potter, my fiancé."

"Dinner is served," said Phipps, the butler.

It was in a sort of trance that my nephew Brancepeth sat through the meal which followed. He toyed listlessly with his food and contributed so little to the conversation that a casual observer, entering the room, would have supposed him to be a deaf-mute who was on a diet. Nor can we fairly blame him for this, for he had had a severe shock. Few things are more calculated to jar an ardent lover and upset his poise than the sudden announcement by the girl he loves that she is engaged to somebody else, and Muriel's words had been like a kick in the stomach from an army mule. And in addition to suffering the keenest mental anguish, Brancepeth was completely bewildered.

It was not as if this Edwin Potter had been Clark Gable or somebody. Studying him closely, Brancepeth was unable to discern in him any of those qualities which win girls' hearts. He had an ordinary, meaningless face, disfigured by an eyeglass, and was plainly a boob of the first water. Brancepeth could make nothing of it. He resolved at the earliest possible moment to get hold of Muriel and institute a probe.

It was not until the next day before luncheon that he found an opportunity of doing so. His morning had been spent in making preliminary sketches of her father. This task concluded, he came out into the garden and saw her reclining in a hammock slung between two trees at the edge of the large lawn.

He made his way towards her with quick, nervous strides. He was feeling jaded and irritated. His first impressions of Lord Bromborough had not misled him. Painting his portrait, he saw, was going to prove, as he had feared it would prove, a severe test of his courage and strength. There seemed so little about Lord Bromborough's face for an artist to get hold of. It was as if he had been commissioned to depict a client who, for reasons of his own, insisted on lying hid behind a haystack.

His emotions lent acerbity to his voice. It was with a sharp intonation that he uttered the preliminary "Hoy!"

The girl sat up.

"Oh, hullo," she said.

"Oh, hullo, yourself, with knobs on," retorted Brancepeth. "Never mind the 'Oh, hullo.' I want an explanation."

"What's puzzling you?"

"This engagement of yours."

"Oh, that?"

"Yes, that. A nice surprise that was to spring on a chap, was it not? A jolly way of saying 'Welcome to

Rumpling Hall,' I don't think." Brancepeth choked. "I came here thinking that you loved me . . ."

"So I do."

"What!"

"Madly. Devotedly."

"Then why the dickens do I find you betrothed to this blighted Potter?"

Muriel sighed.

"It's the old, old story."

"What's the old, old story?"

"This is. It's all so simple, if you'd only understand. I don't suppose any girl ever worshipped a man as I worship you, Brancepeth, but Father hasn't a bean . . . you know what it's like owning land nowadays. Between ourselves, while we're on the subject, I'd stipulate for a bit down in advance on that portrait, if I were you . . ."

Brancepeth understood.

"Is this Potter rotter rich?"

"Rolling. Sir Preston was Potter's Potted Table Delicacies."

There was a silence.

"H'm," said Brancepeth.

"Exactly. You see now. Oh, Brancepeth," said the girl, her voice trembling, "why haven't you money? If you only had the merest pittance—enough for a flat in Mayfair and a little week-end place in the country somewhere and a couple of good cars and a villa in the South of France and a bit of trout fishing on some decent river, I would risk all for love. But as it is . . ."

Another silence fell.

"What you ought to do," said Muriel, "is invent

some good animal for the movies. That's where the money is. Look at Walt Disney."

Brancepeth started. It was as if she had read his thoughts. Like all young artists nowadays, he had always held before him as the goal of his ambition the invention of some new comic animal for the motion pictures. What he burned to do, as Velasquez would have burned to do if he had lived today, was to think of another Mickey Mouse and then give up work and just sit back and watch the money roll in.

"It isn't so easy," he said sadly.

"Have you tried?"

"Of course I've tried. For years I have followed the gleam. I thought I had something with Hilda the Hen and Bertie the Bandicoot, but nobody would look at them. I see now that they were lifeless, uninspired. I am a man who needs the direct inspiration."

"Doesn't Father suggest anything to you?"

Brancepeth shook his head.

"No. I have studied your father, alert for the slightest hint . . ."

"Walter the Walrus?"

"No. Lord Bromborough looks like a walrus, yes, but unfortunately not a funny walrus. That moustache of his is majestic rather than diverting. It arouses in the beholder a feeling of awe, such as one gets on first seeing the pyramids. One senses the terrific effort behind it. I suppose it must have taken a lifetime of incessant toil to produce a cascade like that?"

"Oh no. Father hadn't a moustache at all a few years ago. It was only when Sir Preston began to grow one and rather flaunt it at him at District Council meetings that he buckled down to it. But why," demanded the girl passionately, "are we wasting time talking about moustaches? Kiss me, Brancepeth. We have just time before lunch."

Brancepeth did as directed, and the incident closed.

I do not propose (resumed Mr Mulliner, who had broken off his narrative at this point to request Miss Postlethwaite, our able barmaid, to give him another hot scotch and lemon) to dwell in detail on the agony of spirit endured by my nephew Brancepeth in the days that followed this poignant conversation. The spectacle of a sensitive artist soul on the rack is never a pleasant one. Suffice it to say that as each day came and went it left behind it an increased despair.

What with the brooding on his shattered romance and trying to paint Lord Bromborough's portrait and having his nerves afflicted by the incessant bickering that went on between Lord Bromborough and Sir Preston Potter and watching Edwin Potter bleating round Muriel and not being able to think of a funny animal for the movies, it is little wonder that his normally healthy complexion began to shade off to a sallow pallor and that his eyes took on a haunted look. Before the end of the first week he had become an object to excite the pity of the tenderhearted.

Phipps, the butler, was tenderhearted, and had been since a boy. Brancepeth excited his pity, and he yearned to do something to ameliorate the young man's lot. The method that suggested itself to him was to take a bottle of champagne to his room. It might prove a palliative rather than a cure, but he was convinced that it would, if only temporarily, bring the roses back to Brancepeth's cheeks. So he took a bottle of champagne to his room on the fifth night of my nephew's visit, and found him lying on his bed in striped pajamas and a watered silk dressing gown, staring at the ceiling.

The day that was now drawing to a close had been a particularly bad one for Brancepeth. The weather was unusually warm, and this had increased his despondency, so that he had found himself chafing beneath Lord Bromborough's moustache in a spirit of sullen rebellion. Before the afternoon sitting was over, he had become conscious of a vivid feeling of hatred for the thing. He longed for the courage to get at it with a hatchet after the manner of a pioneer in some wild country hewing a clearing in the surrounding jungle. When Phipps found him, his fists were clenched and he was biting his lower lip.

"I have brought you a little champagne, sir," said Phipps, in his kindly, silver-haired way. "It occurred to me that you might be in need of a restorative."

Brancepeth was touched. He sat up, the hard glare in his eyes softening.

"That's awfully good of you," he said. "You are quite right. I could do with a drop or two from the old bin. I am feeling rather fagged. The weather, I suppose."

A gentle smile played over the butler's face as he watched the young man put away a couple quick.

"No sir. I do not think it is the weather. You may be quite frank with me, sir. I understand. It must be a very wearing task, painting his lordship. Several artists have had to give it up. There was a young fellow here in the spring of last year who had to be removed to the cottage hospital. His manner had been strange and moody for some days, and one night we found him on a ladder in the nude, tearing and tearing away at the ivy on the west wall. His lordship's moustache had been too much for him."

Brancepeth groaned and refilled his glass. He knew just how his brother brush must have felt.

"The ironical thing," continued the butler, "is that conditions would be just as bad were the moustache nonexistent. I have been in service at the Hall for a number of years, and I can assure you that his lordship was fully as hard on the eye when he was clean shaven. Well, sir, when I tell you that I was actually relieved when he began to grow a moustache, you will understand."

"Why, what was the matter with him?"

"He had a face like a fish, sir."

"A fish?"

"Yes sir."

Something resembling an electric shock shot through Brancepeth, causing him to quiver in every limb.

"A funny fish?" he asked in a choking voice.

"Yes sir. Extremely droll."

Brancepeth was trembling like a saucepan of boiling milk at the height of its fever. A strange, wild thought had come into his mind. A funny fish . . .

There had never been a funny fish on the screen. Funny mice, funny cats, funny dogs . . . but not a funny fish. He stared before him with glowing eyes.

"Yes sir, when his lordship began to grow a moustache, I was relieved. It seemed to me that it must be a change for the better. And so it was at first. But now . . . you know how it is, sir. . . . I often find myself wishing those old, happy days were back again. We never know when we are well off, sir, do we?"

"You would be glad to see the last of Lord Bromborough's moustache?"

"Yes sir. Very glad."

"Right," said Brancepeth. "Then I'll shave it off."

In private life, butlers relax that impassive gravity which the rules of their union compel them to maintain in public. Spring something sensational on a butler when he is chatting with you in your bedroom, and he will leap and goggle like any ordinary man. Phipps did so now.

"Shave it off, sir?" he gasped quaveringly.

"Shave it off," said Brancepeth, pouring out the last of the champagne.

"Shave off his lordship's moustache?"

"This very night. Leaving not a wrack behind."

"But, sir . . ."

"Well?"

"The thought that crossed my mind, sir, was—how?"

Brancepeth clicked his tongue impatiently.

"Quite easy. I suppose he likes a little something last thing at night? Whisky or what not?"

"I always bring his lordship a glass of warm milk to the smoking room."

"Have you taken it to him yet?"

"Not yet, sir. I was about to do so when I left you."

"And is there anything in the nature of a sleeping draught in the house?"

"Yes sir. His lordship is a poor sleeper in the hot weather and generally takes a tablet of Slumberola in his milk."

"Then, Phipps, if you are the pal I think you are, you will slip into his milk tonight not one tablet but four tablets."

"But, sir . . ."

"I know, I know. What you are trying to say, I presume, is—What is there in it for you? I will tell you, Phipps. There is a packet in it for you. If Lord Bromborough's face in its stark fundamentals is as you describe it, I can guarantee that in less than no time I shall be bounding about the place trying to evade supertax. In which event, rest assured that you will get your cut. You are sure of your facts? If I make a clearing in the tangled wildwood, I shall come down eventually to a face like a fish?"

"Yes sir."

"A fish with good comedy values?"

"Oh yes, sir. Till it began to get me down, many is the laugh I have had at the sight of it."

"That is all I wish to know. Right. Well, Phipps, can I count on your co-operation? I may add, before you speak, that this means my life's happiness. Sit in, and I shall be able to marry the girl I adore. Refuse to do your bit, and I drift through the remainder of my life a soured, blighted bachelor."

The butler was plainly moved. Always kindly and silver-haired, he looked kindlier and more silver-haired than ever before.

"It's like that, is it, sir?"

"It is."

"Well, sir, I wouldn't wish to come between a young gentleman and his life's happiness. I know what it means to love."

"You do?"

"I do indeed, sir. It is not for me to boast, but there was a time when the girls used to call me Saucy George."

"And so——"

"I will do as you request, sir."

"I knew it, Phipps," said Brancepeth with emotion. "I knew that I could rely on you. All that remains, then, is for you to show me which is Lord Bromborough's room." He paused. A disturbing thought had struck him. "I say! Suppose he locks his door?"

"It is quite all right, sir," the butler reassured him. "In the later summer months, when the nights are sultry, his lordship does not sleep in his room. He reposes in a hammock slung between two trees on the large lawn."

"I know the hammock," said Brancepeth tenderly. "Well, that's fine, then. The thing's in the bag. Phipps," said Brancepeth, grasping his hand. "I don't know how to express my gratitude. If everything develops as I expect it to; if Lord Bromborough's face gives me the inspiration which I anticipate and I clean up big, you, I repeat, shall share my riches. In due season there will call at your pantry elephants laden with gold, and camels bearing precious stones and rare spices. Also apes, ivory and peacocks. And . . . you say your name is George?"

"Yes sir."

"Then my eldest child shall be christened George. Or, if female, Georgiana."

"Thank you very much, sir."

"Not at all," said Brancepeth. "A pleasure."

Brancepeth's first impression on waking next morning was that he had had a strange and beautiful dream. It was a vivid, lovely thing, all about stealing out of the house in striped pajamas and a watered silk dressing gown, armed with a pair of scissors, and stooping over the hammock where Lord Bromborough lay and razing his great moustache Joyeuse to its foundations. And he was just heaving a wistful sigh and wishing it were true, when he found that it was. It all came back to him—the furtive sneak downstairs, the wary passage of the lawn, the snip snip snip of the scissors blending with a strong man's snores in the silent night. It was no dream. The thing had actually occurred. His host's upper lip had become a devastated area.

It was not Brancepeth's custom, as a rule, to spring from his bed at the beginning of a new day, but he did so now. He was consumed with a burning eagerness to gaze upon his handiwork, for the first time to see Lord Bromborough steadily and see him whole. Scarcely ten minutes had elapsed before he was in his clothes and on his way to the breakfast room. The other, he knew, was an early riser, and even so great a bereavement as he had suffered would not deter him from getting at the coffee and kippers directly he caught a whiff of them.

Only Phipps, however, was in the breakfast room.

He was lighting wicks under the hot dishes on the sideboard. Brancepeth greeted him jovially.

"Good morning, Phipps. What ho, what ho, with a hey nonny nonny and a hot cha-cha."

The butler was looking nervous, like Macbeth interviewing Lady Macbeth after one of her visits to the spare room.

"Good morning, sir. Er—might I ask, sir . . ."

"Oh yes," said Brancepeth. "The operation was a complete success. Everything went according to plan."

"I am very glad to hear it, sir."

"Not a hitch from start to finish. Tell me, Phipps," said Brancepeth, helping himself buoyantly to a fried egg and a bit of bacon, and seating himself at the table, "what sort of a fish did Lord Bromborough look like before he had a moustache?"

The butler reflected.

"Well, sir, I don't know if you have seen Sidney the Sturgeon?"

"Eh?"

"On the pictures, sir. I recently attended a cinematographic performance at Norwich—it was on my afternoon off last week—and," said Phipps, chuckling gently at the recollection, "they were showing a most entertaining new feature, 'The Adventures of Sidney the Sturgeon.' It came on before the big picture, and it was all I could do to keep a straight face. This sturgeon looked extremely like his lordship in the old days."

He drifted from the room and Brancepeth stared after him, stunned. His air castles had fallen about him in ruins. Fame, fortune and married bliss were as far away from him as ever. All his labour had been in vain.

If there was already a funny fish functioning on the silver screen, it was obvious that it would be mere waste of time to do another. He clasped his head in his hands and groaned over his fried egg. And, as he did so, the door opened.

"Ha!" said Lord Bromborough's voice. "Good morning, good morning."

Brancepeth spun round with a sharp jerk which sent a piece of bacon flying off his fork as if it had been shot from a catapult. Although his host's appearance could not affect his professional future now, he was consumed with curiosity to see what he looked like. And, having spun round, he sat transfixed. There before him stood Lord Bromborough, but not a hair of his moustache was missing. It flew before him like a banner in all its pristine luxuriance.

"Eh, what?" said Lord Bromborough, sniffing. "Kedgeree? Capital, capital."

He headed purposefully for the sideboard. The door opened again, and Edwin Potter came in, looking more of a boob than ever.

In addition to looking like a boob, Edwin Potter seemed worried.

"I say," he said, "my father's missing."

"On how many cylinders?" asked Lord Bromborough. He was a man who liked his joke of a morning.

"I mean to say," continued Edwin Potter, "I can't find him. I went to speak to him about something just now, and his room was empty and his bed had not been slept in."

Lord Bromborough was dishing out kedgeree on to a plate.

"That's all right," he said. "He wanted to try my hammock last night, so I let him. If he slept as soundly as I did, he slept well. I came over all drowsy as I was finishing my glass of hot milk and I woke this morning in an armchair in the smoking room. Ah, my dear," he went on, as Muriel entered, "come along and try this kedgeree. It smells excellent. I was just telling our young friend here that his father slept in my hammock last night."

Muriel's face was wearing a look of perplexity.

"Out in the garden, do you mean?"

"Of course I mean out in the garden. You know where my hammock is. I've seen you lying in it."

"Then there must be a goat in the garden."

"Goat?" said Lord Bromborough, who had now taken his place at the table and was shovelling kedgeree into himself like a stevedore loading a grain ship. "What do you mean, goat? There's no goat in the garden. Why should there be a goat in the garden?"

"Because something has eaten off Sir Preston's moustache."

"What!"

"Yes. I met him outside, and the shrubbery had completely disappeared. Here he is. Look."

What seemed at first to Brancepeth a total stranger was standing in the doorway. It was only when the newcomer folded his arms and began to speak in a familiar rasping voice that he recognised Sir Preston Potter, Bart., of Wapleigh Towers.

"So!" said Sir Preston, directing at Lord Bromborough a fiery glance full of deleterious animal magnetism.

Lord Bromborough finished his kedgeree and looked up.

"Ah, Potter," he said. "Shaved your moustache, have you? Very sensible. It would never have amounted to anything, and you will be happier without it."

Flame shot from Sir Preston Potter's eye. The man was plainly stirred to his foundations.

"Bromborough," he snarled, "I have only five things to say to you. The first is that you are the lowest, foulest fiend that ever disgraced the pure pages of Debrett; the second that your dastardly act in clipping off my moustache shows you a craven, who knew that defeat stared him in the eye and that only thus he could hope to triumph; the third that I intend to approach my lawyer immediately with a view to taking legal action; the fourth is good-bye forever; and the fifth——"

"Have an egg," said Lord Bromborough.

"I will not have an egg. This is not a matter which can be lightly passed off with eggs. The fifth thing I wish to say——"

"But, my dear fellow, you seem to be suggesting that I had something to do with this. I approve of what has happened, yes. I approve of it heartily. Norfolk will be a sweeter and better place to live in now that this has occurred. But it was none of my doing. I was asleep in the smoking room all night."

"The fifth thing I wish to say——"

"In an armchair. If you doubt me, I can show you the armchair."

"The fifth thing I wish to say is that the engagement between my son and your daughter is at an end."

"Like your moustache. Ha, ha!" said Lord Bromborough, who had many good qualities but was not tactful.

"Oh, but Father!" cried Edwin Potter. "I mean, dash it!"

"And *I* mean," thundered Sir Preston, "that your engagement is at an end. You have my five points quite clear, Bromborough?"

"I think so," said Lord Bromborough, ticking them off on his fingers. "I am a foul fiend, I'm a craven, you are going to institute legal proceedings, you bid me good-bye forever, and my daughter shall never marry your son. Yes, five in all."

"Add a sixth. I shall see that you are expelled from all your clubs."

"I haven't got any."

"Oh?" said Sir Preston, a little taken aback. "Well, if ever you make a speech in the House of Lords, beware. I shall be up in the gallery, booing."

He turned and strode from the room, followed by Edwin, protesting bleatingly. Lord Bromborough took a cigarette from his case.

"Silly old ass," he said. "I expect that moustache of his was clipped off by a body of public-spirited citizens. Like the Vigilantes they have in America. It is absurd to suppose that a man could grow a beastly, weedy caricature of a moustache like Potter's without inflaming popular feeling. No doubt they have been lying in wait for him for months. Lurking. Watching their opportunity. Well, my dear, so your wedding's off. A nuisance in a way, of course, for I'd just bought a new pair of trousers to give you away in. Still, it can't be helped."

"No, it can't be helped," said Muriel. "Besides there will be another one along in a minute."

She shot a tender smile at Brancepeth, but on his lips there was no answering simper. He sat in silence, crouched over his fried egg.

What did it profit him, he was asking himself bitterly, that the wedding was off? He himself could never marry Muriel. He was a penniless artist without prospects. He would never invent a comic animal for the movies now. There had been an instant when he had hoped that Sir Preston's uncovered face might suggest one, but the hope had died at birth. Sir Preston Potter, without his moustache, had merely looked like a man without a moustache.

He became aware that his host was addressing him. "I beg your pardon?"

"I said, 'Got a light?' "

"Oh, sorry," said Brancepeth.

He took out his lighter and gave it a twiddle. Then, absently, he put the flame to the cigarette between his host's lips.

Or, rather, for preoccupation had temporarily destroyed his judgment of distance, to the moustache that billowed above and around it. And the next moment there was a sheet of flame and a cloud of acrid smoke. When this had cleared away, only a little smouldering stubble was left of what had once been one of Norfolk's two most outstanding eyesores.

A barely human cry rent the air, but Brancepeth hardly heard it. He was staring like one in a trance at the face that confronted him through the shredding mists, fascinated by the short, broad nose, the bulging eyes, the mouth that gaped and twitched. It was only when his host made a swift dive across the table with bared teeth and clutching hands that Prudence returned to its throne. He slid under the table and came out on the other side.

"Catch him!" cried the infuriated peer. "Trip him up! Sit on his head!"

"Certainly not," said Muriel. "He is the man I love."

"Is he!" said Lord Bromborough, breathing heavily as he crouched for another spring. "Well, he's the man I am going to disembowel with my bare hands. When I catch him."

"I think I should nip through the window, darling," said Muriel gently.

Brancepeth weighed the advice hastily and found it good. The window, giving on to the gravel drive, was, he perceived, open at the bottom. The sweet summer air floated in, and an instant later he was floating out. As he rose from the gravel, something solid struck him on the back of the head. It was a coffeepot.

But coffeepots, however shrewdly aimed, mattered little to Brancepeth now. This one had raised a painful contusion, and he had in addition skinned both hands and one of his knees. His trousers, moreover, a favourite pair, had a large hole in them. Nevertheless, his heart was singing within him.

For Phipps had been wrong. Phipps was an ass. Phipps did not know a fish when he saw one. Lord Bromborough's face did not resemble that of a fish at all. It suggested something much finer, much fuller of screen possibilities, much more box office than a fish. In that one blinding instant of illumination before he had dived under the table, Brancepeth had seen Lord Bromborough for what he was—Ferdinand the Frog.

He turned, to perceive his host in the act of hurling a cottage loaf.

"Muriel!" he cried.

"Hullo?" said the girl, who had joined her father at the window and was watching the scene with great interest.

"I love you, Muriel."

"Same here."

"But for the moment I must leave you."

"I would," said Muriel. She glanced over her shoulder. "He's gone to get the kedgeree." And Brancepeth saw that Lord Bromborough had left his butt. "He is now," she added, "coming back."

"Will you wait for me, Muriel?"

"To all eternity."

"It will not be necessary," said Brancepeth. "Call it six months or a year. By that time I shall have won fame and fortune."

He would have spoken further, but at this moment Lord Bromborough reappeared, poising the kedgeree. With a loving smile and a wave of the hand, Brancepeth leaped smartly to one side. Then, turning, he made his way down the drive, gazing raptly into a future of Rolls Royces, caviare and silk underclothing made to measure.

THE MASKED TROUBADOUR

A YOUNG MAN came out of the Drones Club and paused on the steps to light a cigarette. As he did so, there popped up—apparently through the pavement, for there had been no sign of him in the street a moment before—a seedy individual who touched his hat and smiled ingratiatingly. The young man seemed to undergo a brief inward struggle; then he felt in his pocket, pressed a coin into the outstretched palm, and passed on.

It was a pretty, heart-warming little scene, the sort of thing you see in full-page pictures in the Christmas numbers, but the only emotion it excited in the bosoms of the two Beans who had witnessed it from the window of the smoking room was amazement.

"Well, stap my vitals," said the first Bean. "If I hadn't seen it with my own eyes I wouldn't have believed it."

"Nor me," said the second Bean.

"Believed what?" asked a Crumpet, who had come up behind them.

The two Beans turned to him as one Bean and spoke in alternate lines, like a Greek chorus.

"Freddie Widgeon——"

"—was outside there a moment ago——"

"—and a chap came up and touched his hat——"

"—and then he touched Freddie."

"And Freddie, though he was on the steps at the time——"

"—and so had only to leap backwards in order to win to safety——"

"—stood there and let the deal go through."

The Crumpet clicked his tongue.

"What sort of a looking chap was he? Small and a bit greasy?"

"Quite fairly greasy."

"I thought as much," said the Crumpet. "I know the bird. He's a fellow named Waterbury, a pianist by profession. He's a sort of pensioner of Freddie's. Freddie is always slipping him money,—here a tanner, there a bob."

The astonishment of the two Beans deepened.

"But Freddie's broke," said the senior Bean.

"True," said the Crumpet. "He can ill spare these bobs and tanners, but that old noblesse oblige spirit of his has cropped up again. He feels that he must allow himself to be touched, because this greasy bird has a claim on him. He saved his life."

"The greasy bird saved Freddie's life?"

"No. Freddie saved the greasy bird's life."

"Then Freddie ought to be touching the greasy bird."

"Not according to the code of the Widgeons." The Crumpet sighed. "Poor old Freddie—it's a shame, this constant drain on his meagre resources, after all he's been through."

"What's he been through?" asked the junior Bean.

"You would not be far out," replied the Crumpet gravely, "if you said that he had been through the furnace."

At the time when this story opens (said the Crumpet) Freddie was feeling a bit low. His heart had just been broken, and that always pulls him down. He had loved Dahlia Prenderby with every fibre of his being, and she had handed him the horse's laugh. He was, therefore, as you may suppose, in no mood for social gaiety: and when he got a note from his uncle, old Blicester, asking him to lunch at the Ritz, his first impulse was to refuse.

But as Lord Blicester was the source from which proceeded his quarterly allowance, he couldn't do that, of course. The old boy's invitations were commands. So he turned up at the eating house and was sitting in the lobby, thinking long, sad thoughts of Dahlia Prenderby, when his host walked in.

"Ha, Frederick," he said, having eased his topper and umbrella off on to a member of the staff. "Glad you were able to come. I want to have a serious talk with you. I've been thinking a lot about you lately."

"Have you, Uncle?" said Freddie, touched.

"Yes," said old Blicester. "Wondering why you were such a blasted young blot on the escutcheon and trying to figure out some way of stopping you from being the world's worst ass and pest. And I think I've found the solution. It would ease the situation very much, in my opinion, if you got married. Don't puff like that. What the devil are you puffing for?"

"I was sighing, Uncle."

"Well, don't. Good God! I thought you'd got

asthma. Yes," said Lord Blicester, "I believe that if you were married and settled down, things might brighten considerably all round. I've known bigger . . . well, no, scarcely that, perhaps . . . I've known very nearly as big fools as you improve out of all recognition by marriage. And here is what I wanted to talk to you about. You will, no doubt, have been wondering why I am buying you a lunch in an infernally expensive place like this. I will tell you. My old friend, Lady Pinfold, is joining us in a few minutes with her daughter Dora. I have decided that she is the girl you shall marry. Excellent family, plenty of money of her own, and sense enough for two—which is just the right amount. So mind you make yourself attractive, if that is humanly possible, to Dora Pinfold."

A weary, mirthless smile twisted Freddie's lips.

"All this——" he began.

"And let me give you a warning. She is not one of your fast modern girls, so bear in mind when conversing with her that you are not in the smoking room of the Drones Club. Only carefully selected stories, and no limericks whatsoever."

"All this——" began Freddie again.

"Don't drink anything at lunch. She is strict in her views about that. And, talking of lunch, when the waiter comes round with the menu, don't lose your head. Keep an eye on the prices in the right-hand column."

"All this," said Freddie, at last getting a word in, "is very kind of you, Uncle, and I appreciate it. Your intentions are good. But I cannot marry this girl."

Old Blicester nodded intelligently.

"I see what you mean. You feel it would be a shabby trick to play on any nice girl. True. There is much in what you say. But somebody has got to suffer in this world. You can't make an omelette without breaking eggs. So never mind the ethics of the thing. You go ahead and fascinate her, or I'll . . . Sh. Here they come."

He got up and started to stump forward to greet a stout, elderly woman who was navigating through the doorway, and Freddie, following, suddenly halted in his tracks and nearly took a toss. He was looking at the girl floating along in the wake of the stout woman. In a blinding flash of revelation he saw that he had been all wrong in supposing that he had loved Dahlia Prenderby and all the other girls who had turned him down. Just boyish infatuations, he could see now. This was his soul mate. There was none like her, none. Freddie, as you know, always falls in love at first sight, and he had done so on this occasion with a wallop.

His knees were wobbling under him as he went in to lunch, and he was glad to be able to sit down and take the weight off them.

The girl seemed to like him. Girls always do like Freddie at first. It is when the gruelling test of having him in their hair for several weeks comes that they throw in the towel. Over the fish and chips he and this Dora Pinfold fraternised like billy-o. True, it was mostly a case of her telling him about her dreams and ideals and his saying, "Oh, ah" and "Oh, absolutely," but that did not alter the fact that the going was good.

So much so that with the cheese Freddie, while not actually pressing her hand, was leaning over towards her at an angle of forty-five and saying why shouldn't they lap up their coffee quick at the conclusion of the meal and go and see a picture or something. And she said she would have loved it, only she had to be in Notting Hill at a quarter to three.

"I'm interested in a sort of mission there," she said.

"Great Scott!" said Freddie. "Cocoa and good works, do you mean?"

"Yes. We are giving an entertainment this afternoon, to the mothers."

Freddie nearly choked over his Camembert. A terrific idea had come to him.

If, he reflected, he was going to meet this girl again only at dinners and dances—the usual social round, I mean to say—all she would ever get to know about him was that he had a good appetite and indiarubber legs. Whereas, if he started frequenting Notting Hill in her company, he would be able to flash his deeper self on her. He could be suave, courteous, the *preux chevalier,* and shower her with those little attentions which make a girl sit up and say to herself, "What ho!"

"I say," he said, "couldn't I come along?"

"Oh, it would bore you."

"Not a bit. I could hover round and shove the old dears into their seats and so on. I'm good at that. I've been an usher at dozens of weddings."

The girl reflected.

"I'll tell you what you can do, if you really want to help," she said. "We are a little short of talent. Can you sing?"

"Rather!"

"Then will you sing?"

"Absolutely."

"That would be awfully kind of you. Any old song will do."

"I shall sing," said Freddie, directing at her a glance which he rather thinks—though he is not sure—made her blush in modest confusion, "a number entitled, 'When the Silver of the Moonlight Meets the Love-light in Your Eyes.'"

So directly lunch was over, off they popped, old Blicester beaming on Freddie and very nearly slapping him on the back—and no wonder, for his work had unquestionably been good—and as the clocks were striking three-thirty Freddie was up on the platform with the vicar and a union jack behind him, the girl Dora at the piano at his side, and about two hundred Notting Hill mothers in front of him, letting it go like a Crosby.

He was a riot. Those mothers, he tells me, just sat back and ate it up. He did two songs, and they wanted a third. He did a third, and they wanted an encore. He did an encore, and they started whistling through their fingers till he came on and bowed. And when he came on and bowed, they insisted on a speech. And it was at this point, as he himself realises now, that Freddie lost his cool judgment. He allowed himself to be carried away by the intoxication of the moment and went too far.

Briefly, what happened was that in a few cordial words he invited all those present to be his guests at a binge to be held in the mission hall that day week.

"Mothers," said Freddie, "this is on me. I shall expect you to the last mother. And if any mothers here have mothers of their own, I hope they will bring them along. There will be no stint. Buns and cocoa will flow like water. I thank you one and all."

And it was only when he got home, still blinking from the bright light which he had encountered in the girl Dora's eyes as they met his, and still half-deafened by the rousing cheers which had greeted his remarks, that he remembered that all he had in the world was one pound, three shillings and fourpence.

Well, you can't entertain a multitude of mothers in slap-up style on one pound, three and fourpence, so it was obvious that he would be obliged to get into somebody's ribs for something substantial. And the only person he could think of who was good for the sum he required—twenty quid seemed to him about the figure —was old Blicester.

It would not be an easy touch. He realised that. The third Earl of Blicester was a man who, though well blessed with the world's goods, hated loosening up. Moths had nested in his pocketbook for years and raised large families. However, one of the fundamental facts of life is that you can't pick and choose when you want twenty quid—you have to go to the man who's got twenty quid. So he went round to tackle the old boy.

There was a bit of a lull when he got to the house. Some sort of by-election, it appeared, was pending down at Bottleton in the East End, and Lord Blicester had gone off there to take the chair at a meeting in the Conservative interest. So Freddie had to wait. But eventually he appeared, a bit hoarse from addressing the proletariat, but in excellent fettle. He was very bucked at the way Freddie had shaped at the luncheon table.

"You surprised me, my boy," he said. "I am really beginning to think that if you continue as you have begun and are careful, when you propose, to do it in a dim light so that she can't get a good look at you, you may win that girl."

"And you want me to win her, don't you, Uncle?"

"I do, indeed."

"Then will you give me twenty pounds?"

The sunlight died out of Lord Blicester's face.

"Twenty pounds? What do you want twenty pounds for?"

"It is vital that I acquire that sum," said Freddie. And in a few words he explained that he had pledged himself to lush up the mothers of Notting Hill on buns and cocoa a week from that day, and that if he welshed and failed to come through, the girl would never forgive him—and rightly.

Lord Blicester listened with growing gloom. He had set his heart on this union, but the overhead made him quiver. The thought of parting with twenty pounds was like a dagger in his bosom.

"It won't cost twenty pounds."

"It will."

"You can do it on much less than that."

"I don't see how. There must have been fully two hundred mothers present. They will bring friends and relations. Add gate crashers, and I can't budget for less than four hundred. At a bob a nob."

Lord Blicester pshawed.

"Preposterous!" he cried. "A bob a nob, forsooth! Cocoa's not expensive."

"But the buns. You are forgetting the buns."

"Buns aren't expensive, either."

"Well, how about hard-boiled eggs? Have you reflected, Uncle, that there may be hard-boiled eggs?"

"Hard-boiled eggs? Good God, boy, what is this thing you're planning? A Babylonian orgy? There will be no question of hard-boiled eggs."

"Well, all right. Then let us return to the buns. Allowing twelve per person . . ."

"Don't be absurd. Twelve, indeed! These are simple, God-fearing English mothers you are entertaining, not tapeworms. I'll give you ten pounds. Ten is ample."

And nothing that Freddie could say would shake him. It was with a brace of fivers in his pocket that he left the other's presence, and every instinct in him told him that they would not be enough. Fifteen quid, in his opinion, was the irreducible minimum. He made his way to the club in pensive mood, his brain darting this way and that in the hope of scaring up some scheme for adding to his little capital. He was still brooding on a problem which seemed to grow each moment more hopeless of solution, when he entered the smoking room and found a group of fellows there, gathered about a kid in knickerbockers. And not only were they gathered about this kid—they were practically fawning on him.

This surprised Freddie. He knew that a chap has to have something outstanding about him to be fawned upon at the Drones', and nothing in this child's appearance suggested that he was in any way exceptional. The only outstanding thing about him was his ears.

"What's all this?" he asked of Catsmeat Potter-Pirbright, who was hovering on the outskirts of the group.

"It's Barmy Phipps's cousin Egbert from Harrow," said Catsmeat. "Most remarkable chap. You see that catapult he's showing those birds. Well, he puts a Brazil nut in it and whangs off at things and hits them every time. It's a great gift, and you might think it would make him conceited. But no, success has not spoiled him. He is still quite simple and unaffected. Would you like his autograph?"

Freddie frankly did not believe the story. The whole nature of a Brazil nut, it being nobbly and of a rummy semicircular shape, unfits it to act as a projectile. The thing, he felt, might be just barely credible, perhaps, of one who was receiving his education at Eton, but Catsmeat had specifically stated that this lad was at Harrow, and his reason revolted at the idea of a Harrovian being capable of such a feat.

"What rot!" he said.

"It isn't rot," said Catsmeat Potter-Pirbright, stung. "Only just now he picked off a passing errand boy as clean as a whistle."

"Pure fluke."

"Well, what 'll you bet he can't do it again?"

A thrill ran through Freddie. He had found a way.

"A fiver!" he cried.

Well, of course, Catsmeat hadn't got a fiver, but he swiftly formed a syndicate to cover Freddie's money, and the stakes were deposited with the chap behind the bar and a Brazil nut provided for the boy Egbert at the club's expense. And it was as he fitted nut to elastic that Catsmeat Potter-Pirbright said, "Look!

"Look!" said Catsmeat Potter-Pirbright. "There's a taxi just drawing up with a stout buffer in it. Will you make this stout buffer the test? Will you bet that Egbert here doesn't knock off his topper as he pays the cabby?"

"Certainly," said Freddie.

The cab stopped. The buffer alighted, his top hat gleaming in the sunshine. The child Egbert with incredible nonchalance drew his bead. The Brazil nut sang through the air. And the next moment Freddie was staggering back with his hands to his eyes, a broken man. For the hat, struck squarely abaft the binnacle, had leaped heavenwards and he was down five quid.

And the worst was yet to come. About a minute later he was informed that Lord Blicester had called to see him. He went to the small smoking room and found his uncle standing on the hearth rug. He was staring in a puzzled sort of way at a battered top hat which he held in his hand.

"Most extraordinary thing," he said. "As I was getting out of my cab just now, something suddenly came whizzing out of the void and knocked my hat off. I think it must have been a small meteor. I am going to write to *The Times* about it. But never mind that. What I came for was to get fifty shillings from you."

Freddie had already tottered on discovering that it was old Blicester who had been the victim of the boy Egbert's uncanny skill. These words made him totter again. That his uncle should be touching him instead of him touching his uncle gave him a sort of gooseflesh feeling as if he were rubbing velvet the wrong way.

"Fifty shillings?" he bleated.

"Two pounds ten," said old Blicester, making it clear to the meanest intelligence. "After you left me, I was dissatisfied with your figures, so I went and consulted my cook, a most capable woman, as to the market price of buns and cocoa, and what she told me convinces me that you can do the whole thing comfortably on seven pounds ten. So I hurried here to recover the fifty shillings which I overpaid you. I can give you change."

Five minutes later, Freddie was at a writing table with pen and paper, trying to work out how he stood. Of his original capital, two pounds ten shillings remained. According to his uncle, who had it straight from the cook's mouth, buns and cocoa could be provided for four hundred at a little over fourpence a head. It seemed incredible, but he knew that his uncle's cook, a levelheaded woman named Bessemer, was to be trusted implicitly on points of this kind. No doubt the explanation was that a considerable reduction was given for quantity. When you buy your buns by the ton, you get them cheaper.

Very well, then. The deficit to be made up appeared still to be five pounds. And where he was to get it was more than he could say. He couldn't very well go back to old Blicester and ask for a further donation, giving as his reason the fact that he had lost a fiver betting that a kid with windjammer ears wouldn't knock his, old Blicester's, hat off with a Brazil nut.

Then what to do? It was all pretty complex, and I am not surprised that for the next two or three days Freddie was at a loss.

During these days he continued to haunt Notting Hill. But though he was constantly in the society of the girl Dora, and though he was treated on all sides as the young Lord Bountiful, he could not bring himself to buck up and be fizzy. Wherever he went, the talk was all of this forthcoming beano of his, and it filled him with a haunting dread. Notting Hill was plainly planning to go for the buns and cocoa in a big way, and who—this was what he asked himself—who was going to foot the bill?

The ironical thing, he saw now, was that his original capital would have seen him through. There had been no need whatsoever for him to go plunging like that in the endeavour to bump up the kitty. When he reflected that, but for getting his figures twisted he would now have been striding through Notting Hill with his chin up and his chest out and not a care on his mind, he groaned in spirit. He told me so himself. "I groaned in spirit," he said.

And then one afternoon, after he had explored every possible avenue, as he thought, without getting a bite, he suddenly stumbled on one that promised to bring home the gravy. Other avenues had let him down with a bump, but this one really did look the goods.

For what happened was that he learned that on that very evening the East Bottleton Palace of Varieties was holding its monthly Amateur Night and that the prize of victory—he reeled as he read the words—was a handsome five-pound note.

At the moment when he made this discovery, things had been looking their darkest. Freddie, in fact, was so up against it that he had come to the conclusion that the only thing to do, if he was to fulfil his honourable obligations, was to go to his uncle, confess all, and try to tap him again.

The old boy, apprised of the facts in the matter of his ruined topper, would unquestionably want to disembowel him, but he was so keen on the wedding coming off that it might just conceivably happen that he would confine himself to harsh words and at the end of a powerful harangue spring the much-needed.

Anyway, it was his only chance. He rang up the Blicester residence and was informed that the big chief was again down at Bottleton East presiding at one of those political meetings. At the Bottleton Palace of Varieties, said the butler. So, though he would much have preferred to go to Whipsnade and try to take a mutton chop away from a tiger, Freddie had a couple of quick ones, ate a clove and set off.

I don't suppose you are familiar with Bottleton East, except by name. It is a pretty tough sort of neighbourhood, rather like Limehouse, only with fewer mysterious Chinamen. The houses are small and grey, cats abound, and anyone who has a bit of old paper or a piece of orange peel throws it on the pavement. It depressed Freddie a good deal, and he was feeling pretty well down among the wines and spirits when a burst of muffled cheering came to his ears and he found that he was approaching the Bottleton Palace of Varieties.

And he was just toddling round to send in his name to old Blicester when he saw on the wall this poster announcing the Grand Amateur Night and the glittering reward offered to the performer who clicked.

It altered the whole aspect of things in a flash. What it meant was that that distressing interview with Lord Blicester could now be pigeonholed indefinitely. Here was the fiver he needed, as good as in his pocket.

This gay confidence on his part may surprise you. But you must remember that it was only a day or two since he had burned up the Notting Hill mothers with his crooning. A man who could put over a socko like that had little to fear, he felt, from any opposition a place like Bottleton East could bring against him.

There was just one small initial difficulty. He would require an accompanist, and it was rather a problem to see where he was to get one. At Notting Hill, you will recall, the girl Dora had tinkled the ivories on his behalf, but he could scarcely ask her to officiate on the present occasion, for—apart from anything else—secrecy was of the essence. For the same reason he could not get anyone from the Drones. The world must never know that Frederick Widgeon had been raising the wind by performing at amateur nights in the East End of London.

He walked on, musing. It was an annnoying little snag to crop up just as everything looked nice and smooth.

However, his luck was in. Halfway down a grubby little street he saw a card in a window announcing that Jos. Waterbury gave piano lessons on those premises; and rightly reasoning that a bloke who could teach the piano would also know how to accompany, he knocked at the door. And after he had been subjected to a keen scrutiny by a mysterious eye through the keyhole, the door opened and he found himself *vis-à-vis* with the greasy bird whom you saw outside there just now.

The first few minutes of the interview were given up to mutual explanations. Freddie handed the greasy bird his card. The greasy bird said that he would not have kept Freddie waiting, only something in the timbre of his knock had given him the idea that he was Ginger Murphy, a gentleman friend of his with whom he had had a slight difference and who had expressed himself desirous of seeing the colour of his insides. Freddie explained that he wanted the greasy bird to accompany him on the piano at Amateur Night. And the greasy bird said that Freddie couldn't have made a wiser move, because he was an expert accompanist and having him with you on such an occasion was half the battle.

After this, there was a bit of haggling about terms, but in the end it was arranged that Freddie should pay the greasy bird five bob—half-a-crown down and the rest that night, and that they should meet at the stage door at eight sharp.

"If I'm not there," said the greasy bird, "you'll find me in the public bar of the Green Goose round the corner."

"Right ho," said Freddie. "I shall sing 'When the Silver of the Moonlight Meets the Lovelight in Your Eyes.' "

"Ah well," said the greasy bird, who seemed a bit of a philosopher, "I expect worse things happen at sea."

Freddie then pushed off, on the whole satisfied with the deal. He hadn't liked this Jos. Waterbury much. Not quite the accompanist of his dreams. He would have felt kindlier towards him if he had bathed more recently and had smelled less strongly of unsweetened gin. Still, he was no doubt as good as could be had at the price. Freddie was not prepared to go higher than five bob, and that ruled out the chaps who play at Queen's Hall.

Having completed the major preliminary arrangements, Freddie now gave thought to make-up and appearance. The other competitors, he presumed, would present themselves to their public more or less aziz, but their circumstances were rather different from his own. In his case, a certain caution was indicated. His uncle appeared to be making quite a stamping ground of Bottleton East just now, and it would be disastrous if he happened to come along and see him doing his stuff. So, though it was not likely that Lord Blicester would attend Amateur Night at the Palace of Varieties, he thought it best to be on the safe side and adopt some rude disguise.

After some meditation, he decided to conceal his features behind a strip of velvet and have himself announced as The Masked Troubadour.

He dined lightly at the club off oysters and a pint of stout, and at eight o'clock, after an afternoon spent in gargling throat tonic and saying "Mi-mi-mi" to limber up the larnyx, he arrived at the stage door.

Jos. Waterbury was there, wearing the unmistakable air of a man who has been more or less submerged in unsweetened gin for several hours, and, half-a-crown having changed hands, they proceeded to the wings together to await their turn.

It was about a quarter of an hour before they were called upon, and during this quarter of an hour Freddie tells me that his spirits soared heavenwards. It was so patently absurd, he felt, as he watched the local talent perform, to suppose that there could be any question of his ability to cop the gage of victory. He didn't know how these things were decided—by popular acclamation, presumably—but whatever system of marking might prevail it must inevitably land him at the head of the poll.

These Bottleton songbirds were well meaning—they spared no pains and gave of their best—but they had nothing that could by the remotest stretch of the word be described as Class. Five of them preceded him, and not one of the five could have held those Notting Hill mothers for a minute, let alone have wowed them as he had wowed them. These things are a matter of personality and technique. Either you have got personality and technique or you haven't. These chaps hadn't. He had. His position, he saw, was rather that of a classic horse put up against a lot of selling platers.

So, as I say, he stood there for a quarter of an hour, muttering "Mi-mi-mi" and getting more and more above himself; and finally, after a cove who looked like a plumber's mate had finished singing "Just Break the News to Mother" and had gone off to sporadic applause, he saw the announcer jerking his thumb at him and realised that the moment had come.

He was not a bit nervous, he tells me. From what he had heard of these amateur nights, he had rather supposed that he might for the first minute or so have to quell and dominate a pretty tough audience. But the house seemed in friendly mood, and he walked onto the stage, adjusting his mask, with a firm and confident tread.

The first jarring note was struck when the announcer turned to enquire his name. He was a stout, puffy man with bags under his eyes and a face the colour of a damson, and on seeing Freddie he shied like a horse. He backed a step or two, throwing up his arms, as he did so, in a defensive sort of way.

"It's all right," said Freddie.

The man seemed reassured. He gulped once or twice, but became calmer.

"What's all this?" he asked.

"It's quite all right," said Freddie. "Just announce me as The Masked Troubadour."

"Coo! You gave me a nasty shock. Masked what?"

"Troubadour," said Freddie, spacing the syllables carefully.

He walked over to the piano, where Jos. Waterbury had seated himself and was playing chords.

"Ready?" he said.

Jos. Waterbury looked up, and a slow look of horror began to spread itself over his face. He shut his eyes, and his lips moved silently. Freddie thinks he was praying.

"Buck up," said Freddie sharply. "We're just going to kick off."

Jos. Waterbury opened his eyes.

"Gawd!" he said. "Is that you?"

"Of course it's me."

"What have you done to your face?"

This was a point which the audience, also, seemed to wish threshed out. Interested voices made themselves heard from the gallery.

"Wot's all this, Bill?"

"It's a masked trebudder," said the announcer.

"Wot's a trebudder?"

"This is." The damson-faced man seemed to wash his hands of the whole unpleasant affair. "Don't blame me, boys," he begged. "That's what he says he is."

Jos. Waterbury bobbed up again. For the last few moments he had been sitting muttering to himself.

"It isn't right," said Jos. Waterbury. "It isn't British. It isn't fair to lead a man on and then suddenly turn round on him——"

"Shut up!" hissed Freddie. All this, he felt, was subversive. Getting the audience into a wrong mood. Already the patrons' geniality was beginning to ebb. He could sense a distinct lessening of that all-pals-together spirit. One or two children were crying.

"Laydeezun-gennelmun," bellowed the damson-faced man, "less blinking noise, if you please. I claim your kind indulgence for this 'ere trebudder."

"That's all right," said Jos. Waterbury, leaving the piano and coming downstage. "He may be a trebudder or he may not, but I appeal to this fair-minded audience—is it just, is it ethical, for a man suddenly to pop out on a fellow who's had a couple——"

"Come on," cried the patrons. "Less of it." And a voice from the gallery urged Jos. Waterbury to put his head in a bucket.

"All right," said Jos. Waterbury, who was plainly in dark mood. "All right. But you haven't heard the last of this by any means."

He reseated himself at the piano, and Freddie began to sing "When the Silver of the Moonlight Meets the Lovelight in Your Eyes."

The instant he got going, he knew that he had never

been in better voice in his life. Whether it was the oysters or the stout or the throat tonic, he didn't know, but the notes were floating out as smooth as syrup. It made him feel a better man to listen to himself.

And yet there was something wrong. He spotted it almost from the start. For some reason he was falling short of perfection. And then suddenly he got on to it. In order to make a song a smash, it is not enough for the singer to be on top of his form. The accompanist, also, must do his bit. And the primary thing a singer expects from his accompanist is that he shall play the accompaniment of the song he is singing.

This Jos. Waterbury was not doing, and it was this that was causing the sweet-bells-jangled effect which Freddie had observed. What the greasy bird was actually playing, he could not say, but it was not the twiddly bits to "When the Silver of the Moonlight Meets the Lovelight in Your Eyes."

It was obviously a case for calling a conference. A bit of that interoffice communication stuff was required. He made a sideways leap to the piano, encouraging some of the audience to suppose that he was going into his dance.

"*There is silver in the moonlight* . . . What the hell are you playing?" sang Freddie.

"Eh?" said Jos. Waterbury.

"*But its silver tarnished seems* . . . You're playing the wrong song."

"What are you singing?"

"*When it meets the golden lovelight* . . . I'm singing 'When the Silver of the Moonlight Meets the Lovelight in Your Eyes,' you silly ass."

"Coo!" said Jos. Waterbury. "I thought you told me 'Top Hat, White Tie and Tails.' All right, cocky, now we're off."

He switched nimbly into the correct channels, and Freddie was able to sing *"In your eyes that softly beams"* without that set-your-teeth-on-edge feeling that he had sometimes experienced when changing gears unskilfully in his two-seater. But the mischief had been done. His grip on his audience had weakened. The better element on the lower floor were still sticking it out like men, but up in the gallery a certain liveliness had begun to manifest itself. The raspberry was not actually present, but he seemed to hear the beating of its wings.

To stave it off, he threw himself into his warbling with renewed energy. And such was his magnetism and technique that he very nearly put it over. The muttering died away. One of the crying children stopped crying. And though another was sick, Freddie thinks this must have been due to something it had eaten. He sang like one inspired.

Oh, the moon is bright and radiant,
But its radiance fades and dies
When the silver of the moonlight
Meets the lovelight in your eyes.

It was when he had reached this point, with that sort of lingering, caressing, treacly tremolo on the "eyes" which makes all the difference, that the mothers of Notting Hill, unable to restrain themselves any longer, had started whooping and stamping and whistling through their fingers. And there is little doubt, he tells me, that ere long these Bottletonians would have begun expressing themselves in similar fashion, had not Jos. Waterbury, who since the recent conference had been as good as gold, at this moment recognised an acquaintance in the front row of the stalls.

This was a large, red-haired man in a sweater and corduroy trousers who looked as if he might be in some way connected with the jellied eel industry. His name was Murphy, and it was he who, as Jos. Waterbury had informed Freddie at their first meeting, wished to ascertain the colour of the accompanist's insides.

What drew Jos. Waterbury's attention to this eel-jellier, if eel-jellier he was, was the circumstance of the latter at this juncture throwing an egg at him. It missed its mark, but it had the effect of causing the pianist to stop playing and rise and advance to the footlights. There was a cold look of dislike in his eyes. It was plain that there was imperfect communion of spirit between these two men. He bent over and asked:

"Did you throw that egg?"

To which the red-haired man's reply was:

"R."

"You did, did you?" said Jos. Waterbury. "Well, what price sausage and mashed?"

Freddie says he cannot understand these East End blokes. Their psychology is a sealed book to him. It is true that Jos. Waterbury had spoken in an unpleasant sneering manner, but even so he could see nothing in his words to stir the passions and cause a human being to lose his kinship with the divine. Personally, I am inclined to think that there must have been some hidden significance in them, wounding the eel-jellier's pride, so that when Jos. Waterbury said, "What price sausage and mashed?" the phrase did not mean to him what it would to you or me, but something deeper. Be that as it may, it brought the red-haired chap to his feet, howling like a gorilla.

The position of affairs was now as follows: The red-haired chap was saying wait till he got Jos. Waterbury outside. Jos. Waterbury was saying that he could eat the red-haired chap for a relish with his tea. Three more children had begun to cry, and the one who had stopped crying had begun again. Forty, perhaps—or it may have been fifty—voices were shouting, "Oy!" The announcer was bellowing, "Order, please, order!" Another infant in the gallery was being sick. And Freddie was singing verse two of "When the Silver of the Moonlight Meets the Lovelight in Your Eyes."

Even at Queen's Hall I don't suppose this sort of thing could have gone on long. At the Bottleton Palace of Varieties the pause before the actual outbreak of Armageddon was only of a few seconds' duration. Bottleton East is crammed from end to end with costermongers dealing in tomatoes, potatoes, Brussels sprouts and fruits in their season, and it is a very negligent audience there that forgets to attend a place of entertainment with full pockets.

Vegetables of all kinds now began to fill the air, and Freddie, abandoning his Art as a washout, sought refuge behind the piano. But this move, though shrewd, brought him only a temporary respite. No doubt this audience had had to deal before with singers who hid behind pianos. It took them perhaps a minute to find the range, and then some kind of a dried fish came dropping from the gallery and caught him in the eye.

Very much the same thing, if you remember, happened to King Harold at the battle of Hastings.

Forty seconds later, he was in the wings, brushing a tomato off his coat.

In circumstances like these, you might suppose that Freddie's soul would have been a maelstrom of mixed emotions. This, however, was not the case. One emotion only gripped him. He had never been more single-minded in his life. He wanted to get hold of Jos. Waterbury and twist his head off and stuff it down his throat. It is true that the red-haired chap had started the final mix-up by throwing an egg, but an accompanist worth his salt, felt Freddie, should have treated a mere egg with silent disdain, not deserted his post in order to argue about the thing. Rightly or wrongly, he considered that it was to Jos. Waterbury that his downfall was due. But for that sozzled pianist, he held, a triumph might have been his, as outstanding as his furore at Notting Hill.

Jos. Waterbury had disappeared, but fortunately Freddie was now not unfamiliar with his habits. His first act, on reaching the stage door and taking a Brussels sprout out of his hair, was to ask to be directed to the Green Goose. And there, a few moments later, he came upon the man he sought. He was standing at the counter drinking an unsweetened gin.

Now, just before the tiger of the jungle springs upon its prey, I am told by chaps who know tigers of the jungle, there is always a moment when it pauses, flexing its muscles and rubbing its feet in the resin. It was so with Freddie at this point. He did not immediately leap upon Jos. Waterbury, but stood clenching and unclenching his fists, while his protruding eyes sought out soft spots in the man. His ears were red and he breathed heavily.

The delay was fatal. Other people were familiar with Jos. Waterbury's habits. Just as he was about to take off, the swing door flew open violently, disclosing the red-haired man. And a moment later the red-haired man, pausing only to spit on his hands, had gone into action.

The words we speak in our heat seldom stand the acid test. In the very first seconds of the encounter it would have become plain to the poorest judge of form that in stating that he could eat the red-haired man for a relish with his tea Jos. Waterbury had overestimated his powers. He put up the rottenest kind of show, being as chaff before the red-haired bloke's sickle. Almost before the proceedings had begun, he had stopped a stinker with his chin and was on the sawdust.

In places like Bottleton East, when you are having a scrap and your antagonist falls, you don't wait for anyone to count ten—you kick him in the slats. This is a local rule. And it was so obvious to Freddie that this was what the red-haired bird was planning to do that he did not hesitate, but with a passionate cry rushed into the fray. He isn't a chap who goes out of his way to get mixed up in barroom brawls, but the sight of this red-haired fellow murdering the bounder he wanted to murder himself seemed to him to give him no option. He felt that his claim was being jumped, and his generous spirit resented it.

And so moved was he by the thought of being done

out of his rights that he might have put up a very pretty fight indeed, had not the chucker out attached to the premises intervened.

When the summons for his professional services reached him, the honest fellow had been enjoying a pint and a bit of bread and cheese in a back room. He now came in, wiping his mouth.

These chuckers out are no fools. A glance showed this one that a big, beefy, dangerous-looking chap was having a spot of unpleasantness with a slim, slight, slender chap, and with swift intelligence and sturdy common sense he grabbed the slim, slender chap. To pick Freddie up like a sack of coals and carry him to the door and hurl him out into the great open spaces was with him the work of a moment.

And so it came about that Lord Blicester, who was driving home after one of his meetings in the Conservative interest, became aware of stirring doings afoot off stage left, and the next moment perceived his nephew Frederick coming through the air like a shooting star.

He signalled to the chauffeur to stop and poked his head out of the window.

"Frederick!" he called—not, as you may well suppose, quite grasping the gist.

Freddie did not reply. Already he was re-entering the swing door in order to take up the argument at the point where it had been broken off. He was by now a bit stirred. Originally he had wanted to assassinate Jos. Waterbury, but since then his conception had broadened, if you know what I mean. He now wished to blot out the red-haired chap as well—also the chucker out and anybody else who crossed his path.

Old Blicester emerged from the car, just in time to see his flesh and blood come popping out again.

"Frederick!" he cried. "What is the meaning of this?" And he seized him by the arm.

Well, anybody could have told him he was asking for it. This was no time to seize Freddie by the arm. There was an arm left over which old Blicester hadn't seized, and with this Freddie smote him a snappy one in the midriff. Then, passing a weary hand over his brow, he made for the swing door again.

The catch about all this sort of thing—running amuck, I mean, and going berserk, or whatever they call it—is that there inevitably comes a morning after. The following morning found Freddie in bed, and so did old Blicester. He appeared as early as nine A. M., rousing Freddie from a troubled sleep, and what he wanted, it seemed, was a full explanation. And when Freddie, who was too weak for polished subterfuge, had given him a full explanation, not omitting the incident of the Brazil nut and the top hat, he put on the black cap.

He had changed his mind about that marriage. It was not right, he said—it was not human—to inflict a fool like Freddie on so sweet a girl, or on any girl, for that matter. After a powerful passage in which he pointed this out, he delivered sentence. Freddie was to take the afternoon train to Blicester Regis, repair by the station cab to Blicester Towers, and at Blicester Towers to remain secluded till further notice. Only thus, in his opinion, could the world be rendered safe for the human race. So there was nothing for Freddie to do but ring up the girl Dora and inform her that the big binge was off.

The statement was not very well received.

"Oh dear!" she said, and Freddie, reading between the lines, could see that what she really meant was "Oh hell!" "Why?"

Freddie explained that he had got to go down to the country that afternoon till further notice. The girl's manner changed. Her voice, which had been sniffy, brightened.

"Oh, but that's all right!" she said. "We shall all miss you, of course, but I can send you the bill."

"Something in that," said Freddie. "Only the trouble is, you see, I can't pay it."

"Why not?"

"I haven't any money."

"Why haven't you any money?"

Freddie braced himself.

"Well, the fact is that in a mistaken moment of enthusiasm, thinking—wrongly, as it turned out—that I was on a pinch, I betted——"

And in broken accents he told her the whole story. Wasted, of course, because she had hung up with a sharp cry at the word "betted." And about ten minutes later, after saying "Hullo, hullo!" a good many times, he, too, hung up—sombrely, because something told him that one more girl whom he had loved had gone out of his life.

And no sooner had he left his rooms and tottered into the street, his intention—and a very sound one—being to make his way to the club and have a few before it was too late, something small and greasy nipped out from the shadows. To cut a long story short, Jos. Waterbury.

And Freddie was just about to summon up all that remained of his frail strength after last night's doings and let him have it right in the eyeball, when Jos. Waterbury began to thank him for saving his life.

Well, you can't swat a man who is thanking you for saving his life, not if your own is ruled by the noblesse oblige code of the Widgeons. And when he tells you that times are hard and moots the possibility of your being able to spare a trifle, you cannot pass on unheeding. It was a bob that time, and on Freddie's return to London some three weeks later—the very day, oddly enough, when he read in the *Morning Post* that a marriage had been arranged and would shortly take place between Percival Alexander, eldest son of Gregory Hotchkiss, Esq., and Mrs Hotchkiss, and Dora, only daughter of the late Sir Ramsworthy Pinfold and Lady Pinfold—it was two, Freddie not having anything smaller on him. And there you are.

There was a thoughtful silence.

"And so it goes on," said the Crumpet.

"So it goes on," said the senior Bean.

The junior Bean agreed that so it went on.

ROMANCE AT DROITGATE SPA

IT HAS BEEN rightly said—and it is a fact on which we pride ourselves—that in the bar parlour of the Angler's Rest distinctions of class are unknown. Double Best Ports hobnob on terms of the easiest affability with humble Ginger Ales, and I myself have heard a Draught Beer in a Pewter call a Half Bottle of Champagne "old chap" and be addressed in his turn as "old fellow." Once inside that enchanted room, we are all brothers, all equals, from the highest to the lowest.

It was with distress and embarrassment, therefore, that we had watched the Plain Vichy snubbing the friendly overtures of a meek little Milk and Soda, high-hatting him so coldly and persistently that in the end he gave it up and slunk out. Soon afterwards the Vichy also left, explaining that his doctor had warned him not to be out of bed after ten o'clock at night, and as the door closed behind him we settled down to discuss the unfortunate affair. The Small Bass who had introduced the two men to one another scratched his head ruefully.

"I can't understand it," he said. "I thought they'd have got on so well together. Twin souls, I thought they'd have been."

Mr Mulliner stirred his hot scotch and lemon.

"What made you think that?"

"Well, they've both just had operations, and they both like talking about them."

"Ah," said Mr Mulliner, "but what you are forgetting is that while one has been operated on for duodenal ulcer, the other has merely had his tonsils removed."

"What difference would that make?"

"Every difference. There is no sphere of life in which class-consciousness is so rampant as among invalids. The ancient Spartans, I believe, were a little standoffish towards their Helots, but not so standoffish as the man who has been out in Switzerland taking insulin for his diabetes towards the man who is simply undergoing treatment from the village doctor for an ingrowing toenail. This is particularly so, of course, in those places where invalids collect in gangs—Bournemouth, for example, or Buxton, or Droitgate Spa. In such resorts the atmosphere is almost unbelievably clique-y. The old aristocracy, the topnotchers with maladies that get written up in the medical journals, keep themselves to themselves pretty rigidly, I can assure you, and have a very short way with the smaller fry."

Mention of Droitgate Spa (said Mr Mulliner, having ordered a second hot scotch and lemon) recalls to my mind the romance of my distant connection, Frederick Fitch-Fitch, whose uncle, Major General Sir Aylmer Bastable, lived there. It was at Droitgate Spa that the story had its setting, and I have always thought it one that throws a very interesting light on conditions in the class of the community of which we have been speaking.

Frederick at that time was a young man of pleasing manners and exterior who supported life on a small private income, the capital of which was held in trust for him by his uncle, Sir Aylmer; and it was his great desire to induce the other to release this capital, so that he could go into the antique business.

For that was where Frederick's heart was. He wanted to buy a half interest in some good Olde Shoppe in the Bond Street neighbourhoode and start selling walnutte tables and things. So every once in a while he would journey down to Droitgate Spa and plead for the stuff, but every time he did so he went away with his dreams shattered. For circumstances had unfortunately so ordered themselves as to make this uncle of his a warped, soured uncle.

Major General Sir Aylmer Bastable, you see, had had an unpleasant shock on coming to settle in Droitgate Spa. The head of a fine old family and the possessor of a distinguished military record, he had expected upon his arrival to be received with open arms by the best people and welcomed immediately into the inner set. But when it was discovered that all he had wrong with him was the gout in the right foot, he found himself cold-shouldered by the men who mattered and thrust back on the society of the asthma patients and the fellows with slight liver trouble.

This naturally soured his disposition a good deal, and his ill humour reacted upon his nephew. Every time Freddie came asking for capital to invest in antique shoppes, he found his uncle smarting from a snub from some swell whom the doctors had twice given up for dead, and so in no mood to part.

And then one day a more serious issue forced itself onto the agenda paper. At a charity matinée Freddie for the first time set eyes on Annabel Purvis. She was the assistant of The Great Boloni, a conjurer who had been engaged to perform at the entertainment, her duties being to skip downstage from time to time, hand him a bowl of goldfish, beam at the audience, do a sort of dance step, and skip back again. And with such winsome grace did she do this that Freddie fell in love at first sight.

It is not necessary for me to describe in detail how my distant connection contrived to make the girl's acquaintance, nor need I take you step by step through his courtship. Suffice it to say that during the cheese and celery course of a luncheon *à deux* some few weeks later Freddie proposed and was accepted. So now it became even more imperative than before that he induce his uncle to release his capital.

It was with a certain uneasiness that he travelled down to Droitgate Spa, for he was fully alive to the fact that the interview might prove a disagreeable one. However, his great love bore him on, and he made the journey and was shown into the room where the old man sat nursing a gouty foot.

"Hullo-ullo-ullo, Uncle!" he cried, for it was always his policy on these occasions to be buoyant till thrown out. "Good morning, good morning, good morning."

"Gaw!" said Sir Aylmer, with a sort of long, shuddering sigh. "It's you, is it?"

And he muttered something which Freddie did not

quite catch, though he was able to detect the words "last straw."

"Well," he went on, "what do you want?"

"Oh, I just looked in," said Freddie. "How's everything?"

"Rotten," replied Sir Aylmer. "I've just lost my nurse."

"Dead?"

"Worse. Married. The clothheaded girl has gone off and got spliced to one of the *canaille*—a chap who's never even had so much as athlete's foot. She must be crazy."

"Still, one sees her point of view."

"No, one doesn't."

"I mean," said Freddie, who felt strongly on this subject, "it's love that makes the world go round."

"It isn't anything of the kind," said Sir Aylmer. Like so many fine old soldiers, he was inclined to be a little literal-minded. "I never heard such dashed silly nonsense in my life. What makes the world go round is . . . Well, I've forgotten at the moment, but it certainly isn't love. How the deuce could it?"

"Oh, right ho. I see what you mean," said Freddie. "But put it another way. Love conquers all. Love's all right, take it from me."

The old man looked at him sharply.

"Are you in love?"

"Madly."

"Of all the young cuckoos! And I suppose you've come to ask for money to get married on?"

"Not at all. I just dropped round to see how you were. Still, as the subject has happened to crop up——"

Sir Aylmer brooded for a moment, snorting in an undertone.

"Who's the girl?" he demanded.

Freddie coughed, and fumbled with his collar. The crux of the situation, he realised, had now been reached. He had feared from the first that this was where the good old snag might conceivably sidle into the picture. For his Annabel was of humble station, and he knew how rigid were his relative's views on the importance of birth. No bigger snob ever swallowed a salicylate pill.

"Well, as a matter of fact," he said, "she's a conjurer's stooge."

"A *what?*"

"A conjurer's assistant, don't you know. I saw her first at a charity matinée. She was abetting a bloke called The Great Boloni."

"In what sense, abetting?"

"Well, she stood there upstage, don't you know, and every now and then she would skip downstage, hand this chap a bowl of goldfish or something, beam at the audience, do a sort of dance step and skip back again. You know the kind of thing."

A dark frown had come into Sir Aylmer's face.

"I do," he said grimly. "So! My only nephew has been ensnared by a bally, beaming goldfish-hander! Ha!"

"I wouldn't call it ensnared exactly," said Freddie deferentially.

"I would," said Sir Aylmer. "Get out of here."

"Right," said Freddie, and caught the 2:35 express

back to London. And it was during the journey that an idea flashed upon him.

The last of the Fitch-Fitches was not a great student of literature, but he occasionally dipped into a magazine; and everybody who has ever dipped into a magazine has read a story about a hardhearted old man who won't accept the hero's girl at any price, so what do they do but plant her on him without telling him who she is and, by Jove, he falls under her spell completely and then they tear off their whiskers and there they are. There was a story of this nature in the magazine which Freddie had purchased at the newsstand at Droitgate Spa station, and, as he read it, he remembered what his uncle had told him about his nurse handing in her portfolio.

By the time the train checked in at Paddington, his plans were fully formed.

"Listen," he said to Annabel Purvis, who had met him at the terminus, and Annabel said, "What?"

"Listen," said Freddie, and Annabel again said "What?"

"Listen," said Freddie, clasping her arm tenderly and steering her off in the direction of the refreshment room, where it was his intention to have a quick one. "To a certain extent I am compelled to admit that my expedition has been a washout . . ."

Annabel caught her breath sharply.

"No blessing?"

"No blessing."

"And no money?"

"No money. The old boy ran entirely true to stable form. He listened to what I had to say, snorted in an unpleasant manner and threw me out. The old routine. But what I'm working round to is that the skies are still bright and the bluebird on the job. I have a scheme. Could you be a nurse?"

"I used to nurse my uncle Joe."

"Then you shall nurse my uncle Aylmer. The present incumbent, he tells me, has just tuned out, and he needs a successor. I will phone him that I am despatching immediately a red-hot nurse whom he will find just the same as Mother makes, and you shall go down to Droitgate Spa and ingratiate yourself."

"But how?"

"Why, cluster round him. Smooth his pillow. Bring him cooling drinks. Coo to him, and give him the old oil. Tell him you are of gentle birth, if that's the expression I want. And when the time is ripe, when you have twined yourself about his heart and he looks upon you as a daughter, shoot me a wire and I'll come down and fall in love with you and he will give us his consent, blessing and the stuff. I guarantee this plan. It works."

So Annabel went to Droitgate Spa, and about three weeks later a telegram arrived for Freddie, running as follows:

HAVE INGRATIATED SELF COME AT ONCE LOVE AND KISSES ANNABEL

Within an hour of its arrival, Freddie was on his way to Podagra Lodge, his uncle's residence.

He found Sir Aylmer in his study. Annabel was sitting by his side, reading aloud to him from a recently published monograph on certain obscure ailments of the medulla oblongata. For the old man, though a mere gout patient, had pathetic aspirations towards higher things. There was a cooling drink on the table, and as Freddie entered the girl paused in her reading to smooth her employer's pillow.

"Gaw!" said Sir Aylmer. "You again?"

"Here I am," said Freddie.

"Well, by an extraordinary chance, I'm glad to see you. Leave us for a moment, Miss Purvis. I wish to speak to my nephew here, such as he is, on a serious and private matter. Did you notice that girl?" he said, as the door closed.

"I did, indeed."

"Pretty."

"An eyeful."

"And as good," said Sir Aylmer, "as she is beautiful. You should see her smooth pillows. And what a cooling drink she mixes! Excellent family, too, I understand. Her father is a colonel. Or, rather, was. He's dead."

"Ah well, all flesh is as grass."

"No, it isn't. It's nothing of the kind. The two things are entirely different. I've seen flesh and I've seen grass. No resemblance whatever. However, that is not the point at issue. What I wanted to say was that if you were not a damned fool, that's the sort of girl you would be in love with."

"I am."

"A damned fool?"

"No. In love with that girl."

"What! You have fallen in love with Miss Purvis? Already?"

"I have."

"Well, that's the quickest thing I ever saw. What about your beaming goldfish?"

"Oh, that's all over. A mere passing boyish fancy."

Sir Aylmer took a deep swig at his cooling drink, and regarded him in silence for a moment.

"Well," he said at length, breathing heavily, "if that's the airy, casual way in which you treat life's most sacred emotions, the sooner you are safely married and settled down, the better. If you're allowed to run around loose much longer, indulging those boyish fancies of yours, I foresee the breach-of-promise case of the century. However, I'm not saying I'm not relieved. I am relieved. I suppose she wore tights, this goldfish girl?"

"Pink."

"Disgusting. Thank God it's all over. Very good, then. You are free, I understand, to have a pop at Miss Purvis. Do you propose to do so?"

"I do."

"Excellent. You get that sweet, refined, most-suitable-in-all-respects girl to marry you, and I'll hand over that money of yours, every penny of it."

"I will start at once."

"Heaven speed your wooing." said Sir Aylmer.

And ten minutes later Freddie was able to inform his uncle that his whirlwind courtship had been successful, and Sir Aylmer said that when he had asked heaven to speed his wooing he had had no notion that it would speed it to quite that extent. He congratulated Freddie warmly and said he hoped that he appreciated his good fortune, and Freddie said he certainly did, because his love was like a red, red rose, and Sir Aylmer said, No, she wasn't, and when Freddie added that he was walking on air Sir Aylmer said he couldn't be, the thing was physically impossible.

However, he gave his blessing and promised to release Freddie's capital as soon as the necessary papers were drawn up, and Freddie went back to London to see his lawyer about this.

His mood, as the train sped through the quiet countryside, was one of perfect tranquillity and happiness. It seemed to him that his troubles were now definitely ended. He looked down the vista of the years and saw nothing but joy and sunshine. If somebody had told Frederick Fitch-Fitch at that moment that even now a V-shaped depression was coming along which would shortly blacken the skies and lower the general temperature to freezing point, he would not have believed him.

Nor when, two days later, as he sat in his club, he was informed that a Mr Rackstraw was waiting to see him in the small smoking room, did he have an inkling that here was the V-shaped depression in person. His heart was still light as he went down the passage, wondering idly, for the name was unfamiliar to him, who this Mr Rackstraw might be. He entered the room, and found there a tall, thin man with pointed black moustaches who was pacing up and down, nervously taking rabbits out of his top hat as he walked.

"Mr Rackstraw?"

His visitor spun round, dropping a rabbit. He gazed at Freddie piercingly. He had bright, glittering, sinister eyes.

"That is my name. Mortimer Rackstraw."

Freddie's mind had flown back to the charity matinée at which he had first seen Annabel, and he recognised the fellow now.

"The Great Boloni, surely?"

"I call myself that professionally. So you are Mr Fitch? So *you* are Mr Fitch? Ha! Fiend!"

"Eh?"

"I am not mistaken? You are Frederick Fitch?"

"Frederick Fitch-Fitch."

"I beg your pardon. In that case, I should have said 'Fiend! Fiend!' "

He produced a pack of cards and asked Freddie to take one—any one—and memorise it and put it back. Freddie did so absently. He was considerably fogged. He could make nothing of all this.

"How do you mean—Fiend-Fiend?" he asked.

The other sneered unpleasantly.

"Cad!" he said, twirling his moustache.

"Cad?" said Freddie, mystified.

"Yes sir. Cad. You have stolen the girl I love."

"I don't understand."

"Then you must be a perfect ass. It's quite simple, isn't it? I can't put it any plainer, can I? I say you have stolen . . . Well, look here," said Mortimer Rackstraw. "Suppose this top hat is me. This rabbit," he went on, producing it from the lining, "is the girl I love. You come along and, presto, the rabbit vanishes."

"It's up your sleeve."

"It is not up my sleeve. And if it were, if I had a thousand sleeves and rabbits up every one of them, that would not alter the fact that you have treacherously robbed me of Annabel Purvis."

Freddie began to see daylight. He was able to appreciate the other's emotion.

"So you love Annabel too?"

"I do."

"I don't wonder. Nice girl, what? I see, I see. You worshipped her in secret, never telling your love . . . "

"I did tell my love. We were engaged."

"Engaged?"

"Certainly. And this morning I get a letter from her saying that it's all off, because she has changed her mind and is going to marry you. She has thrown me over."

"Oh, ah? Well, I'm frightfully sorry—deepest sympathy, and all that—but I don't see what's to be done about it, what?"

"I do. There still remains—revenge."

"Oh, I say, dash it! You aren't going to be stuffy about it?"

"I am going to be stuffy about it. For the moment you triumph. But do not imagine that this is the end. You have not heard the last of me. Not by any means. You may have stolen the woman I love with your underhanded chicanery, but I'll fix you."

"How?"

"Never mind how. You will find out how quite soon enough. A nasty jolt you're going to get, my good fiend, and almost immediately. As sure," said Mortimer Rackstraw, illustrating by drawing one from Freddie's back hair, "as eggs are eggs. I wish you a very good afternoon."

He took up his top hat, which in his emotion he had allowed to fall to the ground, brushed it on his coat sleeve, extracted from it a cage of lovebirds and strode out.

A moment later he returned, bowed a few times to right and left and was gone again.

To say that Freddie did not feel a little uneasy as the result of this scene would be untrue. There had been something in the confident manner in which the other had spoken of revenging himself that he had not at all liked. The words had had a sinister ring, and all through the rest of the day he pondered thoughtfully, wondering what a man so trained in the art of having things up his sleeve might have up it now. It was in meditative mood that he dined, and only on the following morning did his equanimity return to him.

Able, now that he had slept on it, to review the disturbing conversation in its proper perspective, he came to the conclusion that the fellow's threats had been mere bluff. What, after all, he asked himself, could this conjurer do? It was not as if they had been living in the Middle Ages, when chaps of that sort used to put spells on you and change you into things.

No, he decided, it was mere bluff, and with his complacency completely restored had just lighted a cigarette and fallen to dreaming of the girl he loved, when a telegram was brought to him.

It ran as follows:

COME AT ONCE ALL LOST RUIN STARES FACE LOVE AND KISSES ANNABEL

Half an hour later, he was in the train, speeding towards Droitgate Spa.

It had been Freddie's intention, on entering the train, to devote the journey to earnest meditation. But, as always happens when one wishes to concentrate and brood during a railway journey, he found himself closeted with a talkative fellow-traveller.

The one who interrupted Freddie's thoughts was a flabby, puffy man of middle age, wearing a red waistcoat, brown shoes, a morning coat and a bowler hat. With such a Grade A bounder, even had his mind been at rest, Freddie would have had little in common, and he sat chafing while the prismatic fellow prattled on. Nearly an hour passed before he was freed from the infliction of the other's conversation, but eventually the man's head began to nod, and presently he was snoring and Freddie was able to give himself up to his reverie.

His thoughts became less and less agreeable as the train rolled on. And what rendered his mental distress so particularly acute was the lack of informative detail in Annabel's telegram. It seemed to him to offer so wide a field for uncomfortable speculation.

"All lost", for instance. A man could do a lot of thinking about a phrase like that. And "Ruin stares face." Why, he asked himself, did ruin stare face? While commending Annabel's thriftiness in keeping the thing down to twelve words, he could not help wishing that she could have brought herself to spring another twopence and be more lucid.

But of one thing he felt certain. All this had something to do with his recent visitor. Behind that mystic telegram he seemed to see the hand of Mortimer Rackstraw, that hand whose quickness deceived the eye, and he knew that in lightly dismissing the other as a negligible force he had been too sangine.

By the time he reached Podagra Lodge, the nervous strain had become almost intolerable. As he rang the bell, he was quivering like some jelly set before a diet patient, and the sight of Annabel's face as she opened the door did nothing to alleviate his perturbation. The girl was obviously all of a twitter.

"Oh, Freddie!" she cried. "The worst has happened."

Freddie gulped.

"Rackstraw?"

"Yes," said Annabel. "But how did you know about him?"

"He came to see me, bubbling over a good deal with veiled menaces and what not," explained Freddie. He frowned and eyed her closely. "Why didn't you tell me you had been engaged to that bird?"

"I didn't think you would be interested. It was just a passing girlish fancy."

"You're sure? You didn't really love this blighted prestidigitator?"

"No, no. I was dazzled for a while, as any girl might have been, when he sawed me in half, but then you came along and I saw that I had been mistaken and that you were the only man in the world for me."

"Good egg," said Freddie, relieved.

He kissed her fondly and, as he did so, there came to

his ears the sound of rhythmic hammering from somewhere below.

"What's that?" he asked.

Annabel wrung her hands.

"It's Mortimer!"

"Is he here?"

"Yes. He arrived on the one-fifteen. I locked him in the cellar."

"Why?"

"To stop him going to the Pump Room."

"Why shouldn't he go to the Pump Room?"

"Because Sir Aylmer has gone there to listen to the band, and they must not meet. If they do, we are lost. Mortimer has hatched a fearful plot."

Freddie's heart seemed to buckle under within him. He had tried to be optimistic, but all along he had known that Mortimer Rackstraw would hatch some fearful plot. He could have put his shirt on it. A born hatcher.

"What plot?"

Annabel wrung her hands again.

"He means to introduce Sir Aylmer to my uncle Joe. He wired to him to come to Droitgate Spa. He had arranged to meet him at the Pump Room, and then he was going to introduce him to Sir Aylmer."

Freddie was a little fogged. It did not seem to him much of a plot.

"Now that I can never be his, all he wants is to make himself unpleasant and prevent our marriage. And he knows that Sir Aylmer will never consent to your marrying me if he finds out that I have an uncle like Uncle Joe."

Freddie ceased to be fogged. He saw the whole devilish scheme now—a scheme worthy of the subtle brain that could put the ace of spades back in the pack, shuffle, cut three times, and then produce it from the inside of a lemon.

"Is he so frightful?" he quavered.

"Look," said Annabel simply. She took a photograph from her bosom and extended it towards him with a trembling hand. "That is Uncle Joe, taken in the masonic regalia of a Grand Exalted Periwinkle of the Mystic Order of Whelks."

Freddie glanced at the photograph and started back with a hoarse cry. Annabel nodded sadly.

"Yes," she said. "That is how he takes most people. The only faint hope I have is that he won't have been able to come. But if he has——"

"He has," cried Freddie, who had been fighting for breath. "We travelled down in the train together."

"What!"

"Yes. He must be waiting at the Pump Room now."

"And at any moment Mortimer will break his way out of the cellar. The door is not strong. What shall we do?"

"There is only one thing to do. I have all the papers . . ."

"You have no time to read now."

"The legal papers, the ones my uncle has to sign in order to release my money. There is just a chance that if I rush to the Pump Room I may get him to put his name on the dotted line before the worst happens."

"Then rush," cried Annabel.

"I will," said Freddie.

He kissed her quickly, grabbed his hat, and was off the mark like a jack rabbit.

A man who is endeavouring to lower the record for the distance between Podagra Lodge, which is in Arterio-Sclerosis Avenue, and the Droitgate Spa Pump Room has little leisure for thinking, but Freddie managed to put in a certain amount as his feet skimmed the pavement. And the trend of his thought was such as to give renewed vigour to his legs. He could scarcely have moved more rapidly if he had been a character in a two-reel film with the police after him.

And there was need for speed. Beyond a question, Annabel had been right when she had said that Sir Aylmer would never consent to their union if he found out that she had an uncle like her uncle Joe. Uncle Joe would get right in amongst him. Let them but meet, and nothing was more certain than that the haughty old man would veto the proposed nuptials.

A final burst of speed took him panting up the Pump Room steps and into the rotunda where all that was best and most refined in Droitgate Spa was accustomed to assemble of an afternoon and listen to the band. He saw Sir Aylmer in a distant seat and hurried towards him.

"Gaw!" said Sir Aylmer. "You?"

Freddie could only nod.

"Well, stop puffing like that and sit down," said Sir Aylmer. "They're just going to play 'Poet and Peasant.' "

Freddie recovered his breath.

"Uncle——" he began. But it was too late. Even as he spoke, there was a crash of brass and Sir Aylmer's face assumed that reverent, doughlike expression of attention so familiar in the rotundas of cure resorts.

"Sh," he said.

Of all the uncounted millions who in their time have listened to bands playing "Poet and Peasant," few can ever have listened with such a restless impatience as did Frederick Fitch-Fitch on this occasion. Time was flying. Every second was precious. At any moment disaster might befall. And the band went on playing as if it had taken on a life job. It seemed to him an eternity before the final oom-pom-pa.

"Uncle," he cried, as the echoes died away.

"Sh," said Sir Aylmer testily, and Freddie, with a dull despair, perceived that they were going to get an encore.

Of all the far-flung myriads who year in and year out have listened to bands playing the "Overture" to *Raymond,* few can ever have chafed as did Frederick Fitch-Fitch now. This suspense was unmanning him, this delay was torture. He took the papers and a fountain pen from his pocket and toyed with them nervously. He wondered dully as he sat there how the opera *Raymond* had ever managed to get itself performed, if the "Overture" was as long as this. They must have rushed it through in the last five minutes of the evening as the audience groped for its hats and wraps.

But there is an end to all things, even to the "Overture" from *Raymond.* Just as the weariest river winds somewhere safe to sea, so does this "Overture" eventually finish. And when it did, when the last notes faded into silence and the conductor stood bowing and smiling with that cool assumption, common to all conductors, that it is they and not the perspiring orchestra who have been doing the work, he started again.

"Uncle," he said, "may I trouble you for a moment . . . These papers."

Sir Aylmer cocked an eye at the documents.

"What papers are those?"

"The ones you have to sign, releasing my capital."

"Oh, those," said Sir Aylmer genially. The music had plainly mellowed him. "Of course, yes. Certainly, certainly. Give me . . ."

He broke off, and Freddie saw that he was looking at a distinguished, silvery-haired man with thin, refined features, who was sauntering by.

"Afternoon, Rumbelow," he said.

There was an unmistakable note of obsequiousness in Sir Aylmer's voice. His face had become pink, and he was shuffling his feet and twiddling his fingers. The man to whom he had spoken paused and looked down. Seeing who it was that had accosted him, he raised a silvery eyebrow. His manner was undisguisedly supercilious.

"Ah, Bastable," he said distantly.

A duller man than Sir Aylmer Bastable could not have failed to detect the cold hauteur in his voice. Freddie saw the flush on his uncle's face deepen. Sir Aylmer mumbled something about hoping that the distinguished-looking man was feeling better today.

"Worse," replied the other curtly. "Much worse. The doctors are baffled. Mine is a very complicated case." He paused for a moment, and his delicately chiselled lip curled in a sneer. "And how is the gout, Bastable? Gout! Ha, ha!"

Without waiting for a reply, he passed on and joined a group that stood chatting close by. Sir Aylmer choked down a mortified oath.

"Snob!" he muttered. "Thinks he's everybody just because he's got telangiecstasis. I don't see what's so wonderful about having telangiecstasis. Anybody could have . . . What on earth are you doing? What the devil's all this you're waving under my nose? Papers? Papers? I don't want any papers. Take them away, sir!"

And before Freddie could burst into the impassioned plea which trembled on his lips, a commotion in the doorway distracted his attention. His heart missed a beat, and he sat there, frozen.

On the threshhold stood Mortimer Rackstraw. He was making some enquiry of an attendant, and Freddie could guess only too well what that enquiry was. Mortimer Rackstraw was asking which of those present was Major General Sir Aylmer Bastable. Attached to his arm, obviously pleading with him and appealing to his better self, Annabel Purvis gazed up into his face with tear-filled eyes.

A moment later, the conjurer strode up, still towing the girl. He halted before Sir Aylmer and threw Annabel aside like a soiled glove. His face was cold and hard and remorseless. With one hand he was juggling mechanically with two billiard balls and a bouquet of roses.

"Sir Aylmer Bastable?"

"Yes."

"I forbid the banns."

"What banns?"

"Their banns," said Mortimer Rackstraw, removing from his lips the hand with which he had been coldly curling his moustache and jerking it in the direction of Annabel and Freddie, who stood clasped in each other's arms, waiting for they knew not what.

"They're not up yet," said Annabel.

The conjurer seemed a little taken aback.

"Oh?" he said. "Well, when they are, I forbid them. And so will you, Sir Aylmer, when you hear all."

Sir Aylmer puffed.

"Who is this tight bounder?" he asked irritably.

Mortimer Rackstraw shook his head and took the two of clubs from it.

"A bounder, maybe," he said, "but not tight. I have come here, Sir Aylmer, in a spirit of altruism to warn you that if you allow your nephew to marry this girl the grand old name of Bastable will be mud."

Sir Aylmer started.

"Mud?"

"Mud. She comes from the very dregs of society."

"I don't," cried Annabel.

"Of course she doesn't," cried Freddie.

"Certainly she does not," assented Sir Aylmer warmly. "She told me herself that her father was a colonel."

Mortimer Rackstraw uttered a short, sneering laugh and took an egg from his left elbow.

"She did, eh? Did she add that he was a colonel in the Salvation Army?"

"What!"

"And that before he saw the light he was a Silver Ring bookie, known to all the heads as Rat-Faced Rupert, the Bermondsey Twister?"

"Good God!"

Sir Aylmer turned to the girl with an awful frown. "Is this true?"

"Of course it's true," said Mortimer Rackstraw. "And if you want further proof of her unfitness to be your nephew's bride, just take a look at her uncle Joe, who is now entering left-centre."

And Freddie, listless now and without hope, saw that his companion of the train was advancing towards them. He heard Sir Aylmer gasp and was aware that Annabel had stiffened in his arms. He was not surprised. The sun, filtering through the glass of the rotunda, lit up the man's flabby puffiness, his morning coat, his red waistcoat and his brown shoes, and rarely, if ever, thought Freddie, could the sun of Droitgate Spa have shone on a more ghastly outsider.

There was nothing, however, in the newcomer's demeanour to suggest that he felt himself out of place in these refined surroundings. His manner had an easy self-confidence. He sauntered up and without *gêne* slapped the conjurer on the back and patted Annabel on the shoulder.

" 'Ullo, Mort. 'Ullo, Annie, my dear."

Sir Aylmer, who had blinked, staggered and finally recovered himself, spoke in a voice of thunder.

"You, sir! Is this true?"

"What's that, old cock?"

"Are you this girl's uncle?"

"That's right."

"Gaw!" said Sir Aylmer.

He would have spoken further, but at this point the band burst into "Pomp and Circumstance" and conversation was temporarily suspended. When it became possible once more for the human voice to make itself heard, it was Annabel's Uncle Joe who took the floor. He had recognised Freddie.

"Why, I've met you," he said. "We travelled down in the train together. Who's this young feller, Annie, that's huggin' and squeezin' you?"

"He is the man I am going to marry," said Annabel.

"He is not the man you are going to marry," said Sir Aylmer.

"Yes, I am the man she is going to marry," said Freddie.

"No, you're not the man she is going to marry," said Mortimer Rackstraw.

Annabel's Uncle Joe seemed puzzled. He appeared not to know what to make of this conflict of opinion.

"Well, settle it among yourselves," he said genially. "All I know is that whoever does marry you, Annie, is going to get a good wife."

"That's me," said Freddie.

"No, it isn't," said Sir Aylmer.

"Yes, it is," said Annabel.

"No, it's not," said Mortimer Rackstraw.

"Because I'm sure no man," proceeded Uncle Joe, "ever had a better niece. I've never forgotten the way you used to come and smooth my pillow and bring me cooling drinks when I was in the hospital."

There was the sound of a sharp intake of breath. Sir Aylmer, who was saying, "It isn't, it isn't, it isn't," had broken off abruptly.

"Hospital?" he said. "Were you ever in a hospital?"

Mr Boffin laughed indulgently.

"Was I ever in a hospital! That's a good 'un. That would make the boys on the medical council giggle. Ask them at St Luke's if Joe Boffin was ever in a hospital. Ask them at St Christopher's. Why, I've spent most of my life in hospitals. Started as a child with Congenital Pyloric Hypertrophy of the Stomach and never looked back."

Sir Aylmer was trembling violently. A look of awe had come into his face, the look which a small boy wears when he sees a heavyweight champion of the world.

"Did you say your name was Joe Boffin?"

"That's right."

"Not *the* Joe Boffin? Not the man there was that interview with in the Christmas number of *The Lancet?*"

"That's me."

Sir Aylmer started forward impulsively.

"May I shake your hand?"

"Put it there."

"I am proud to meet you, Mr Boffin. I am one of your greatest admirers."

"Nice of you to say so, ol' man."

"Your career has been an inspiration to me. Is it really true that you have Thrombosis of the Heart *and* Vesicular Emphysema of the Lungs?"

"That's right."

"And that your temperature once went up to 107.5?"

"Twice. When I had Hyperpyrexia."

Sir Aylmer sighed.

"The best I've ever done is 102.2."

Joe Boffin patted him on the back.

"Well, that's not bad," he said. "Not bad at all."

"Excuse me," said a well-bred voice.

It was the distinguished-looking man with the silvery hair who had approached them, the man Sir Aylmer had addressed as Rumbelow. His manner was diffident. Behind him stood an eager group, staring and twiddling their fingers.

"Excuse me, my dear Bastable, for intruding on a private conversation, but I fancied . . . and my friends fancied . . ."

"We all fancied," said the group.

"That we overheard the name Boffin. Can it be, sir, that you are Mr *Joseph* Boffin?"

"That's right."

"Boffin of St Luke's?"

"That's right."

The silvery-haired man seemed overcome by a sudden shyness. He giggled nervously.

"Then may we say—my friends and I—how much . . . We felt we would just like . . . Unwarrantable intrusion, of course, but we are all such great admirers . . . I suppose you have to go through a good deal of this sort of thing, Mr Boffin . . . people coming up to you, I mean, and . . . perfect strangers, I mean to say . . ."

"Quite all right, old man, quite all right. Always glad to meet the fans."

"Then may I introduce myself? I am Lord Rumbelow. These are my friends, the Duke of Mull, the Marquis of Peckham, Lord Percy . . ."

" 'Ow are you, 'ow are you? Come and join us, boys. My niece, Miss Purvis."

"Charmed."

"The young chap she's going to marry."

"How do you do?"

"And his uncle, Sir Aylmer Bastable."

All heads were turned towards the Major General. Lord Rumbelow spoke in an awed voice.

"Is this really so, Bastable? Your nephew is actually going to marry Mr Boffin's niece? I congratulate you, my dear fellow. A most signal honor." A touch of embarrassment came into his manner. He coughed. "We were just talking about you, oddly enough, Bastable, my friends and I. Saying what a pity it was that we saw so little of you. And we were wondering—it was the Duke's suggestion—if you would care to become a member of a little club we have—quite a small affair—rather exclusive, we like to feel—the Twelve Jolly Stretcher Cases. . . ."

"My dear Rumbelow!"

"We have felt for a long time that our company was incomplete without you. So you will join us? Capital, capital! Perhaps you will look in there tonight? Mr Boffin, of course," he went on deprecatingly, "would, I am afraid, hardly condescend to allow himself to be entertained by so humble a little circle. Otherwise——"

Joe Boffin slapped him affably on the back.

"My dear feller, I'd be delighted. There's nothing stuck-up about me."

"Well, really! I hardly know what to say . . ."

"We can't all be Joe Boffins. That's the way I look at it."

"The true democratic spirit."

"Why, I was best man at a chap's wedding last week, and all he'd got was emotional dermatitis."

"Amazing! Then you and Sir Aylmer will be with us tonight? Delightful. We can give you a bottle of lung tonic which I think you will appreciate. We pride ourselves on our cellar."

A babble of happy chatter had broken out, almost drowning the band, which was now playing the "Overture" to *William Tell,* and Mr Boffin, opening his waistcoat, was showing the Duke of Mull the scar left by his first operation. Sir Aylmer, watching them with a throbbing heart, was dizzily aware of a fountain pen being thrust into his hand.

"Eh?" he said. "What? What's this? What, what?"

"The papers," said Freddie. "The merry old documents in the case. You sign here, where my thumb is."

"Eh? What? Eh? Ah yes, to be sure. Yes, yes, yes," said Sir Aylmer, absently affixing his signature.

"Thank you, Uncle, a thousand——"

"Quite, quite. But don't bother me now, my boy. Busy. Got a lot to talk about to these friends of mine. Take the girl away and give her a sulphur water."

And, brushing aside Mortimer Rackstraw, who was offering him a pack of cards, he joined the group about Joe Boffin. Freddie clasped Annabel in a fond embrace. Mortimer Rackstraw stood glaring for a moment, twisting his moustache. Then he took the flags of all nations from Annabel's back hair and with a despairing gesture strode from the room.

ALL'S WELL WITH BINGO

A BEAN and a Crumpet were in the smoking room of the Drones Club having a quick one before lunch, when an Egg who had been seated at the writing table in the corner rose and approached them.

"How many 'r's' in 'intolerable'?" he asked.

"Two," said the Crumpet. "Why?"

"I am writing a strong letter to the committee," explained the Egg, "drawing their attention to the intolerable . . . Great Scott!" he cried, breaking off. "There he goes again!"

A spasm contorted his face. Outside in the passage a fresh young voice had burst into a gay song with a good deal of vo-de-o-de-o about it. The Bean cocked an attentive ear as it died away in the direction of the dining room.

"Who is this linnet?" he enquired.

"Bingo Little, blast him! He's always singing nowadays. That's what I'm writing my strong letter to the committee about—the intolerable nuisance of this incessant heartiness of his. Because it isn't only his singing. He slaps backs. Only yesterday he came sneaking up behind me in the bar and sloshed me between the shoulder blades, saying 'Aha!' as he did so. Might have choked me. How many 's's' in 'incessant'?"

"Three," said the Crumpet.

"Thanks," said the Egg.

He returned to the writing table. The Bean seemed perplexed.

"Odd," he said. "Very odd. How do you account for young Bingo carrying on like this?"

"Just joie de vivre."

"But he's married. Didn't he marry some female novelist or other?"

"That's right. Rosie M. Banks, authoress of *Only A Factory Girl, Mervyn Keene, Clubman, 'Twas Once In May,* and other works. You see her name everywhere. I understand she makes a packet with the pen."

"I didn't know married men had any joie de vivre."

"Not many, of course. But Bingo's union has been an exceptionally happy one. He and the other half of the sketch have hit it off from the start like a couple of lovebirds."

"Well, he oughtn't to slap backs about it."

"You don't know the inside facts. Bingo is no mere wanton backslapper. What has made him that way at the moment is the fact that he recently had a most merciful escape. There was within a toucher of being very serious trouble in the home."

"But you said they were like a couple of lovebirds."

"Quite. But even with lovebirds circumstances can arise which will cause the female lovebird to get above herself and start throwing her weight about. If Mrs Bingo had got on Bingo what at one time it appeared inevitable that she must get on him, it would have kept her in conversation for the remainder of their married lives. She is a sweet little thing, one of the best, but women are women and I think that there can be no doubt that she would have continued to make passing allusions to the affair right up to the golden wedding day. The way Bingo looks at it is that he has escaped the fate that is worse than death, and I am inclined to agree with him."

The thing started one morning when Bingo returned to the love nest for a bite of lunch after taking the Pekingese for a saunter. He was in the hall trying to balance an umbrella on the tip of his nose, his habit when at leisure, and Mrs Bingo came out of her study with a wrinkled brow and a couple of spots of ink on her chin.

"Oh, there you are," she said. "Bingo, have you ever been to Monte Carlo?"

Bingo could not help wincing a little at this. Unwittingly, the woman had touched an exposed nerve. The thing he had always wanted to do most in the world was to go to Monte Carlo, for he had a system which couldn't fail to clean out the Casino, but few places, as you are probably aware, are more difficult for a married man to sneak off to.

"No," he said with a touch of moodiness. Then, recovering his usual sunny aplomb, "Look," he said. "Watch, old partner in sickness and in health. I place the umbrella so. Then, maintaining a perfect equilibrium . . ."

"I want you to go there at once," said Mrs Bingo.

Bingo dropped the umbrella. You could have knocked

him down with a toothpick. For a moment, he tells me, he thought that he must be dreaming some beautiful dream.

"It's for my book. I can't get on without some local colour."

Bingo grasped the gist. Mrs Bingo had often discussed this business of local colour with him, and he had got the strength of it. Nowadays, he knew, if you are providing wholesome fiction for the masses, you have simply got to get your atmosphere right. The customers have become cagey. They know too much. Chance your arm with the *mise en scène,* and before you can say, "What ho", you've made some bloomer and people are writing you nasty letters, beginning, "Dear Madam: Are you aware . . ."

"And I can't go myself. There's the Pen and Ink Dinner on Friday, and on Tuesday the Writers Club is giving a luncheon to Mrs Carrie Melrose Bopp, the American novelist. And any moment now I shall be coming to the part where Lord Peter Shipbourne breaks the bank. So do you think you could possibly go, Bingo darling?"

Bingo was beginning to understand how the Israelites must have felt when that manna started descending in the wilderness.

"Of course I'll go, old egg," he said heartily. "Anything I can——"

His voice trailed away. A sudden thought had come, biting into his soul like acid. He had remembered that he hadn't a bean to his name. He had lost every penny he possessed two weeks before on a horse called Bounding Beauty which was running—if you could call it running—in the two-thirty at Haydock Park.

The trouble with old Bingo is that he will allow his cooler judgment to be warped by dreams and omens. Nobody had known better than he that by the ruling of the form book Bounding Beauty hadn't a chance; but on the eve of the race he had a nightmare in which he saw his uncle Wilberforce dancing the rumba in the nude on the steps of the National Liberal Club and, like a silly ass, accepted this as a bit of stable information. And bang, as I say, had gone every penny he had in the world.

For a moment he reeled a bit. Then he brightened. Rosie, he reasoned, would scarcely expect him to undertake an irksome job like sweating all the way over to Monte Carlo without financing the tedious expedition.

"Of course, of course, of course," he said. "Yes, rather! I'll start tomorrow. And about expenses. I suppose a hundred quid would see me through, though two would be still better, and even three wouldn't hurt . . ."

"Oh no, that's all right," said Mrs Bingo. "You won't need any money."

Bingo gulped like an ostrich swallowing a brass doorknob.

"Not . . . need . . . any . . . money?"

"Except a pound or two for tips and so on. Everything is arranged. Dora Spurgeon is at Cannes, and I'm going to phone her to get you a room at the Hôtel de Paris at Monte Carlo, and all the bills will be sent to my bank."

Bingo had to gulp a couple more times before he was able to continue holding up his end of the duologue.

"But I take it," he said in a low voice, "that you want me to hobnob with the international spies and veiled women and so forth and observe their habits carefully, don't you? This will run into money. You know what international spies are. It's champagne for them every time, and no half bots, either."

"You needn't bother about the spies. I can imagine them. All I want is the local colour. An exact description of the Rooms and the Square and all that. Besides, if you had a lot of money, you might be tempted to gamble."

"What!" cried Bingo. "Gamble? Me?"

"No, no," said Mrs Bingo remorsefully. "I'm wronging you, of course. Still, I think I'd sooner we did it the way I've arranged."

So there you have the position of affairs, and you will not be surprised to learn that poor old Bingo made an indifferent lunch, toying with the minced chicken and pushing the roly-poly pudding away untasted. His manner during the meal was distrait, for his brain was racing like a dynamo. Somehow he had got to get the stuff. But how? How?

Bingo, you see, is not a man who finds it easy to float a really substantial loan. People know too much about his financial outlook. He will have it in sackfuls some day, of course, but until he realises on his uncle Wilberforce—who is seventy-six and may quite easily go to par—the wolf, as far as he is concerned, will always be in or about the vestibule. The public is aware of this, and it makes the market sluggish.

It seemed to him, brooding over the thing, that his only prospect for the sort of sum he required was Oofy Prosser. Oofy, while not an easy parter, is a millionaire, and a millionaire was what he required. So round about cocktail time he buzzed off to the club, only to be informed that Oofy was abroad. The disappointment was so severe that he was compelled to go to the smoking room and have a restorative. I was there when he came in, and so haggard and fishlike was his demeanour that I asked him what was up, and he told me all.

"You couldn't lend me between twenty and twenty-five or, better still, thirty quid, could you?" he said.

I said, No, I couldn't, and he heaved a long, low, quivering sigh.

"And so it goes on," he said. "That's life. Here I am with this unique opportunity of making a stupendous fortune, and crippled for lack of the essential capital. Did you ever hear of a chap called Garcia?"

"No."

"Skinned the Monte Carlo administration of a hundred thousand quid in his day. Ever hear of a chap called Darnborough?"

"No."

"Eighty-three thousand of the best was what he pocketed. Did you ever hear of a chap called Owers?"

"No."

"His winning streak lasted for more than twenty years. These three birds of whom I speak simply went to Monte Carlo and lolled back in their chairs with fat cigars and the Casino just thrust the money on them. And I don't suppose any of them had a system like mine. Oh hell, oh blast, oh damn, a thousand curses!" said Bingo.

Well, there isn't much you can say when a fellow's in the depths like that. The only thing I could suggest was that he should put some little trinket up the spout temporarily. His cigarette case, for instance, I said, and it was then that I learned that that cigarette case of his is not the solid gold we have always imagined. Tin, really. And except for the cigarette case, it appeared, the only trinket he had ever possessed was a diamond brooch which, being in funds at the moment as the result of a fortunate speculation at Catterick Bridge, he had bought Mrs Bingo for a birthday present.

It all seemed pretty hopeless, accordingly, so I merely offered him my heartfelt sympathy and another snootful. And next morning he steamed off on the eleven-o'clock express, despair in his soul and in his pocket a notebook, four pencils, his return ticket, and about three pounds for tips and so on. And shortly before lunch on the following day he was alighting at Monte Carlo station.

I don't know if you remember a song some years ago that went "Ti-um-ti-um-ti-um-ti-um, ti-um-ti-um-ti-ay," and then, after a bit more of that, finished up:

> "*Ti-um-ti-um-ti-um-ti*-um,
> *The curse of an aching heart.*"

You don't hear it much nowadays, but at one time you were extraordinarily apt to get it shot at you by basses at smoking concerts and entertainments in aid of the Church Organ Fund in the old village hall. They would pause for a moment after the *"um"* and take a breath that came up from their anklebones, and then:

"It's the curse of an a-ching heart."

Most unpleasant, of course, the whole thing, and I wouldn't have mentioned it, only the phrase absolutely puts in a nutshell the way poor old Bingo felt during his first two days at Monte Carlo. He had an aching heart, and he cursed like billy-o. And I'm not surprised, poor chap, for he was suffering severe torments.

All day long, though it was like twisting the knife in the wound, he would wander through the Rooms, trying out that system of his on paper; and the more he tried it out, the more ironclad it revealed itself. Simply couldn't lose.

By bedtime on the second night he found that, if he had been playing in hundred-franc chips, he would have been no less than two hundred and fifty pounds ahead—just like that. In short, there was all that stuff—his for the picking up, as you might say—and he couldn't get it.

Garcia would have got it. Darnborough would have got it. So would Owers. But he couldn't. Simply, mark you, for lack of a trifling spot of initial capital which a fellow like Oofy Prosser could have slipped him and never felt it. Pretty bitter.

And then, on the third morning, as he sat glancing through the continental New York *Herald* over the breakfast table, he saw a news item which brought him up in his chair with a jerk, choking over his coffee.

Among recent arrivals at the Hotel Magnifique at

Nice, it said, were their serene highnesses, the Prince and Princess of Graustark, His Majesty the ex-King of Ruritania, Lord Percy Poffin, the Countess of Goffin, Major General Sir Everard Slurk, K.V.O., and Mr Prosser.

Well, of course, it might be some other brand of Prosser, but Bingo didn't think so. A hotel where serene highnesses were to be found was just the place for which a bally snob like Oofy would have made a beeline. He rushed to the telephone and was presently in communication with the concierge.

"Hullo? Yes?" said the concierge. "This is the Hotel Magnifique. Hall porter speaking."

"Dites-moi," said Bingo. "Esker-vous avez dans votre hotel un monsieur nommé Prosser?"

"Yes sir. Quite correct. There is a Mr Prosser staying in the hotel."

"Est-il un oiseau avec beaucoup de . . . Oh hell, what's the French for 'pimples'?"

"The word you are trying to find is *bouton,*" said the concierge. "Yes sir, Mr Prosser is liberally pimpled."

"Then put me through to his room," said Bingo. And pretty soon he heard a sleepy and familiar voice hullo-ing.

"Hullo, Oofy, old man," he cried. "This is Bingo Little."

"Oh God!" said Oofy, and something in his manner warned Bingo that it would be well to proceed with snakiness and caution.

There were, he knew, two things which rendered Oofy Prosser a difficult proposition for the ear biter. In the first place, owing to his habit of mopping it up at late parties, he nearly always had a dyspeptic headache. In the second place, his position as the official moneyed man of the Drones Club had caused him to become shy and wary, like a bird that's been a good deal shot over. You can't touch a chap like that on the telephone at ten in the morning. It would, he perceived, if solid results were to be obtained, be necessary to sweeten Oofy.

"I just this minute saw in the paper that you were in these parts, Oofy, old man. A wonderful surprise it was. Gosh, I said. Golly, I said. Dear old Oofy, I said. Well, well, well!"

"Get on with it," said Oofy. "What do you want?"

"Why, to give you lunch, of course, old chap," said Bingo.

Yes, he had made the great decision. That money which he had been earmarking for tips must be diverted to another end. It might lead to his having to sneak out of the hotel at the conclusion of his visit with his face scarlet and his ears hanging down, but the risk had to be taken. Nothing venture, nothing have.

At the other end of the telephone he heard a sort of choking gasp.

"There must be something wrong with this wire," said Oofy. "It sounds just as if you were saying you want to give me lunch."

"So I am."

"*Give* me lunch?"

"That's right."

"What, pay the bill?"

"Yes."

There was a silence.

"I must send this to Ripley," said Oofy.

"Ripley?"

"The 'Believe-it-or-not' man."

"Oh?" said Bingo. He was not quite sure that he liked Oofy's attitude, but he remained sunny. "Well, where and when? What time? What place?"

"We may as well lunch here. Come fairly early, because I'm going to the races this afternoon."

"Right," said Bingo. "I'll be on the mat at one sharp."

And at one sharp there he was, his little all in his pocket. His emotions, he tells me, as he drove in on the Monte Carlo–Nice bus, were mixed. One moment, he was hoping that Oofy would have his usual dyspeptic headache, because that would blunt his appetite and enable him to save something out of the wreck; the next, he was reminding himself that an Oofy with dull, shooting pains about the temples would be less likely to come across. It was all very complex.

Well, as it turned out, Oofy's appetite was the reverse of blunted. The extraordinary position in which he found himself—guest and not host to a fellow member of the Drones—seemed to have put an edge on it. It is not too much to say that from the very outset he ate like a starving python. The light, casual way in which he spoke to the headwaiter about hothouse grapes and asparagus froze Bingo to the marrow. And when—from force of habit, no doubt—he called for the wine list and ordered a nice, dry champagne, it began to look to Bingo as if the bill for this binge was going to resemble something submitted to Congress by President Roosevelt in aid of the American farmer.

However, though once or twice—notably when Oofy started wading into the caviare—he had to clench his fists and summon up all his iron self-control, he did not on the whole repine. Each moment, as the feast proceeded, he could see his guest becoming more and more mellow. It seemed merely a question of time before the milk of human kindness would come gushing out of him as if the dam had burst. Feeling that a cigar and liqueur ought just about to do the trick, Bingo ordered them; and Oofy, unbuttoning the last three buttons of his waistcoat, leaned back in his chair.

"Well," said Oofy, beaming, "this will certainly be something to tell my grandchildren. I mean, that I once lunched with a member of the Drones Club and didn't get stuck with the bill. Listen, Bingo, I'd like to do something for you in return."

Bingo felt like some great actor who has received his cue. He leaned forward and relighted Oofy's cigar with a loving hand. He also flicked a speck of dust off his coatsleeve.

"And what I'm going to do is this. I'm going to give you a tip. On these races this afternoon. Back Spotted Dog for the Prix Honoré Sauvan. A sure winner."

"Thanks, Oofy, old man," said Bingo. "That's splendid news. If you will lend me a tenner, then, Oofy, old boy, I'll put it on."

"What do you want me to lend you a tenner for?"

"Because, after I've paid the lunch bill, Oofy, old chap, I shan't have any money."

"You won't need any money," said Oofy, and Bingo wondered how many more people were going to make this blithering remark to him. "My London bookie is staying here. He will accommodate you in credit, seeing that you are a friend of mine."

"But doesn't it seem a pity to bother him with a lot of extra bookkeeping, Oofy, old fellow?" said Bingo, flicking another speck of dust off Oofy's other coat sleeve. "Much better if you would just lend me a tenner."

"Joking aside," said Oofy, "I think I'll have another kümmel."

And it was at this moment, when the conversation appeared to have reached a deadlock, and there seemed no hope of finding a formula, that a stout, benevolent-looking man approached their table. From the fact that he and Oofy at once began to talk odds and figures, Bingo deduced that this must be the bookie from London.

"And my friend, Mr Little," said Oofy, in conclusion, "wants a tenner on Spotted Dog for the Prix Honoré Sauvan."

And Bingo was just about to shake his head and say that he didn't think his wife would like him to bet, when the glorious Riviera sunshine, streaming in through the window by which they sat, lit up Oofy's face and he saw that it was a perfect mass of spots. A moment later, he perceived that the bookie had a pink spot on his nose and the waiter, who was now bringing the bill, a bountifully spotted forehead. A thrill shot through him. These things, he knew, are sent to us for a purpose.

"Right ho," he said. "A tenner at the current odds."

And then they all went off to the races. The Prix

Honoré Sauvan was the three o'clock. A horse called Lilium won it. Kerry second, Maubourget third, Ironside fourth, Irresistible fifth, Sweet and Lovely sixth, Spotted Dog seventh. Seven ran. So there was Bingo owing ten quid to this bookie and not a chance of a happy ending unless the fellow would consent to let the settlement stand over for a bit.

So he buttonholed the bookie and suggested this, and the bookie said, certainly.

"Certainly," said the bookie. He put his hand on Bingo's shoulder and patted it. "I like you, Mr Little," he said.

"Do you?" said Bingo, putting his hand on the bookie's and patting that. "Do you, old pal?"

"I do, indeed," said the bookie. "You remind me of my little boy Percy, who took the knock the year Worcester Sauce won the Jubilee Handicap. Bronchial trouble. So when you ask me to wait for my money, I say, of course I'll wait for my money. Suppose we say till next Friday?"

Bingo blenched a bit. The period he had had in mind had been something more along the lines of a year or eighteen months.

"Well," he said, "I'll try to brass up then . . . but you know how it is . . . you mustn't be disappointed if . . . this world-wide money shortage . . . circumstances over which I have no control . . ."

"You think you may not be able to settle?"

"I'm a bit doubtful."

The bookie pursed his lips.

"I do hope you will," he said, "and I'll tell you why. It's silly to be superstitious, I know, but I can't help remembering that every single bloke that's ever done me down for money has had a nasty accident occur to him. Time after time I've seen it happen."

"Have you?" said Bingo, beginning to exhibit symptoms of bronchial trouble like the late Percy.

"I have, indeed," said the bookie. "Time after time after time. It almost seems like some kind of fate. Only the other day there was a fellow with a ginger moustache named Watherspoon. Owed me fifty for Plumpton and pleaded the gaming act. And would you believe it, less than a week later he was found unconscious in the street—must have got into some unpleasantness of some kind—and had to have six stitches."

"Six!"

"Seven. I was forgetting the one over his left eye. Makes you think, that sort of thing does. Hoy, Erbut," he called.

A frightful plug-ugly appeared from nowhere, as if he had been a djinn and the bookie had rubbed a lamp.

"Erbut," said the bookie, "I want you to meet Mr Little, Erbut. Take a good look at him. You'll remember him again?"

The plug-ugly drank Bingo in. His eye was cold and gray, like a parrot's.

"Yus," he said. "Yus, I won't forget him."

"Good," said the bookie. "That will be all, Erbut. Then about that money, Mr Little, we'll say Friday without fail, shall we?"

Bingo tottered away and sought out Oofy.

"Oofy, old man," he said, "it is within your power to save a human life."

"Well, I'm jolly well not going to," said Oofy, who

had now got one of his dyspeptic headaches. "The more human lives that aren't saved, the better I shall like it. I loathe the human race. Any time it wants to stand in front of the Cornish Express, it will be all right with me."

"If I don't get a tenner by Friday, a fearful bounder named Erbut is going to beat me into a pulp."

"Good," said Oofy, brightening a little. "Capital. Splendid. That's fine."

Bingo then caught the bus back to Monte Carlo.

That night, he dressed for dinner moodily. He was unable to discern the bluebird. In three months from now he would be getting another quarter's allowance, but a fat lot of good that would be. In far less than three months, if he had read aright the message in Erbut's eyes, he would be in some hospital or nursing home with stitches all over him. How many stitches, time alone could tell. He fell to musing on Watherspoon. Was it, he wondered, to be his fate to lower that ginger-moustached man's melancholy record?

His thoughts were still busy with the stitch outlook, when the telephone rang.

"Hullo," said a female voice. "Is that Rosie?"

"No," said Bingo, and might have added that the future was not, either. "I'm Mr Little."

"Oh, Mr Little, this is Dora Spurgeon. Can I speak to Rosie?"

"She isn't here."

"Well, when she comes in, will you tell her that I'm just off to Corsica in some people's yacht. We leave in an hour, so I shan't have time to come over and see her, so will you give her my love and tell her I am sending the brooch back."

"Brooch?"

"She lent me her brooch when I left London. I think it's the one you gave her on her birthday. She told me to take special care of it, and I don't feel it's safe having it with me in Corsica—so many brigands about—so I am sending it by registered post to the Hôtel de Paris. Good-bye, Mr Little. I must rush."

Bingo hung up the receiver and sat down on the bed to think this over. Up to a point, of course, the situation was clear. Dora Spurgeon, a muddleheaded poop if ever there was one, obviously supposed that Mrs Bingo had accompanied him to Monte Carlo. No doubt Mrs Bingo had gone to some pains in her telephone call to make it thoroughly clear that she was remaining in London, but it was no good trying to drive things into a head like Dora Spurgeon's by means of the spoken word. You needed a hammer. The result was that on the morrow that brooch which he had given Mrs Bingo would arrive at the hotel.

So far, as I say, Bingo found nothing to perplex him. But what he could not make up his mind about was this: should he, after he had pawned the brooch, send the proceeds straight to that bookie? Or should he take the money and go and have a whack at the Casino?

Far into the silent night he pondered without being able to reach a decision, but next morning everything seemed to clarify, as is so often the way after a night's sleep, and he wondered how he could ever have been in doubt. Of course he must have a whack at the Casino.

The catch about sending the money to the bookie was that, while this policy would remove from his future the dark shadow of Erbut, it would not make for contentment and happiness in the home. When Mrs Bingo discovered that he had shoved her brooch up the spout in order to pay a racing debt, friction would ensue. He unquestionably had a moral claim on the brooch—bought with his hard-earned money—the thing, you might say, was really his to do what he liked with—nevertheless, something told him that friction would ensue.

By going and playing his system he would avoid all unpleasantness. It was simply a matter of strolling into the Rooms and taking the stuff away.

And, as it turned out, he couldn't have paid off Erbut's bookie, anyway, because the local popshop would only give him a fiver on the brooch. He pleaded passionately for more, but the cove behind the counter was adamant. So, taking the fiver, he lunched sparingly at a pub up the hill, and shortly after two o'clock was in the arena, doing his stuff.

I have never been able quite to get the hang of that system of Bingo's. He has explained it to me a dozen times, but it remains vague. However, the basis of it, the thing that made it so frightfully ingenious, was that instead of doubling your stake when you lost, as in all these other systems, you doubled it when you won. It involved a lot of fancywork with a pencil and a bit of paper, because you had to write down figures and add figures and scratch figures out, but that, I gathered, was the nub of the thing—you doubled up when you won, thus increasing your profits by leaps and bounds and making the authorities look pretty sick.

The only snag about it was that in order to do this you first had to win, which Bingo didn't.

I don't suppose there is anything—not even Oofy Prosser—that has a nastier disposition than the wheel at Monte Carlo. It seems to take a sinister pleasure in doing down the common people. You can play mentally by the hour and never get a losing spin, but once you put real money up the whole aspect of things alters. Poor old Bingo hadn't been able to put a foot wrong so long as he stuck to paper punting, but he now found himself in the soup from the start.

There he stood, straining like a greyhound at the leash, waiting for his chance of doubling up, only to see all his little capital raked in except one solitary hundred-franc chip. And when with a weary gesture he bunged this on black, up came zero and it was swept away.

And scarcely had he passed through this gruelling spiritual experience, when a voice behind him said, "Oh, there you are!" and, turning, he found himself face to face with Mrs Bingo.

He stood gaping at her, his heart bounding about inside him like an adagio dancer with nettle rash. For an instant, he tells me, he was under the impression that this was no flesh and blood creature that stood before him, but a phantasm. He thought that she must have been run over by a bus or something in London, and that this was her spectre looking in to report, as spectres do.

"You!" he said, like someone in a play.

"I've just arrived," said Mrs Bingo, very merry and bright.

"I—I didn't know you were coming."

"I thought I would surprise you," said Mrs Bingo, still bubbling over with joyous animation. "You see, what happened was that I was talking to Millie Pringle about my book, and she said that it was no use getting local colour about the Rooms, because a man like Lord Peter Shipbourne would never go to the Rooms—he would do all his playing at the Sporting Club. And I was just going to wire you to go there, when Mrs Carrie Melrose Bopp trod on a banana skin in the street and sprained her ankle, and the luncheon was postponed, so there was nothing to prevent me coming over, so I came. Oh, Bingo darling, isn't this jolly!"

Bingo quivered from cravat to socks. The adjective "jolly" was not the one he would have selected. And it was at this point that Mrs Bingo appeared to observe for the first time that her loved one was looking like a corpse that has been left out in the rain for a day or two.

"Bingo!" she cried. "What's the matter?"

"Nothing," said Bingo. "Nothing. Matter? How do you mean?"

"You look . . ." A wifely suspicion shot through Mrs Bingo. She eyed him narrowly. "You haven't been gambling?"

"No, no," said Bingo. He is a fellow who is rather exact in his speech, and the word "gambling", to his mind, implied that a chap had a chance of winning. All that he had done, he felt, had been to take his little bit of money and give it to the administration. You couldn't describe that as gambling. More like making a donation to a charity. "No, no," he said. "Rather not."

"I'm so glad. Oh, by the way, I found a letter from Dora Spurgeon at the hotel. She said she was sending my brooch. I suppose it will arrive this afternoon."

Bingo's gallant spirit was broken. It seemed to him that this was the end. It was all over, he felt, except the composition of the speech in which he must confess everything. And he was just turning over in his mind a few opening remarks, beginning with the words "Listen, darling", when his eye fell on the table, and there on black was a pile of chips, no less than three thousand, two hundred francs worth in all—or, looking at it from another angle, about forty quid. And as he gazed at them, wondering which of the lucky stiffs seated round the board had got ahead of the game to that extent, the croupier at the bottom of the table caught his eye and smirked congratulatingly, as croupiers do when somebody has won a parcel and they think that there is going to be something in it for them in the way of largesse.

And Bingo, tottering on his base, suddenly realised that this piled-up wealth belonged to him. It was the increment accruing from that last hundred francs of his.

What he had forgotten, you see, was that though, when zero turns up, those who have betted on numbers, columns and what not get it in the neck, stakes on the even chances aren't scooped up—they are what is called put in prison. I mean, they just withdraw into the background for the moment, awaiting the result of the next spin. And, if that wins, out they come again.

Bingo's hundred francs had been on black, so zero

had put it in prison. And then, presumably, black must have turned up, getting it out again. And, as he hadn't taken it off, it had of course stayed on black. And then, while he was immersed in conversation with Mrs Bingo about brooches, the wheel, from being a sort of mechanical Oofy Prosser, had suddenly turned into a Santa Claus. Seven more times it had come up black, putting Bingo in the position in which that system of his ought to have put him—viz. of doubling up when he won. And the result, as I say, was that the loot now amounted to the colossal sum of forty quid, more than double what he required in order to be able to pay off all his obligations and look the world in the eye again.

The relief was so terrific that Bingo tells me he came within a toucher of swooning. And it was only as he was about to snatch the stuff up and trouser it and live happily ever after—he had, indeed, actually poised himself for the spring—that he suddenly saw that there was a catch. To wit, that if he did, all must be discovered. Mrs Bingo would know that he had been gambling; she would speedily ascertain the source whence had proceeded the money he had been gambling with, and the home, if not actually wrecked, would unquestionably become about as hot for him as the inside of a baked potato.

And yet, if he left the doubloons where they were, the next spin might see them all go down the drain.

I expect you know the expression "A man's crossroads." Those were what Bingo was at, at this juncture.

There seemed just one hope—to make a face at the croupier and do it with such consummate skill that the other would see that he wanted those thirty-two hundred francs taken off the board and put on one side till he was at liberty to come and collect. So he threw his whole soul into a face, and the croupier nodded intelligently and left the money on. Bingo, he saw, was signalling to him to let the works ride for another spin, and he admired his sporting spirit. He said something to the other croupier in an undertone—no doubt "Quel homme!" or "Epatant!" or something of that kind.

And the wheel, which now appeared definitely to have accepted the role of Bingo's rich uncle from Australia, fetched up another black.

Mrs Bingo was studying the gamesters. She didn't seem to think much of them.

"What dreadful faces these people have," she said.

Bingo did not reply. His own face at this moment was nothing to write home about, resembling more than anything else that of an anxious fiend in hell. He was watching the wheel revolve.

It came up black again, bringing his total to twelve thousand eight hundred.

And now at last it seemed that his tortured spirit was to be at rest. The croupier, having shot another smirk in his direction, was leaning forward to the pile of chips and had started scooping. Yes, all was well. At the eleventh hour the silly ass had divined the message of that face of his and was doing the needful.

Bingo drew a deep, shuddering breath. He felt like one who has passed through the furnace and, though a bit charred in spots, can once more take up the burden of life with an easy mind. Twelve thousand eight hundred francs . . . Gosh! It was over a hundred and fifty quid, more than he had ever possessed at one time since the Christmas, three years ago, when his uncle Wilberforce had come over all Dickensy as the result of lemon punch and had given him a cheque on which next day he had vainly tried to stop payment. There was a froust in the Rooms which you could have cut with a knife, but he drew it into his lungs as if it had been the finest ozone. Birds seemed to be twittering from the ceiling and soft music playing everywhere.

And then the world went to pieces again. The wheel had begun to spin, and there on black lay twelve thousand francs. The croupier, though he had scooped, hadn't scooped enough. All he had done was to remove from the board the eight hundred. On that last coup, you see, Bingo had come up against the limit. You can't have more than twelve thousand on an even chance.

And, of course, eight hundred francs was no use to him whatever. It would enable him to pay off Erbut and the bookie, but what of the brooch?

It was at this point that he was aware that Mrs Bingo was saying something to him. He came slowly out of his trance with a where-am-I look.

"Eh?" he said.

"I said, 'Don't you think so?' "

"Think so?"

"I was saying that it didn't seem much good wasting any more time in here. Millie Pringle was quite right. Lord Peter Shipbourne would never dream of coming to a place like this. He would never stand the smell, for one thing. I have drawn him as a most fastidious man. So shall I go on to the Sporting Club . . . Bingo?"

Bingo was watching the wheel, tense and rigid. He

was tense and rigid, I mean, not the wheel. The wheel was spinning.

"Bingo!"

"Hullo?"

"Shall I go on to the Sporting Club and pay our entrance fees?"

A sudden bright light came into Bingo's face, rendering it almost beautiful. His brow was bedewed with perspiration and he rather thought his hair had turned snowy white, but the map was shining like the sun at noon, and he beamed as he had seldom beamed before.

For the returns were in. The wheel had stopped. And once again black had come up, and even now the croupier was removing twelve thousand francs from the pile and adding them to the eight hundred before him.

"Yes do," said Bingo. "Do. Yes do. That 'll be fine. Splendid. I think I'll just stick on here for a minute or two. I like watching these weird blokes. But you go on and I'll join you."

Twenty minutes later he did so. He walked into the Sporting Club a little stiffly, for there were forty-eight thousand francs distributed about his person, some of it in his pockets, some of it in his socks, and quite a good deal tucked inside his shirt. He did not see Mrs Bingo at first; then he caught sight of her sitting over in the bar with a bottle of vittel in front of her.

"What ho, what ho," he said, lumbering up.

Then he paused, for it seemed to him that her manner was rummy. Her face was sad and set, her eyes dull. She gave him an odd look, and an appalling suspicion struck him amidships. Could it be, he asked himself, was it possible that somehow, by some mysterious wifely intuition . . .

"There you are," he said. He sat down beside her, hoping that he wasn't going to crackle. "Er—how's everything?" He paused. She was still looking rummy. "I've got that brooch," he said.

"Oh?"

"Yes. I—er—thought you might like to have it, so I —ah—nipped out and got it."

"I'm glad it arrived safely . . . Bingo!" said Mrs Bingo.

She was staring sombrely before her. Bingo's apprehension increased. He now definitely feared the worst. It was as if he could feel the soup plashing about his ankles. He took her hand in his and pressed it. It might, he felt, help. You never knew.

"Bingo," said Mrs Bingo, "we always tell each other everything, don't we?"

"Do we? Oh yes. Yes."

"Because when we got married, we decided that that was the only way. I remember your saying so on the honeymoon."

"Yes," said Bingo, licking his lips and marvelling at the depths of fatheadedness to which men can sink on their honeymoons.

"I'd hate to feel that you were concealing anything from me. It would make me wretched."

"Yes," said Bingo.

"So if you had been gambling, you would tell me, wouldn't you?"

Bingo drew a deep breath. It made him crackle all over, but he couldn't help that. He needed air. Besides, what did it matter now if he crackled like a forest fire? He threw his mind back to those opening sentences which he had composed.

"Listen, darling," he began.

"So I must tell you," said Mrs Bingo. "I've just made the most dreadful fool of myself. When I came in here, I went over to that table there to watch the play, and suddenly something came over me . . ."

Bingo uttered a snort which rang through the Sporting Club like a bugle.

"You didn't have a pop?"

"I lost over two hundred pounds in ten minutes. Oh, Bingo, can you ever forgive me?"

Bingo had still got hold of her hand, for he had been relying on the soothing effects of hanging on to it during the remarks which he had outlined. He squeezed it lovingly. Not immediately, however, because for perhaps half a minute he had felt so boneless that he could not have squeezed a grape.

"There, there!" he said.

"Oh, Bingo!"

"There, there, there!"

"You do forgive me?"

"Of course. Of course."

"Oh, Bingo," cried Mrs Bingo, her eyes like twin stars, and damp ones at that, "there's nobody like you in the world."

"Would you say that?"

"You remind me of Sir Galahad. Most husbands——"

"Ah," said Bingo, "but I understand these sudden impulses. I don't have them myself, but I understand them. Not another word. Good gosh, what's a couple of hundred quid, if it gave you a moment's pleasure?"

His emotions now almost overpowered him, so strenuously did they call for an outlet. He wanted to shout, but he couldn't shout—the croupiers would object. He wanted to give three cheers, but he couldn't give three cheers—the barman wouldn't like it. He wanted to sing, but he couldn't sing—the customers would complain.

His eye fell on the bottle of vittel.

"Ah!" said Bingo. "Darling!"

"Yes, darling?"

"Watch, darling," said Bingo. "I place the bottle so. Then, maintaining a perfect equilibrium . . ."

TRIED IN THE FURNACE

THE annual smoking-concert of the Drones Club had just come to an end, and it was the unanimous verdict of the little group assembled in the bar for a last quick one that the gem of the evening had been item number six on the programme, the knockabout cross-talk act of Cyril ("Barmy") Fotheringay-Phipps and Reginald ("Pongo") Twistleton-Twistleton. Both Cyril, in the red beard, and Reginald, in the more effective green whiskers, had shown themselves, it was agreed, at the very peak of their form. With sparkling repartee and vigorous byplay they had gripped the audience from the start.

"In fact," said an Egg, "it struck me that they were even better than last year. Their art seemed to have deepened somehow."

A thoughtful Crumpet nodded.

"I noticed the same thing. The fact is, they passed through a soul-testing experience not long ago and it has left its mark upon them. It also dashed nearly wrecked the act. I don't know if any of you fellows are aware of it, but at one time they had definitely decided to scratch the fixture and not give a performance at all."

"What!"

"Absolutely. They were within a toucher of failing to keep faith with their public. Bad blood had sprung up between them. Also pique and strained relations. They were not on speaking terms."

His hearers were frankly incredulous. They pointed out that the friendship between the two artistes had always been a byword or whatever you called it. A well-read Egg summed it up by saying that they were like Thingummy and What's-his-name.

"Nevertheless," insisted the Crumpet, "what I am telling you is straight, official stuff. Two weeks ago, if Barmy had said to Pongo: 'Who was that lady I saw you coming down the street with?' Pongo would not have replied: 'That was no lady, that was my wife,' —he would simply have raised his eyebrows coldly and turned away in a marked manner."

It was a woman, of course (proceeded the Crumpet), who came between them. Angelica Briscoe was her name, and she was the daughter of the Rev. P. P. Briscoe, who vetted the souls of the local peasantry at a place called Maiden Eggesford down in Somersetshire. This hamlet is about half-a-dozen miles from the well-known resort, Bridmouth-on-Sea, and it was in the establishment of the Messrs. Thorpe and Widgery, the popular grocers of that town, that Barmy and Pongo first set eyes on the girl.

They had gone to Bridmouth partly for a splash of golf, but principally to be alone and away from distractions, so that they would be able to concentrate on the rehearsing and building up of this cross-talk act which we have just witnessed. And on the morning of which I speak they had strolled into the Thorpe and Widgery emporium to lay in a few little odds and ends, and there, putting in a bid for five pounds of streaky bacon, was a girl so lovely that they congealed in their tracks. And as they stood staring she said to the bloke behind the counter:

"That's the lot. Send them to Miss Angelica Briscoe, the Vicarage, Maiden Eggesford."

She then pushed off, and Barmy and Pongo, feeling rather as if they had been struck by lightning, bought some sardines and a segment of certified butter in an overwrought sort of way and went out.

They were both pretty quiet for the rest of the day, and after dinner that night Pongo said to Barmy:

"I say, Barmy."

And Barmy said:

"Hullo?"

And Pongo said:

"I say, Barmy, it's a bally nuisance, but I'll have to buzz up to London for a day or two. I've suddenly remembered some spots of business that call for my personal attention. You won't mind my leaving you?"

Barmy could scarcely conceal his bracedness. Within two minutes of seeing that girl, he had made up his mind that somehow or other he must repair to Maiden Eggesford and get to know her, and the problem which had been vexing him all day had been what to do with the body—viz., Pongo's.

"Not a bit," he said.

"I'll be back as soon as I can."

"Don't hurry," said Barmy heartily. "As a matter

of fact, a few days' layoff will do the act all the good in the world. Any pro. will tell you that the worst thing possible is to over-rehearse. Stay away as long as you like."

So next morning—it was a Saturday—Pongo climbed on to a train, and in the afternoon Barmy collected his baggage and pushed off to the Goose and Grasshopper at Maiden Eggesford. And, having booked a room there and toddled into the saloon bar for a refresher with the love light in his eyes, the first thing he saw was Pongo chatting across the counter with the barmaid.

Neither was much bucked. A touch of constraint about sums it up.

"Hullo!" said Barmy.

"Hullo!" said Pongo.

"You here?"

"Yes. You here?"

"Yes."

"Oh."

There was a bit of a silence.

"So you didn't go to London?" said Barmy.

"No," said Pongo.

"Oh," said Barmy.

"And you didn't stick on at Bridmouth?" said Pongo.

"No," said Barmy.

"Oh," said Pongo.

There was some more silence.

"You came here, I see," said Pongo.

"Yes," said Barmy. "I see *you* came here."

"Yes," said Pongo. "An odd coincidence."

"Very odd."

"Well, skin off your nose," said Pongo.

"Fluff in your latchkey," said Barmy.

He drained his glass and tried to exhibit a light-hearted nonchalance, but his mood was sombre. He was a chap who could put two and two together and sift and weigh the evidence and all that sort of thing, and it was plain to him that love had brought Pongo also to this hamlet, and he resented the fact. Indeed, it was at this instant, he tells me, that there came to him the first nebulous idea of oiling out of that cross-talk act of theirs. The thought of having to ask a beastly, butting-in blighter like Reginald Twistleton-Twistleton if he was fond of mutton broth and being compelled to hit him over the head with a rolled-up umbrella when he replied "No, Mutt and Jeff," somehow seemed to revolt his finest feelings.

Conversation languished after this, and presently Pongo excused himself in a somewhat stiff manner and went upstairs to his room. And it was while Barmy was standing at the counter listening in a distrait kind of way to the barmaid telling him what cucumber did to her digestive organs that a fellow in plus fours entered the bar and Barmy saw that he was wearing the tie of his old school.

Well, you know how it is when you're in some public spot and a stranger comes in wearing the old school tie. You shove a hasty hand over your own and start to sidle out before the chap can spot it and grab you and start gassing. And Barmy was just doing this when the barmaid uttered these sensational words:

"Good evening, Mr Briscoe."

Barmy stood spellbound. He turned to the barmaid and spoke in a hushed whisper.

"Did you say 'Briscoe'?"

"Yes sir."

"From the Vicarage?"

"Yes sir."

Barmy quivered like a jelly. The thought that he had had the amazing luck to find in the brother of the girl he loved an old schoolmate made him feel boneless. After all, he felt, as he took his hand away from his tie, there is no bond like that of the old school. If you meet one of the dear old school in a public spot, he meant to say, why, you go straight up to him and start fraternizing.

He made a beeline for the chap's table.

"I say," he said, "I see you're wearing a . . ."

The chap's hand had shot up to his tie with a sort of nervous gesture, but he evidently realized that the time had gone by for protective measures. He smiled a bit wryly.

"Have a drink," he said.

"I've got one, thanks," said Barmy. "I'll bring it along to your table, shall I? Such a treat meeting someone from the dear old place, what?"

"Oh, rather."

"I think I'd have been a bit after your time, wouldn't I?" said Barmy, for the fellow was well stricken in years—twenty-eight, if a day. "Fotheringay-Phipps is more or less my name. Yours is Briscoe, what?"

"Yes."

Barmy swallowed a couple of times.

"Er . . . Ah . . . Um . . . I think I saw your sister yesterday in Bridmouth," he said, blushing prettily.

So scarlet, indeed, did his countenance become that the other regarded him narrowly, and Barmy knew that he had guessed his secret.

"You saw her in Bridmouth yesterday, eh?"

"Yes."

"And now you're here."

"Er—yes."

"Well, well," said the chap, drawing his breath in rather thoughtfully.

There was a pause, during which Barmy's vascular motors continued to do their bit.

"You must meet her," said the chap.

"I should like to," said Barmy. "I only saw her for a moment buying streaky bacon, but she seemed a charming girl."

"Oh, she is."

"I scarcely noticed her, of course, but rather attractive she struck me as."

"Quite."

"I gave her the merest glance, you understand, but I should say at a venture that she has a great white soul. In fact," said Barmy, losing his grip altogether, "you wouldn't be far out in describing her as divine."

"You must certainly meet her," said the chap. Then he shook his head. "No, it wouldn't be any good."

"Why not?" bleated Barmy.

"Well, I'll tell you," said the chap. "You know what girls are. They have their little enthusiasms and it hurts them when people scoff at them. Being a parson's daughter, Angelica is wrapped up at present in the annual village School Treat. I can see at a glance the sort of fellow you are—witty, mordant, ironical. You would get off one of your devastating epigrams at the expense of the School Treat, and, while she might laugh at the wit, she would be deeply wounded by the satire."

"But I wouldn't dream . . ."

"Ah, but if you didn't, if you spoke approvingly of the School Treat, what then? The next thing that would happen would be that she would be asking you to help her run it. And that would bore you stiff."

Barmy shook from stem to stern. This was better even than he had hoped.

"You don't mean she would let me help her with the School Treat?"

"Why, you wouldn't do it, would you?"

"I should enjoy it above all things."

"Well, if that's the way you feel, the matter can easily be arranged. She will be here any moment now to pick me up in her car."

And, sure enough, not two minutes later there floated through the open window a silvery voice, urging the fellow, who seemed to answer to the name of "Fathead," to come out quick, because the voice did not intend to remain there all night.

So the fellow took Barmy out, and there was the girl, sitting in a two-seater. He introduced Barmy. The girl beamed. Barmy beamed. The fellow said that Barmy was anxious to come and help with the School Treat. The girl beamed again. Barmy beamed again. And presently the car drove off, the girl's last words being a reminder that the binge started at two sharp on the Monday.

That night, as they dined together, Barmy and Pongo put in their usual spot of rehearsing. It was their practice to mould and shape the act during meals, as they found that mastication seemed to sharpen their intellect. But tonight it would have been plain to an observant spectator that their hearts were not in it. There was an unmistakable coolness between them. Pongo said he had an aunt who complained of rheumatism, and Barmy said, "Well, who wouldn't?" And Barmy said his father could not meet his creditors, and Pongo said, "Did he want to?" But the old fire and sparkle were absent. And they had relapsed into a moody silence when the door opened and the barmaid pushed her head in.

"Miss Briscoe has just sent over a message, Mr Phipps," said the barmaid. "She says she would like you to be there a little earlier than two, if you can manage it. One-fifteen if possible, because there's always so much to do."

"Oh, right," said Barmy, a bit rattled, for he had heard the sharp hiss of his companion's indrawn breath.

"I'll tell her," said the barmaid.

She withdrew, and Barmy found Pongo's eyes resting on him like a couple of blobs of vitriol.

"What's all this?" asked Pongo.

Barmy tried to be airy.

"Oh, it's nothing. Just the local School Treat. The vicar's daughter here—a Miss Briscoe—seems anxious that I should drop round on Monday and help her run it."

Pongo started to grind his teeth, but he had a chunk of potato in his mouth at the moment and was hampered. But he gripped the table till his knuckles stood out white under the strain.

"Have you been sneaking round behind my back and inflicting your beastly society on Miss Briscoe?" he demanded.

"I do not like your tone, Reginald."

"Never mind about my tone. I'll attend to my tone. Of all the bally low hounds that ever stepped you are the lowest. So this is what the friendship of years amounts to, is it? You crawl in here and try to cut me out with the girl I love."

"Well, dash it . . ."

"That is quite enough."

"But, dash it . . ."

"I wish to hear no more."

"But, dash it, I love her, too. It's not my fault if you happen to love her, too, is it? I mean to say, if a fellow loves a girl and another fellow loves her, too, you can't expect the fellow who loves the girl to edge out because he happens to be acquainted with the fellow who loves her, too. When it comes to love, a chap has got to look out for his own interests, hasn't he? You didn't find Romeo or any of those chaps easing away from the girl just to oblige a pal, did you? Certainly not. So I don't see . . ."

"Please!" said Pongo.

A silence fell.

"Might I trouble you to pass the mustard, Fotheringay-Phipps," said Pongo coldly.

"Certainly, Twistleton-Twistleton," replied Barmy, with equal hauteur.

It is always unpleasant not to be on speaking terms with an old friend. To be cooped up alone in a mouldy village pub with an old friend with whom one has ceased to converse is simply rotten. And this is especially so if the day happens to be a Sunday.

Maiden Eggesford, like so many of our rural hamlets, is not at its best and brightest on a Sunday. When you have walked down the main street and looked at the Jubilee Watering-Trough, there is nothing much to do except go home and then come out again and walk down the main street once more and take another look at the Jubilee Watering-Trough. It will give you some rough idea of the state to which Barmy Fotheringay-Phipps had been reduced by the end of the next day when I tell you that the sound of the church bells ringing for evensong brought him out of the Goose and Grasshopper as if he had heard a fire engine. The thought that at last something was going to happen in Maiden Eggesford in which the Jubilee Watering-Trough *motif* was not stressed, stirred him strangely. He was in his pew in three jumps. And as the service got under way he began to feel curious emotions going on in his bosom.

There is something about evening church in a village in the summertime that affects the most hard boiled. They had left the door open, and through it came the scent of lime trees and wallflowers and the distant hum of bees fooling about. And gradually there poured over Barmy a wave of sentiment. As he sat and listened to the First Lesson he became a changed man.

The Lesson was one of those chapters of the Old Testament all about how Abimelech begat Jazzbo and Jazzbo begat Zachariah. And, what with the beauty of the words and the peace of his surroundings, Barmy suddenly began to become conscious of a great remorse.

He had not done the square thing, he told himself, by dear old Pongo. Here was a chap, notoriously one of the best, as sound an egg as ever donned a heliotrope sock, and he was deliberately chiselling him out of the girl he loved. He was doing the dirty on a fellow whom he had been pally with since their Eton-jacket days—a bloke who time and again had shared with him his last bar of almond rock. Was this right? Was this just? Would Abimelech have behaved like that to Jazzbo or—for the matter of that—Jazzbo to Zachariah? The answer, he could not disguise it from himself, was in the negative.

It was a different, stronger Barmy, a changed, chastened Cyril Fotheringay-Phipps, who left the sacred edifice at the conclusion of the vicar's fifty-minute sermon. He had made the great decision. It would play the dickens with his heart and probably render the rest of his life a blank, but nevertheless he would retire from the unseemly struggle and give the girl up to Pongo.

That night, as they cold-suppered together, Barmy cleared his throat and looked across at Pongo with a sad, sweet smile.

"Pongo," he said.

The other glanced distantly up from his baked potato.

"There is something you wish to say to me, Fotheringay-Phipps?"

"Yes," said Barmy. "A short while ago I sent a note to Miss Briscoe, informing her that I shall not be attending the School Treat and mentioning that you will be there in my stead. Take her, Pongo, old man. She is yours. I scratch my nomination."

Pongo stared. His whole manner changed. It was as if he had been a Trappist monk who had suddenly decided to give Trappism a miss and become one of the boys again.

"But, dash it, this is noble!"

"No, no."

"But it is! It's . . . Well, dash it, I hardly know what to say."

"I hope you will be very, very happy."

"Thanks, old man."

"Very, very, very happy."

"Rather! I should say so. And I'll tell you one thing. In the years to come there will always be a knife and fork for you at our little home. The children shall be taught to call you Uncle Barmy."

"Thanks," said Barmy. "Thanks."

"Not at all," said Pongo. "Not at all."

At this moment the barmaid entered with a note for Barmy. He read it and crumpled it up.

"From her?" asked Pongo.

"Yes."

"Saying she quite understands, and so forth?"

"Yes."

Pongo ate a piece of cheese in a meditative manner. He seemed to be pursuing some train of thought.

"I should think," he said, "that a fellow who married a clergyman's daughter would get the ceremony performed at cut rates, wouldn't he?"

"Probably."

"If not absolutely on the nod?"

"I shouldn't wonder."

"Not," said Pongo, "that I am influenced by any consideration like that, of course. My love is pure and flamelike, with no taint of dross. Still, in times like these, every little helps."

"Quite," said Barmy. "Quite."

He found it hard to control his voice. He had lied to his friend about that note. What Angelica Briscoe had really said in it was that it was quite all right if he wanted to edge out of the School Treat, but that she would require him to take the Village Mothers for their Annual Outing on the same day. There had to be some responsible person with them, and the curate had sprained his ankle tripping over a footstool in the vestry.

Barmy could read between the lines. He saw what this meant. His fatal fascination had done its deadly work, and the girl had become infatuated with him. No other explanation would fit the facts. It was absurd to suppose that she would lightly have selected him for this extraordinarily important assignment. Obviously it was the big event of the village year. Anyone would do to mess about at the School Treat, but Angelica Briscoe would place in charge of the Mothers' Annual Outing only a man she trusted . . . respected . . . loved.

He sighed. What must be, he felt, must be. He had done his conscientious best to retire in favour of his friend, but Fate had been too strong.

I found it a little difficult (said the Crumpet) to elicit from Barmy exactly what occurred at the annual outing of the Village Mothers of Maiden Eggesford. When telling me the story, he had the air of a man whose old wound is troubling him. It was not, indeed, till the fourth cocktail that he became really communicative. And then, speaking with a kind of stony look in his eye, he gave me a fairly comprehensive account. But even then each word seemed to hurt him in some tender spot.

The proceedings would appear to have opened in a quiet and orderly manner. Sixteen females of advanced years assembled in a motor coach, and the expedition was seen off from the vicarage door by the Rev. P. P. Briscoe in person. Under his eye, Barmy tells me, the Beauty Chorus was demure and docile. It was a treat to listen to their murmured responses. As nice and respectable a bunch of mothers, Barmy says, as he had ever struck. His only apprehension at this point, he tells me, was lest the afternoon's proceedings might possibly be a trifle stodgy. He feared a touch of ennui.

He needn't have worried. There was no ennui.

The human cargo, as I say, had started out in a spirit of demureness and docility. But it was amazing what a difference a mere fifty yards of the high road made to these Mothers. No sooner were they out of sight of the vicarage than they began to effervesce to an almost unbelievable extent. The first intimation Barmy had that the binge was going to be run on lines other than those which he had anticipated was when a very stout Mother in a pink bonnet and a dress covered with bugles suddenly picked off a passing cyclist with a well-directed tomato, causing him to skid into a ditch. Upon which, all sixteen Mothers laughed like fiends in hell, and it was plain that they considered that the proceedings had now been formally opened.

Of course, looking back at it now in a calmer spirit, Barmy tells me that he can realize that there is much to be said in palliation of the exuberance of these ghastly female pimples. When you are shut up all the year round in a place like Maiden Eggesford, with nothing to do but wash underclothing and attend Divine Service, you naturally incline to let yourself go a bit at times of festival and holiday. But at the moment he did not think of this, and his spiritual agony was pretty pronounced.

If there's one thing Barmy hates it's being conspicuous, and conspicuous is precisely what a fellow cannot fail to be when he's in a motor coach with sixteen women of mature ages who alternate between singing ribald songs and hurling volleys of homely chaff at passers-by. In this connection, he tells me, he is thinking particularly of a Mother in spectacles and a Homburg hat, which she had pinched from the driver of the vehicle, whose prose style appeared to have been modelled on that of Rabelais.

It was a more than usually penetrating sally on the part of this female which at length led him to venture a protest.

"I say! I mean, I say. I say, dash it, you know. I mean, dash it," said Barmy, feeling, even as he spoke, that the rebuke had not been phrased as neatly as he could have wished.

Still, lame though it had been, it caused a sensation which can only be described as profound. Mother looked at Mother. Eyebrows were raised, breath drawn in censoriously.

"Young man," said the Mother in the pink bonnet, who seemed to have elected herself forewoman, "kindly keep your remarks to yourself."

Another Mother said: "The idea!" and a third described him as a kill-joy.

"We don't want none of *your* impudence," said the one in the pink bonnet.

"Ah!" agreed the others.

"A slip of a boy like that!" said the Mother in the Homburg hat, and there was a general laugh, as if the meeting considered that the point had been well taken.

Barmy subsided. He was wishing that he had yielded to the advice of his family and become a curate after coming down from the University. Curates are specially trained to handle this sort of situation. A tough, hard-boiled curate, spitting out of the corner of his mouth, would soon have subdued these Mothers, he reflected. He would have played on them as on a stringed instrument—or, rather, as on sixteen stringed instruments. But Barmy, never having taken orders, was helpless.

So helpless, indeed, that when he suddenly discovered that they were heading for Bridmouth-on-Sea he felt that there was nothing he could do about it. From the vicar's own lips he had had it officially that the programme was that the expedition should drive to the neighbouring village of Bottsford Mortimer, where there were the ruins of an old abbey, replete with interest; lunch among these ruins; visit the local museum (founded and presented to the village by the late Sir Wandesbury Pott, J.P.); and, after filling in with a bit of knitting, return home. And now the whole trend of the party appeared to be towards the Amusement Park on the Bridmouth pier. And, though Barmy's whole soul shuddered at the thought of these sixteen Bacchantes let loose in an Amusement Park, he hadn't the nerve to say a word.

It was at about this point, he tells me, that a vision rose before him of Pongo happily loafing through the summer afternoon amid the placid joys of the School Treat.

Of what happened at the Amusement Park Barmy asked me to be content with the sketchiest of outlines. He said that even now he could not bear to let his memory dwell upon it. He confessed himself perplexed by the psychology of the thing. These Mothers, he said, must have had mothers of their own and at those mothers' knees must have learned years ago the difference between right and wrong, and yet . . . Well, what he was thinking of particularly, he said, was what occurred on the Bump the Bumps apparatus. He refused to specify exactly, but he said that there was one woman in a puce mantle who definitely seemed to be living for pleasure alone.

It was a little unpleasantness with the proprietor of this concern that eventually led to the expedition leaving the Amusement Park and going down to the beach. Some purely technical point of finance, I understand—he claiming that a Mother in bombazine had had eleven rides and only paid once. It resulted in Barmy getting lugged into the brawl and rather roughly handled—which was particularly unfortunate, because the bombazined Mother explained on their way down to the beach that the whole thing had been due to a misunderstanding. In actual fact, what had really happened was that she had had twelve rides and paid twice.

However, he was so glad to get his little troupe out of the place that he counted an eye well blacked as the price of deliverance, and his spirits, he tells me, had definitely risen when suddenly the sixteen Mothers gave a simultaneous whoop and made for a sailing-boat which was waiting to be hired, sweeping him along with them. And the next moment they were off across the bay, bowling along before a nippy breeze which, naturally, cheesed it abruptly as soon as it had landed them far enough away from shore to make things interesting for the unfortunate blighter who had to take to the oars.

This, of course, was poor old Barmy. There was a man in charge of the boat, but he, though but a rough, untutored salt, had enough sense not to let himself in for a job like rowing this Noah's Ark home. Barmy did put it up to him tentatively, but the fellow said that he had to attend to the steering, and when Barmy said that he, Barmy, knew how to steer, the fellow said that he, the fellow, could not entrust a valuable boat to an amateur. After which, he lit his pipe and lolled back in the stern sheets with rather the air of an ancient Roman banqueter making himself cosy among the cushions. And Barmy, attaching himself to a couple of oars of about the size of those served out to galley slaves in the old trireme days, started to put his back into it.

For a chap who hadn't rowed anything except a light

canoe since he was up at Oxford, he considers he did dashed well, especially when you take into account the fact that he was much hampered by the Mothers. They would insist on singing that thing about "Give yourself a pat on the back," and, apart from the fact that Barmy considered that something on the lines of the Volga Boat Song would have been far more fitting, it was a tune it was pretty hard to keep time to. Seven times he caught crabs, and seven times those sixteen Mothers stopped singing and guffawed like one Mother. All in all, a most painful experience. Add the fact that the first thing the females did on hitting the old homeland again was to get up an informal dance on the sands and that the ride home in the quiet evenfall was more or less a repetition of the journey out, and you will agree with me that Barmy, as he eventually tottered into the saloon bar of the Goose and Grasshopper, had earned the frothing tankard which he now proceeded to order.

He had just sucked it down and was signalling for another, when the door of the saloon bar opened and in came Pongo.

If Barmy had been less preoccupied with his own troubles he would have seen that Pongo was in poorish shape. His collar was torn, his hair dishevelled. There were streaks of chocolate down his face and half a jam sandwich attached to the back of his coat. And so moved was he at seeing Barmy that he started ticking him off before he had so much as ordered a gin and ginger.

"A nice thing you let me in for!" said Pongo. "A jolly job you shoved off on me!"

Barmy was feeling a little better after his ingurgitations, and he was able to speak.

"What are you talking about?"

"I am talking about School Treats," replied Pongo with an intense bitterness. "I am talking about seas of children, all with sticky hands, who rubbed those hands on me. I am talking . . . Oh, it's no good your gaping like a diseased fish, Fotheringay-Phipps. You know dashed well that you planned the whole thing. Your cunning fiend's brain formulated the entire devilish scheme. You engineered the bally outrage for your own foul purposes, to queer me with Angelica. You thought that when a girl sees a man blindfolded and smacked with rolled-up newspapers by smelly children she can never feel the same to him again. Ha!" said Pongo, at last ordering his gin and ginger.

Barmy was stunned, of course, by this violent attack, but he retained enough of the nice sense of propriety of the Fotheringay-Phippses to realize that this discussion could not be continued in public. Already the barmaid's ears had begun to work loose at the roots as she pricked them up.

"I don't know what the dickens you're talking about," he said, "but bring your drink up to my room and we'll go into the matter there. We cannot bandy a woman's name in a saloon bar."

"Who's bandying a woman's name?"

"You are. You bandied it only half a second ago. If you don't call what you said bandying, there are finer-minded men who do."

So they went upstairs, and Barmy shut the door.

"Now, then," he said. "What's all this drivel?"

"I've told you."

"Tell me again."

"I will."

"Right ho. One moment."

Barmy went to the door and opened it sharply. There came the unmistakable sound of a barmaid falling downstairs. He closed the door again.

"Now, then," he said.

Pongo drained his gin and ginger.

"Of all the dirty tricks one man ever played on another," he began, "your sneaking out of that School Treat and letting me in for it is one which the verdict of history will undoubtedly rank the dirtiest. I can read you now like a book, Fotheringay-Phipps. Your motive is crystal clear to me. You knew at what a disadvantage a man appears at a School Treat, and you saw to it that I and not you should be the poor mutt to get smeared with chocolate and sloshed with newspapers before the eyes of Angelica Briscoe. And I believed you when you handed me all that drip about yielding your claim and what not. My gosh!"

For an instant, as he heard these words, stupefaction rendered Barmy speechless. Then he found his tongue. His generous soul was seething with indignation at the thought of how his altruism, his great sacrifice, had been misinterpreted.

"What absolute rot!" he cried. "I never heard such bilge in my life. My motives in sending you to that School Treat instead of me were unmixedly chivalrous. I did it simply and solely to enable you to ingratiate yourself with the girl, not reflecting that it was out of the question that she should ever love a popeyed, pimply-faced poop like you."

Pongo started.

"Popeyed?"

"Popeyed was what I said."

"Pimply-faced?"

"Pimply-faced was the term I employed."

"Poop?"

"Poop was the expression with which I concluded. If you want to know the real obstacle in the way of any wooing you may do now or in the years to come, Twistleton-Twistleton, it is this—that you entirely lack sex appeal and look like nothing on earth. A girl of the sweet, sensitive nature of Angelica Briscoe does not have to see you smeared with chocolate to recoil from you with loathing. She does it automatically, and she does it on her head."

"Is that so?"

"That is so."

"Oh? Well, let me inform you that in spite of what has happened, in spite of the fact that she has seen me at my worst, there is something within me that tells me that Angelica Briscoe loves me and will one day be mine."

"Mine, you mean. I can read the message in a girl's shy, drooping eyes, Twistleton-Twistleton, and I am prepared to give you odds of eleven to four that before the year is out I shall be walking down the aisle with Angelica Fotheringay-Phipps on my arm. I will go further. Thirty-three to eight."

"What in?"

"Tenners."

"Done."

It was at this moment that the door opened.

"Excuse me, gentlemen," said the barmaid.

The two rivals glared at the intruder. She was a well-nourished girl with a kind face. She was rubbing her left leg, which appeared to be paining her. The staircases are steep at the Goose and Grasshopper.

"You'll excuse me muscling in like this, gentlemen," said the barmaid, or words to that effect, "but I happened inadvertently to overhear your conversation, and I feel it my duty to put you straight on an important point of fact. Gentlemen, all bets are off. Miss Angelica Briscoe is already engaged to be married."

You can readily conceive the effect of this announcement. Pongo biffed down into the only chair, and Barmy staggered against the washhand stand.

"What!" said Pongo.

"What!" said Barmy.

The barmaid turned to Barmy.

"Yes sir. To the gentleman you were talking to in my bar the afternoon you arrived."

Her initial observation had made Barmy feel as if he had been punched in the wind by sixteen Mothers, but at this addendum he was able to pull himself together a bit.

"Don't be an ass, my dear old barmaid," he said. "That was Miss Briscoe's brother."

"No sir."

"But his name was Briscoe, and you told me he was at the vicarage."

"Yes sir. He spends a good deal of his time at the

vicarage, being the young lady's second cousin, and engaged to her since last Christmas!"

Barmy eyed her sternly. He was deeply moved.

"Why did you not inform me of this earlier, you chump of a barmaid? With your gift for listening at doors you must long since have become aware that this gentleman here and myself were deeply enamoured of Miss Briscoe. And yet you kept these facts under your hat, causing us to waste our time and experience the utmost alarm and despondencey. Do you realize, barmaid, that, had you spoken sooner, my friend here would not have been subjected to nameless indignities at the School Treat? . . ."

"Yes sir. It was the School Treat that Mr Briscoe was so bent on not having to go to, which he would have had to have done, Miss Angelica insisting. He had a terrible time there last year, poor gentleman. He was telling me about it. And that was why he asked me as a particular favour not to mention that he was engaged to Miss Briscoe, because he said that, if he played his cards properly and a little secrecy and silence were observed in the proper quarters, there was a mug staying at the inn that he thought he could get to go instead of him. It would have done you good, sir, to have seen the way his face lit up as he said it. He's a very nice gentleman, Mr Briscoe, and we're all very fond of him. Well, I mustn't stay talking here, sir. I've got my bar to see to."

She withdrew, and for some minutes there was silence in the room. It was Barmy who was the first to break it.

"After all, we still have our Art," said Barmy.

He crossed the room and patted Pongo on the shoulder.

"Of course, it's a nasty knock, old man. . . ."

Pongo had raised his face from his hands and was fumbling for his cigarette case. There was a look in his eyes as if he had just wakened from a dream.

"Well, *is* it?" he said. "You've got to look at these things from every angle. Is a girl who can deliberately allow a man to go through the horrors of a School Treat worth bothering about?"

Barmy started.

"I never thought of that. Or a girl, for that matter, who could callously throw a fellow to the Village Mothers."

"Remind me some time to tell you about a game called 'Is Mr Smith At Home?' where you put your head in a sack and the younger generation jab you with sticks."

"And don't let me forget to tell you about that Mother in the puce mantle on the Bump the Bumps."

"There was a kid called Horace . . ."

"There was a Mother in a Homburg hat . . ."

"The fact is," said Pongo, "we have allowed ourselves to lose our sober judgment over a girl whose idea of a mate is a mere 'Hey, you,' to be ordered hither and thither at her will, and who will unleash the juvenile population of her native village upon him without so much as a pang of pity—in a word, a parson's daughter. If you want to know the secret of a happy and successful life, Barmy, old man, it is this: Keep away from parsons' daughters."

"Right away," agreed Barmy. "How do you react to

hiring a car and pushing off to the metropolis at once?"

"I am all for it. And if we're to give of our best on the evening of the eleventh *prox.* we ought to start rehearsing again immediately."

"We certainly ought."

"We haven't any too much time, as it is."

"We certainly haven't. I've got an aunt who complains of rheumatism."

"Well, who wouldn't? My father can't meet his creditors."

"Does he want to? My uncle Joe's in very low water just now."

"Too bad. What's he doing?"

"Teaching swimming. Listen, Pongo," said Barmy, "I've been thinking. You take the green whiskers this year."

"No, no."

"Yes, really. I mean it. If I've said it to myself once, I've said it a hundred times—good old Pongo simply must have the green whiskers this year."

"Barmy!"

"Pongo!"

They clasped hands. Tried in the furnace, their friendship had emerged strong and true. Cyril Fotheringay-Phipps and Reginald Twistleton-Twistleton were themselves again.

THE END